CHRISTMAS
CUPCAKE
MURDER

Books by Joanne Fluke

Hannah Swensen Mysteries

CHOCOLATE CHIP COOKIE MURDER
STRAWBERRY SHORTCAKE MURDER
BLUEBERRY MUFFIN MURDER
LEMON MERINGUE PIE MURDER
FUDGE CUPCAKE MURDER
SUGAR COOKIE MURDER
PEACH COBBLER MURDER
CHERRY CHEESECAKE MURDER
KEY LIME PIE MURDER
CANDY CANE MURDER
CARROT CAKE MURDER
CREAM PUFF MURDER
PLUM PUDDING MURDER
APPLE TURNOVER MURDER
DEVIL'S FOOD CAKE MURDER
GINGERBREAD COOKIE MURDER
CINNAMON ROLL MURDER
RED VELVET CUPCAKE MURDER
BLACKBERRY PIE MURDER
DOUBLE FUDGE BROWNIE MURDER
WEDDING CAKE MURDER
CHRISTMAS CARAMEL MURDER
BANANA CREAM PIE MURDER
RASPBERRY DANISH MURDER
CHRISTMAS CAKE MURDER
CHOCOLATE CREAM PIE MURDER
CHRISTMAS SWEETS
COCONUT LAYER CAKE MURDER
CHRISTMAS CUPCAKE MURDER
JOANNE FLUKE'S LAKE EDEN COOKBOOK

Suspense Novels

VIDEO KILL
WINTER CHILL
DEAD GIVEAWAY
THE OTHER CHILD
COLD JUDGMENT
FATAL IDENTITY
FINAL APPEAL
VENGEANCE IS MINE
EYES
WICKED
DEADLY MEMORIES
THE STEPCHILD

Published by Kensington Publishing Corporation

CHRISTMAS CUPCAKE MURDER

JOANNE
FLUKE

KENSINGTON BOOKS
www.kensingtonbooks.com

This book is for Kathy Allen for baking
fabulous cupcakes!

KENSINGTON BOOKS are published by

Kensington Publishing Corp.
119 West 40th Street
New York, NY 10018

Copyright © 2020 by H.L. Swensen, Inc.

All Kensington titles, imprints and distributed lines are available
at special quantity discounts for bulk purchases for sales promo-
tion, premiums, fund-raising, educational or institutional use.
Special book excerpts or customized printings can also be created
to fit specific needs. For details, write or phone the office of the
Kensington Special Sales Manager: Kensington Publishing Corp.,
119 West 40th Street, New York, NY, 10018. Attn. Special Sales
Department. Phone: 1-800-221-2647.

Kensington and the K logo Reg. U.S. Pat. & TM Off.

Library of Congress Card Catalogue Number: 2020937089

ISBN-13: 978-1-4967-2912-5
ISBN-10: 1-4967-2912-9
First Kensington Hardcover Edition: October 2020

ISBN-13: 978-1-4967-2914-9 (e-book)
ISBN-10: 1-4967-2914-5 (e-book)

10 9 8 7 6 5 4 3 2 1

Printed in the United States of America

Acknowledgements:

Many thanks to my extended family for putting up with me while I was writing this book.

Hugs to Trudi Nash and her husband, David, for being brave enough to taste a recipe that might, or might not, have worked.

Thank you to my friends and neighbors: Mel & Kurt, Lyn & Bill, Gina, Dee Appleton, Jay, Richard Jordan, Laura Levine, the real Nancy and Heiti, Dan, Mark & Mandy at Faux Library, Daryl and her staff at Groves Accountancy, Gene and Ron at SDSA, and my friends at HomeStreet Bank.

Hugs to my Minnesota friends: Lois & Neal, Bev & Jim, Val, Ruthann, Lowell, Dorothy & Sister Sue, and Mary & Jim.

Big hugs to John Scognamiglio, editor of genius.
(That's his genius, not mine!)

Hugs for Meg Ruley and the staff at the Jane Rotrosen Agency for their constant support and sage advice.

Thanks to all the wonderful folks at Kensington Publishing who keep Hannah sleuthing and baking yummy goodies.

Thanks to Robin in Production, and Larissa in Publicity. Both of you go above and beyond.

Thanks to Hiro Kimura for his incredible cupcakes on the cover.
I really love that reindeer!

Thank you to Lou Malcangi at Kensington for designing all of Hannah's gorgeous book covers. They're simply wonderful.

A special thank you to Julie Gulik from *My Food and Family* by Kraft Heinz for letting Hannah use the White Chocolate

Eggnog Cupcake recipe. Baking these cupcakes is the perfect way to taste Christmas any time of the year! More of Julie's Kraft Heinz recipes are at www.MyFoodAndFamily.com.

Thanks to John at *Placed4Success* for Hannah's movie and TV placements, his presence on Hannah's social media platforms, and for being my son.

Thanks to Tami Chase for designing and managing my website at **wwwJoanneFluke.com** and for giving support to Hannah's social media.

Thank you to Kathy Allen for the final testing of every single recipe in this book!

A big hug to JQ for helping Hannah and me for so many years.

Kudos to Beth, from Up In Stitches, and her phalanx of sewing machines for her gorgeous embroidery on our hats, visors, aprons, and tote bags.

Thank you to food stylist, friend, and media guide Lois Brown for her expertise with the launch parties at Poisoned Pen in Scottsdale, AZ and baking for the TV food segments I do at KPNX in Phoenix.
Thanks also to Destry, the lovely, totally unflappable producer and host of *Arizona Midday*.

Hugs to Debbie Risinger and everyone else on Team Swensen.

Thank you to Dr. Rahhal, Dr. Umali, Dr. and Cathy Line, Dr. Levy (especially for telling me about T.B.I.), Dr. Koslowski, and Drs. Ashley and Lee for answering my book-related medical and dental questions.

Hugs to all the Hannah fans who read the books, share their family recipes, post on my Facebook page, **Joanne Fluke Author**, and enjoy the photos of Sven, my bear-footed dessert chef.

This story takes place before Hannah Swensen, Lake Eden's cookie-baking amateur sleuth, solves her first missing person case. It's also before Hannah's mother, Delores Swensen, opens an antique store with her best friend, Carrie Rhodes.

If you think life must be boring in small town Minnesota, read on!

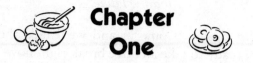

Chapter One

Hannah Swensen was just taking a pan of German Chocolate Cupcakes out of her industrial oven at The Cookie Jar, when there was a knock on the back kitchen door. Hannah quickly slid the pan of cupcakes on a shelf in the bakers rack, and hurried to answer the door. A man was standing there and he stepped back a few feet from the door, a man Hannah had never seen before.

"I'm sorry, but we're not open yet," she said.

"I know that, ma'am. And thank you for answering the door. I saw the closed sign, but I was hoping that someone was here early and they might have some work for me to do. I don't need money. That's not it. But I'd be grateful for a couple of cookies to eat for breakfast."

As the man spoke, Hannah noticed that he was shivering. His coat didn't look very warm and it was cold this early in the morning. She felt a rush of compassion for his situation and she opened the door wider and motioned him closer. "Come in and we'll talk about the work. I'm ready to take a coffee break right now. Would you like to have a cup of coffee with me?"

"Yes, I certainly would, ma'am!" he said immediately, a smile breaking out on his face. "A cup of coffee would be really good."

"Just hang your coat on one of those hooks by the door," she said, walking quickly to the kitchen coffeepot. She'd finished a cup of coffee only minutes before, but it was obvious that the man needed to come in out of the cold, and drink something warm. She was about to offer him cream and sugar, but one glance at his emaciated form when he hung up his coat prompted her to add two more packets of sugar and a generous amount of cream to his coffee.

Hannah carried his coffee to one of the stools by the stainless steel work station and pulled out a stool for him. "Would you like one of the cupcakes I just baked?" she asked. "It's not frosted yet, but it should still be good without frosting."

"Yes, thank you, ma'am!" the man said, giving her a grateful smile. And then he smiled even wider as she delivered the cupcake and he saw that it was chocolate. "I love chocolate. My mother used to say that it was God's gift to mankind."

"Your mother was a wise woman," Hannah said with a smile. "These cupcakes are going to be German chocolate when they're frosted."

"I love German chocolate cake! My mother used to make a German chocolate cake every year for my birthday. It was our family's official birthday cake and my mother was famous for her cake. She copied the recipe on a card and gave it away every time she baked a birthday cake for someone."

Hannah could see that his eyes were wet with unshed tears at the memory. "You'll have to come back here in an hour or so and I'll give you a cupcake that's frosted."

"I'll be back. Thank you, ma'am." He took a bite of his cupcake and swallowed with obvious relish. "These are really good."

"Thank you. Would you like another?"

"Oh, yes! Yes, I would, and thank you, ma'am!"

Hannah went back to the baker's rack and picked up another cupcake. The man was polite and completely non-threatening. Mike Kingston, the chief detective at the Winnetka County Sheriff's Department, would chastise her for opening the door to a stranger, but if he were here and actually met her early-morning visitor, Hannah was sure he would agree with her assessment of the man's character.

"Tell me more about your mother's German chocolate cake," she said, sitting down on a stool directly across from his. "Did you ever watch her make it?"

"Yes, ma'am. I surely did. And when I got old enough, I rode to the store with her to get all the things she needed to bake it."

"Do you remember what they were?"

"I do. She bought German chocolate. She never kept it in the pantry because she said it might get old between birthdays and she wanted it fresh. And she bought coconut, pecans, and cake flour. She wanted those fresh, too. And then we went to the fruit section and she bought one orange."

"An orange?" Hannah asked curiously. An orange wasn't called for in any German chocolate cake recipe that she'd ever seen.

"The orange was for me. After she took off the peel, she cut it into little wheels on a plate. Then she picked out the seeds and gave it to me to eat. She told me that oranges were expensive and orange wheels were part of my birthday present."

"Your birthday was in the winter?" Hannah gave an educated guess since the man was well over twenty years old, and fresh produce, especially fruit that had to be trucked in from warmer climates, was expensive in the winter.

"I don't . . . yes! Yes, my birthday is in the winter. I can remember that Dad had to drive us to town through the snow to buy what she needed for my birthday cake." The man looked sad again, and Hannah was almost sorry she'd asked for more information about his birthday. But after a moment, he began to smile again. "I know what I can do for you, ma'am! I can brush the snow off your car, and scrape the ice from your windshield."

"That would be wonderful," Hannah agreed quickly. It was obvious to her that the man wanted to repay her in some way for giving him coffee and the cupcakes. "And while you're out there, you can unwind the cord from my front bumper and plug in my car. There's a strip of outlets on the side of the building and I forgot to do it when I came to work this morning."

"I'll go do that right now," the man said, standing up quickly. "It's cold out there this morning."

"No, don't go yet," Hannah told him quickly, motioning him back down to his stool. "Stay here and drink some more of your coffee so you'll warm up first. Finish your coffee and your second cupcake, and then I'll show you which car is mine."

The man laughed. It was a nice laugh and Hannah was glad to hear it. From his appearance, she suspected that he hadn't had much to laugh about in recent weeks. "You don't have to tell me which one is yours, ma'am. There's only one vehicle in the parking lot and I figure that red Chevy Suburban must be yours."

"You figured right," Hannah told him. "While you're outside, I'm going to frost those cupcakes. Then you can have a couple of them when you're done."

After the man finished his coffee and cupcake, he went back outside and Hannah not only frosted the cupcakes, she also looked through her lost and found box. She'd been open for two years now and she'd been planning to take the contents of last year's box to Helping Hands, the thrift store across the alley. If there was anything in the lost and found box that would fit, she'd take it out and give it to him. She also decided to pay him five dollars. It wasn't much, but she wanted to give him something so he could buy a meal later in the day.

Twenty minutes later, dressed in the warm sweater and scarf she'd found, the man left, clutching the bag of frosted German Chocolate Cupcakes that she'd given him, along with a promise that he'd stop by the following morning to see if she had any additional work for him.

After he had gone, Hannah began baking again. She felt good as she mixed up the cupcake batter, put it in the cups, and waited for it to bake. She'd helped someone who truly needed help and, since her instincts had been correct and the man had been polite and grateful for her help, it had been the right thing for her to do.

There was another knock at the door, the moment after Hannah had slipped a pan of cupcakes on the revolving racks in her industrial oven. This time it was a knock she recognized and she hurried to the door.

"Hello, Mother," she called out before she even opened the door. There was only one person in town who knocked three times in quick succession, paused for several seconds, and then repeated the pattern.

"Good morning, dear," Delores greeted her. "Do you have time for a quick cup of coffee with me? I really need to discuss something important with you."

Hannah's instincts went on red alert. Her mother usually simply walked in and took a seat on a stool at Hannah's work station without asking. Whatever Delores had to discuss with her must involve some kind of last-minute favor that would mean extra work for Hannah.

"Of course, if you're terribly busy, I can always come back a bit later," Delores offered, obviously noticing her eldest daughter's hesitation.

"No. It's fine, Mother. Just hang up your coat and take a seat. I'll get your coffee, put the rest of my cupcakes in the oven, and be right with you."

"Thank you, dear." Delores took off her coat, hung it on one of the hooks near the back door, and headed for a stool at the stainless steel work station. "Do I smell chocolate?"

"You do." Hannah delivered her mother's coffee and hurried back to her industrial oven to set the timer. "I'm trying out a recipe for German Chocolate Cupcakes that Lisa found in her mother's recipe box."

"They smell divine, dear. I don't suppose any of them are cool enough to . . . ?"

"They are," Hannah said, anticipating the rest of her mother's question. "I'll bring you one just as soon as I'm through here."

"Oh, good! Thank you, dear. That would be lovely. I was running late this morning and I simply didn't have time for my yogurt and wheat toast."

As she glanced over at her mother, a puzzled expression crossed Hannah's face. Her always impeccably-dressed mother was wearing a bulky sweater that did nothing to enhance her flawless figure and an old pair of slacks that had seen better days. For a woman who had never appeared in public in an outfit that was less than designer perfect, this fashion lapse was highly unusual.

"Are you feeling all right this morning?" Hannah

asked, setting an almost-cooled cupcake in front of her mother before she poured her own coffee and took a seat.

"I'm fine, dear." It was Delores's turn to look puzzled. "Why do you ask?"

"Because . . . well . . ." Hannah thought fast and managed to come up with an answer. "Because it's early and you don't usually come in this time of the morning."

"I see. And of course it doesn't have anything to do with the fact that I look as if I bought this outfit at Helping Hands." Delores named the charity thrift store that was just across the alley from her daughter's bakery and coffee shop.

Hannah knew she was about to tread on eggshells, but she had to be truthful. "Well . . . yes, it does. I don't think I've ever seen you appear in public without a designer outfit and full makeup before."

"Of course you haven't." Delores gave a little smile. "I've never appeared in public like this before. But I needed to get here early so that I could catch you while you were still baking."

"I see," Hannah said, even though she didn't.

"I probably should have called, but I thought it was best to ask you in person."

DefCon 4! DefCon 4! her mind alerted, and Hannah came close to groaning. Whatever her mother was about to ask had to be something big. She really didn't want to know what it entailed, but she had to find out. "What do you want to ask me, Mother?"

"I know it's an imposition, but I'm between a rock and a hard place. I need to ask you for a favor . . ." Delores paused and frowned slightly. "Actually, it entails *two* favors," she corrected herself.

"Tell me what you need, Mother." Hannah knew better than to promise to perform a favor for her mother without knowing what it was. She'd learned her lesson years ago when she'd said yes, and risked permanent ear damage by escorting her younger sister, Andrea, and two of her friends to a punk rock concert in Minneapolis.

"I need you to help me find the Christmas decorations I bought three years ago at an estate sale," Delores explained.

"I'll be glad to help you with that," Hannah agreed readily. "Do you have any idea where they are?"

"Yes. They're in the antique shed. I think they might be in back of the mahogany davenport I bought at a farm sale in Grey Eagle. As a matter of fact, I'm almost positive that's where they are. The problem is moving the davenport to look. It's heavy, and Carrie and I can't do that by ourselves."

Hannah nodded. "I can help you move it, Mother. When do you need the decorations?"

"That's another problem. We need them today. We promised Doc we'd decorate the patient rooms and the lobby at the hospital this afternoon."

Hannah turned to glance at the baker's rack. She'd started baking early this morning and it was almost full of baked goods. "No problem, Mother. I finished the baking early and I can help you just as soon as Lisa gets here."

"Oh, good! Thank you, dear. You have no idea how happy this makes me! I was afraid I'd have to call Doc and ask him to reschedule the Jordan High Chorale. They're coming this afternoon to sing Christmas carols for the tree-lighting ceremony."

"I'm glad I can help," Hannah said. The first favor was easy. It just required a bit of heavy lifting. But her mother had said there were two favors and Hannah still didn't know about the second one. "What's the second favor, Mother?"

"It's a bit more complicated." Delores paused to take a sip of her coffee. Then she peeled the paper from the cupcake that Hannah had given her and took a bite. A rapturous expression crossed her face as she tasted it and she gave a little mewl of enjoyment. "Superb!" she pronounced. "These are the best cupcakes I've ever had, dear. They're absolutely marvelous! And I see that you baked a lot of them this morning."

"Yes, I did," Hannah said, watching as Delores eyed the baker's rack. Was her mother mentally calculating the number of cupcakes that Hannah had stored there?

"My, you've been busy this morning!" Delores remarked, turning to smile at her daughter. "Do you really think you'll sell all those marvelous German Chocolate Cupcakes, dear?"

She wants your cupcakes, the suspicious part of Hannah's brain announced.

Hannah began to smile as she realized that the suspicious part of her mind was correct. Her mother's second favor definitely involved the German Chocolate Cupcakes. "How many do you need, Mother?" she asked.

"Oh, dear!" Delores looked properly embarrassed. "Was I *that* transparent?"

I told you she wanted your cupcakes! the suspicious part of Hannah's brain congratulated itself.

"How did you know, dear?" Delores asked.

"It was just a guess," Hannah said quickly. "You told me that you and Carrie are decorating for Doc today and I thought the patients and nurses might like a little sweet treat during the annual tree-lighting ceremony."

"You're absolutely right, dear. How clever of you to think of that! But of course if you don't have time to bake more cupcakes . . ." Delores stopped speaking and gave a little sigh. "Everyone will be very disappointed, but we'll all understand."

Caught like a rat in a trap!! the rational part of Hannah's brain announced. This analysis was quite needless since Hannah already realized it. Delores knew full-well that her daughter wouldn't want to disappoint Doc's hard-working nurses and hospital staff, and deprive the patients who weren't well enough to be home for the holidays.

"I'll find time to bake for you, Mother," Hannah promised, "and now I understand why you're dressed the way you are."

Delores laughed. "You mean, like something the cat dragged in, don't you, dear?"

"Uh . . ." Hannah began to frown as she found herself stuck for words, an unusual circumstance for her. She gave a little nod to acknowledge her mother's question and then she sighed deeply. "I totally understand that you have to dress in old clothes to crawl around the big Christmas tree that Cliff always donates for the hospital lobby, not to mention climbing up ladders to hang ornaments and put on lights. You wouldn't want to damage one of your beautiful outfits."

Delores laughed. "That's a good guess, dear, but these aren't the clothes I'll wear for decorating."

"They're not?"

"No. I have a nice pantsuit for that. I'm wearing this because of the antique shed. Nothing in there has been dusted in ages. And just for your information, I wouldn't dream of going to the hospital and letting Doc Knight and his staff see me like this! Once Carrie and I are ready to go, I'll change into the pantsuit I bought especially for Christmas decorating. This is definitely *not* what I'm wearing! I just hopped in the car and took the chance that I wouldn't see anyone I knew . . . except you, of course. And I knew *you'd* understand."

Because I always look like something the cat dragged in when I wear a sweatshirt and jeans for baking in the mornings? Hannah's mind posed the question, but she was wise enough not to ask it aloud. "How many cupcakes do you think you need, Mother?"

"I called Doc this morning and he thought twelve dozen cookies should do it, but we were figuring on two cookies each. Since cupcakes are bigger, I think six dozen should be fine."

"What time do you need them?"

"At three. That's usually when the patients have a little mid-afternoon snack."

"That won't be a problem, Mother," Hannah said quickly. "I got here early this morning and the cookie baking is all done. I can take care of the cupcakes and have them ready by two, if that's soon enough."

"Perfect!" Delores declared, taking another bite of her cupcake. After she'd finished the confection, she smiled and looked very pleased. "I knew I could count on you, Hannah. You always come through for me in a pinch. I'll ask Doc if he can spare one of the nurses to drive here and pick them up."

"No need. I'll drive them out," Hannah offered quickly. "I'd like to see your decorations, Mother. Christmas is such a beautiful time of the year."

"Yes, it is." Delores stood up with a smile. "I'd better run before the sun comes out and someone sees me like this. And thank you for everything, dear. And . . . I probably shouldn't mention this, but . . ."

Hannah began to smile, anticipating precisely what her mother was struggling to say. "Don't worry, Mother. I'll change clothes before I come out to the hospital."

"Perfect. A little lipstick wouldn't hurt either, dear. And if you could just run a comb through your hair . . ." She gave a little sigh. "Doc explained it to me when you were a baby, but I confess I'm still a bit angry about the fact that you inherited your father's curly red hair." She stopped to sigh again. "Your sister Andrea's blond hair is so perfect, and Michelle's hair is a lovely shade of golden brown. My dark hair would have been wonderful for you, too. Sometimes I blame myself, Hannah, but unruly red hair like yours doesn't run in my family at all."

"It's all right, Mother," Hannah told her. "I really don't mind having hair like Dad's. It was just luck of the draw, I guess."

"You're probably right, but I wish you had my hair color. It's still the same shade it was when I was a teenager."

"Yes, it is," Hannah agreed, not admitting that she knew her mother had a private standing appointment at Bertie's Cut 'n Curl, their local beauty shop, to cover the grey in her hair.

"All right then, dear." Delores finished the last of her cupcake and stood up. "Carrie promised to be at my house by nine and I want to be at the hospital by ten-thirty. Can you meet us at my house by nine-thirty?"

"I'll be there," Hannah promised. "I'll leave for your house right after Lisa comes in. And if we're not too busy today, I'll drive out to the hospital early and help you finish up the decorating."

"Oh, that would be wonderful!" A wide smile spread over Delores's face. "You're so much better on a ladder than either Carrie or I are. Give me a call on my cell phone the moment you know what time you're coming. If it's early enough, Carrie and I will save the top part of the tree in the lobby for you to decorate."

Wonderful! Hannah thought. *That's all I need!*

Delores stood up and slipped into her parka. "Thank you, dear. You're always so sweet about doing these little favors for me."

When the door had shut behind her mother, Hannah headed back to the work station to finish her coffee. Moving a heavy, antique davenport, baking and decorating six dozen more cupcakes, and climbing a ladder to decorate the fourteen-foot tree in the hospital lobby certainly wasn't what she'd planned for today. And her mother had called it a *small favor*?

"One of these days, I'm going to say no," she said as she picked up her coffee cup and took a sip of her lukewarm coffee.

"Were you talking to me?" Lisa asked, pushing through the swinging door that separated the kitchen from the coffee shop just in time to hear Hannah's disgruntled comment.

"No!" Hannah reassured her. "It's just that Mother asked me to bake an extra six dozen cupcakes this morning."

"I thought I saw her car pulling away." Lisa walked to the coffeepot and poured a cup for herself. "And you agreed?"

Hannah gave an exasperated sigh. "Yes, I'm afraid I did. And I also agreed to help her look for Christmas decorations in her antique shed, and to help decorate the Christmas tree in the hospital lobby."

"Wow!" Lisa looked properly shocked. "Did you resist at all?"

Hannah shook her head. "Not really. She just put on that sad puppy dog look and I couldn't say no."

Lisa laughed. "My mother used to use that look whenever she wanted me to clean my room."

"And it worked?"

"Like a charm. I think mothers learn that look right after they have their first baby. How long did you manage to resist before you caved in?"

"No more than a couple of seconds."

"That figures." Lisa walked over to the baker's rack and took a cupcake. "Are these my mother's German Chocolate Cupcakes?"

"Yes. Mother tasted one and loved it. She wants six dozen by this afternoon."

"No problem." Lisa came back to her stool at the work station and peeled the paper from the cupcake. "Rachael is going to be here any minute now and she can bake them for you. My mom taught her to bake the summer she stayed with us."

Hannah was puzzled. "Who's Rachael?"

"My cousin from Cedar Rapids. She's spending the holidays with us and she drove up last night. When does your mother need the cupcakes?"

"I promised to have them ready by two this afternoon. They're having a tree-lighting ceremony in the hospital lobby again this year."

"The way they did last year with the Jordan High Chorale and all?"

"That's right."

"Oh, that's nice! Rachael can drive them out there for you. She's going to nursing school in Cedar Rapids and it'll give her a chance to talk to some of the nurses." Lisa glanced up at the clock. "What time are you going to your mother's house?"

"As soon as everything's organized here. I have to help Mother and Carrie move an antique davenport."

"It'll probably take all three of you. Those old sofas are heavy, especially if they're the kind that lifts out to make a bed. You can go now, Hannah. All I have to do is put up the coffee in the coffee shop and fill the cookie display jars."

"Are you sure?" Hannah found herself feeling a bit guilty about leaving all the work to Lisa.

"I'm sure. It could take you some time to locate those decorations. Your mother once told me she had over a hundred and fifty antiques in that shed."

"Are you sure you don't need me to help you with anything before I leave?"

"Not a thing. I'll have plenty of help. Dad's coming down here, too, if that's all right with you."

"Of course that's all right!" Hannah responded quickly. Lisa's father loved to visit with the customers and everyone had a good time when he was there.

"Go ahead, Hannah. They'll be here any minute."

"All right . . . if you're sure . . ."

"I am. Go help your mother before she decides to try to move that sofa herself and throws out her back."

"You've got a point," Hannah said, getting up from

her stool and carrying her cup to the sink. "If Carrie gets there early, they might decide to do something like that."

"Good luck finding the decorations," Lisa called after her as Hannah headed for the strip of coat hooks by the back door and grabbed her parka. "And don't let your mother and Carrie reposition the treetop angel more than two or three times this year."

GERMAN CHOCOLATE CUPCAKES

Preheat oven to 350 degrees F., rack in the middle position.

2 large eggs
½ cup vegetable oil *(not canola or olive oil)*
½ cup chocolate milk
1 cup of sour cream
1 box chocolate cake mix, with or without pudding in the mix, the kind that makes a 9-inch by 13-inch cake or a 2-layer cake *(I used Duncan Hines Chocolate Fudge)*
5.1-ounce package of instant chocolate pudding *(I used Jell-O, the kind that makes 6 half-cup servings)*
12-ounce (by weight) bag of milk chocolate chips, chopped into smaller pieces

Prepare 2 cupcake pans, the kind that makes 12 cupcakes each, by lining them with cupcake papers.

Hannah's 1st Note: I always use double cupcake papers when I make cupcakes.

Crack the eggs into the bowl of an electric mixer on LOW speed until they are a uniform color.

Pour in the half-cup of vegetable oil and mix on LOW speed until it is combined with the eggs.

Pour in the chocolate milk and mix on LOW speed.

Measure out the cup of sour cream and use a rubber spatula to add that to your mixer bowl. Mix that in on LOW speed.

When everything is well mixed, shut off the mixer and open the box of cake mix. *(Don't bother to read the directions on the box—You won't be using them in these cupcakes.)*

Sprinkle in approximately HALF of the dry cake mix and combine that with the liquid ingredients at LOW speed. Then sprinkle in the rest of the cake mix and mix it all together.

When the cake mix has been thoroughly incorporated, open the box of instant chocolate pudding and sprinkle it into the bowl of your mixer. Mix that in on LOW speed.

If you haven't already done so, chop the milk chocolate chips into smaller pieces. This is most easily done by placing them in the bowl of a food processor and chopping them in an on-and-off motion with the steel blade.

Add the chopped milk chocolate chips to the mixer bowl. Combine them with the other ingredients at LOW speed.

Shut off the mixer, scrape down the sides of the bowl, and remove the bowl from the mixer.

Give the bowl a final stir by hand with a rubber spatula or a wooden spoon.

Use a scoop or a mixing spoon to transfer the German Chocolate Cupcake batter to the pans you've prepared, filling each cupcake paper ¾ full.

Hannah's 2nd Note: These cupcakes are very dense and do not rise very much in the oven.

Bake your cupcakes at 350 degrees F. for 18 to 22 minutes, or until a toothpick inserted a half-inch from the center comes out clean.

Remove from the oven and let cool in the cupcake pans on cold stovetop burners or wire racks.

Let the cupcakes cool completely before frosting with German Chocolate Cupcake Frosting. (Recipe follows)

GERMAN CHOCOLATE CUPCAKE FROSTING

Hannah's 1st Note: This frosting consists of two parts, the Cooked Pecan Coconut Frosting and the Chocolate Buttercream Frosting. Make the cooked frosting first and let it cool while you make the Chocolate Buttercream Frosting.

COOKED PECAN COCONUT FROSTING

1 cup evaporated milk
3 egg yolks, beaten *(just whip them up in a glass with a fork)*
1 cup brown sugar, firmly packed
½ cup *(1 stick, 4 ounces, ¼ pound)* salted butter
1 teaspoon vanilla extract
½ teaspoon coconut extract
1 cup flaked coconut
1 cup pecans *(pieces are fine)*

Place the evaporated milk, egg yolks, brown sugar, and butter in a medium-size saucepan. Turn the burner

22

to MEDIUM heat and stir CONSTANTLY with a wooden spoon until the mixture thickens.

Hannah's 2nd Note: This will take from 12 to 15 minutes.

Pull the saucepan off the heat, shut off the burner, and stir in the vanilla extract and the coconut extract.

Put the cup of flaked coconut and the pecans in the bowl of a food processor. Process in an on-and-off motion with the steel blade until they are chopped into small pieces.

Add the coconut and pecan pieces to the saucepan and stir them in.

Move the saucepan to a cool burner and let it cool until it reaches room temperature while you make the Chocolate Buttercream Frosting.

CHOCOLATE BUTTERCREAM FROSTING

4 ounces softened cream cheese *(half of an 8-ounce package)*

½ cup (1 stick, 4 ounces, ¼ pound) salted butter, softened

½ cup cocoa powder *(unsweetened)*

3 cups confectioners' *(powdered)* sugar

1 teaspoon vanilla extract

Rinse out the bowl of your electric mixer with hot water and dry it with a paper towel. Put it back in the mixer and attach the paddle.

Place the softened cream cheese and the softened, salted butter in the bowl of the mixer.

Beat them together on MEDIUM speed for 5 minutes.

Add the unsweetened cocoa, powdered sugar, and vanilla extract and continue to beat on MEDIUM speed for 3 to 4 additional minutes.

Shut off the mixer and check the consistency of the frosting. If it's too thin, add a bit more powdered sugar and beat for another minute. If it's too thick, add a tea-

spoon or two of heavy cream or milk and beat on MEDIUM speed for another few minutes.

When your Chocolate Buttercream Frosting is of the proper spreading consistency, take the bowl out of the mixer and give it a final stir by hand.

Check the Cooked Pecan Coconut Frosting. If it has cooled to room temperature and your German Chocolate Cupcakes have cooled completely, it is time to frost them.

To frost German Chocolate Cupcakes, start with the Chocolate Buttercream Frosting.

Using a frosting knife, spread frosting generously over the top of the cupcakes, leaving a slight indentation in the center. This is where you will spread the Cooked Pecan Coconut Frosting.

Once all the cupcakes have been frosted with the Chocolate Buttercream Frosting, rinse off your frosting knife and use it to give the saucepan of Cooked Pecan Coconut Frosting a final stir.

Spread approximately a Tablespoon of the cooked frosting in the center of the cupcakes where you left the slight indentation. Use your frosting knife to spread it

out a bit, but make sure there's a visible border of the Chocolate Buttercream Frosting around the top of each cupcake.

These cupcakes can be frozen for up to a month. Thaw in the refrigerator the night before you want to serve them.

Yield: 1 to 1 and ½ dozen cupcakes.

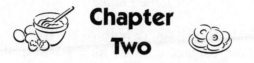

Chapter Two

"**O**h, dear!" Delores gave a little cry of distress as she unlocked the door to her antique shed. "I should have come out here to check this after the first snow."

Hannah gave a nod as she surveyed the blanket of snow on top of the blue plastic drop cloths that covered her mother's antiques. She agreed wholeheartedly with her mother's comment, but it was wiser to maintain her silence.

"Maybe it's not that bad," Carrie said. "The plastic drop cloths kept the snow off and we haven't had any warm days this winter."

"Carrie's right," Hannah agreed. "The snow didn't melt, so there hasn't been any water damage. Let's pull off the drop cloths and shake them off outside. Then we can put them back on again when we find the decorations you bought."

Delores, who had been looking very upset, brightened considerably. "You're both right. There shouldn't be any water damage until we hit a warm spell. And I have to get someone to repair the roof before then."

"There's a board loose on the side of the shed that faces the house," Carrie pointed out. "You'd better get someone to fix that, too."

Working together, the three women managed to pull off the drop cloths and move them outside. Once they'd shaken them clean of snow, they folded them and brought them back into the shed.

"Is that the dining room table you told me about?" Hannah asked her mother, pointing to the table stacked next to the davenport.

"Yes. I was going to refinish it this winter, but it was just too cold out here."

"You can't work out here," Carrie told her, stomping her feet to keep them warm.

"I know, but the table's too big to bring inside the garage and I don't have room to work on it in the house."

Hannah, who had been glancing around at the antique furniture stacked into every square inch of the shed, gave a little sigh. "This shed is a wreck, Mother. I don't think anyone can repair it. And even if someone agrees to tackle the job, you'll have to move all the antiques somewhere while they're working."

"Hannah's right," Carrie said. "You have some beautiful things here, Delores. That grandfather clock", she pointed to the far wall, "is worth a bundle. Were you planning on moving it into your living room?"

Delores shook her head. "No. That was my original plan, but then Lars mentioned that he didn't want to listen to it ticking and chiming. And it needs refinishing, while I have the works repaired."

"This is beautiful," Carrie commented, running her gloved hand over the top of a walnut vanity. "I used to have a maple one like this."

"All it needs is a new mirror," Delores told her. "Would you like it, Carrie?"

Carrie shook her head. "That's sweet of you, Delores, and thank you for offering, but my bedroom's too crowded as it is. I'd like to help you refinish it, though. I love to breathe new life into old wood."

Delores smiled. "So do I! Maybe I should find someone to move it into the garage and we could work on it."

"No," Hannah said quickly. "The garage isn't heated, Mother. And you get only so much ambient heat from the house. You need a place to store your antiques that's heated and has plenty of light."

"You mean," Delores frowned slightly, "a storage locker?"

Hannah shook her head. "No. I was thinking about a deserted storefront with lights and heat. When you're through at the hospital today, why don't you two run into Lake Eden Realty to see Al Percy? He might know of the perfect place to rent."

"That's a good idea," Carrie said immediately. "Delores has some lovely things and it would be a real shame if they got damaged out here because of the weather. The way they're stacked up on top of each other isn't good, either."

"I know," Delores admitted. "I just haven't gotten around to doing anything about it. And the last time I was out here was in the summer. The roof seemed all right then."

Which summer? Hannah's suspicious mind prompted her to ask, but she quickly dismissed that suggestion. "It's okay, Mother," she said, reaching out to pat her mother's shoulder. "It looks as though everything is still okay."

"Yes, it does," Carrie agreed, walking over to run her hand over a mahogany nightstand. "Between your antiques and my antiques, I think we have enough to open our own antique store."

Delores laughed. "You're probably right. Lars kept after me to do exactly that. But opening a store is a lot of work and I never really pursued it seriously."

"But you kept on buying antiques," Hannah pointed out.

Delores gave a heartfelt sigh. "I know. I just love well-made, beautiful, old furniture. Why, I have an antique chair that's held together by wooden peg construction. I checked it out before I bought it, and there's not a speck of glue in it."

"They just don't make things like that anymore," Carrie commented. "Everything now is mass produced. I think that's why it's just a treat to bring old furniture back to life."

Hannah nodded. "I can understand that. I feel the

same way about trying old recipes. Sometimes they're more work than using modern shortcuts, but they can be worth it."

"Unless it comes to angel food cake," Delores said. "I remember the day you and Grandma Ingrid and Great-Grandma Elsa tried baking angel food and chiffon cakes by hand."

Hannah laughed at the memory. "You're right, Mother. My arm was sore for a solid week from whipping those egg whites. Sometimes using modern conveniences like a stand mixer is a lot easier and quicker than making them the old way."

Carrie turned to Delores. "Where do you think you stored those decorations?"

"Behind there," Delores said, pointing to the antique davenport at the side of the shed. "I'm almost positive they're stacked in big boxes behind it."

Carrie walked over and gave the arm of the davenport a little tug. "I don't know, Delores. The three of us might not be able to move it. Do you think I should call Norman and ask him if he can come over to help us? He doesn't have any dental appointments this morning. He's just down there doing billing."

"Maybe. I know it's really heavy. The estate auctioneer recruited four farmers to get it into the truck I rented. And Lars had Cliff and two of his friends help to get it out of the truck and move it in here."

"Let's try it and see if we need help," Hannah suggested. "It would be a shame to get Norman over here if it turns out that we don't need him." She walked over to the davenport, grasped the wooden arm, and gave a trial tug.

"It moved!" Delores said, beginning to smile. "Do you think we can move it far enough so we can look for those boxes?"

"Yes, if we work together. But if you're wrong and the decorations aren't there, we'd better call for more manpower."

"Like Mike and a couple of the deputies?" Carrie asked her.

"Yes, but let's hold off until we're sure we need help."

What ensued, as Hannah later described it to Lisa, was a scene worthy of a Three Stooges comedy. Hannah resorted to counting so they could coordinate their efforts, and finally, by the time they were all nearly exhausted, they got the heavy davenport to slide out far enough so that Delores, the thinnest member of their trio, could slip into the space behind it and look for the boxes.

"Are they there, Mother?" Hannah asked, hoping desperately that they were.

"They're here, but the boxes are too big for me to lift by myself."

"Let me help you," Hannah offered, clambering over the arm of the sofa and stepping in next to her mother. "I think we can do it if we lift together. Let's try to get them over the back of the couch and slide them down to the cushions. Then I can put them in the back of my cookie truck and drive them out to the hospital."

"You're going to help us decorate?" Carrie asked, looking pleased.

"Yes. All I have to do is take a quick shower and change into something . . ."

"Suitable for decorating," Delores interrupted, finishing the sentence for Hannah.

"Yes, Mother," Hannah said.

"I'm home, Moishe!" Hannah called out to the twenty-three pound orange and white cat who shared her apartment. "Where are you?"

There was no answering yowl from her pet and Hannah shrugged out of her parka and went to look for him. There was no sign of him in the laundry room or the kitchen. One glance told her he wasn't on the sofa in the living room, so Hannah headed down the hallway to check the bedrooms.

The guest room was cat-less, even though she checked under the bed, so she headed for her bedroom. Moishe wasn't sleeping in the closet and the bathroom didn't have a feline visitor. This led Hannah to wonder if Moishe could have gotten out somehow, but the door had been locked and all the windows were shut. There was nowhere for him to go except . . .

That was the instant that she spotted the suspicious lump under the quilt on her bed. She slipped back the quilt and began to smile as she saw Moishe curled up into a comfortable-looking ball on the flannel sheets she used on her mattress in the winter.

Moishe looked highly startled for a moment and

then, when he recognized her, he started to purr. Hannah reached out to pet him and he moved closer so she could pick him up.

Lifting Moishe from the bed was no easy task, but Hannah managed. She straightened up and retraced her steps, heading back to the kitchen.

"It's not dinner time yet," she warned him, setting him down next to his food bowl. "I just came home to take a quick shower and then I have to drive out to the hospital to help Mother and Carrie decorate for Christmas."

"Rrrow!" Moishe complained, pawing at his empty food bowl. Then he looked up at her expectantly.

"Oh, all right," Hannah told him, giving in to what she interpreted as a feline plea for food. "I won't fill your bowl right now, but I'll give you a little something to tide you over."

With her feline roommate watching, Hannah opened the cupboard door and took down a can of tuna. As she opened it, she heard Moishe start to purr loudly. He knew what was coming and it was one of his favorite treats.

After a quick trip to the broom closet, where she kept Moishe's large bag of dry cat food, Hannah scooped some in Moishe's bowl and baited the top with the canned tuna. Once the remainder of the can was refrigerated for later, she left Moishe with his head buried in his food bowl and hurried off to take her shower.

Fifteen minutes later, she was back in her cookie

truck, dressed in what her mother would be certain to describe as suitable decorating clothing, and she was on her way to the hospital.

As Hannah drove past fields of unbroken snow, she slipped on her sunglasses. Winter visitors to Minnesota were usually puzzled when they saw drivers wearing sunglasses, until they experienced, first-hand, the sun glaring off a snowy field. Even if they'd heard the term *snow-blind* before, they'd never truly understood it until they experienced the glare coming off white snow.

Hannah breathed a sigh of relief as she turned off the main road and took the county road that led to Doc Knight's hospital. Here the huge pines that lined both sides of the road shielded the snow from the sun. She knew that if she stopped her truck for any reason, she would experience at least a ten-degree drop in temperature now that she was in the shade.

The visitors' section of the hospital parking lot was nearly empty this time of the morning and Hannah found a spot next to her mother's car. She hooked her sunglasses over the rearview mirror, zipped up her parka, slipped on her gloves, grabbed her purse, the one that her mother claimed was as large as a saddlebag, and got out of the truck. Since she planned to be here for several hours, she unwound the extension cord that was wrapped around her front bumper. She plugged it into the outlet and headed for the door leading to the hospital lobby.

The temperature difference was noticeable once she

stepped inside the outer door. Most buildings in Minnesota had both outer and inner doors. This insulated the interior from the freezing cold in the winter and kept in the heat. The same system also worked in the summer to keep out the heat and make sure that the air-conditioning kept the inside of the hospital and all of the patients' rooms at a comfortable temperature.

Once Hannah was inside the inner door, she headed straight for the cloakroom, a term that always amused her since practically no one wore cloaks any longer. She took off her boots, changed to the shoes she'd brought with her, and hung up her parka. Only then did she head for the receptionist desk.

"Hello, Hannah," Becky Summers, the volunteer who was manning the front desk, greeted her. "Your mother and Carrie are in the lobby. You must be here to help them decorate."

"You're right," Hannah admitted, handing over the box of cookies she'd brought with her.

"For me?" Becky looked surprised.

"Yes," Hannah said, playing fast and loose with the truth. She'd brought the cookies for whoever was manning the desk by the door, but it wouldn't hurt to let Becky think they'd been intended just for her. "These are Pink Peppermint Cookies."

"I *love* peppermint!" Becky said reverently. "You must have remembered that it's my favorite! Thank you, Hannah."

"You're welcome. Sorry that I don't have time to stay

and talk, but I'm late and Mother and Carrie are depending on me to help them decorate the Christmas tree."

"Of course," Becky said with a smile. "Stop by when you're through decorating and tell me all the news from town. I'm so busy out here, I just don't have the time to chat with anyone these days."

Right, Hannah thought as she hurried toward the lobby where her mother and Carrie were waiting. She'd managed to escape a conversation with Becky, and that was lucky. Everyone in town knew that Becky loved to gossip and whatever Hannah said would be broadcast by phone to all Becky's friends the moment that Becky got home from her shift at the hospital. Becky was one of the founders of the phone tree that Hannah called the Lake Eden Gossip Hotline. If there were any scandals, near-scandals, or even mildly interesting gossip, it would be reported immediately by phone to five people who would each call five more people. Then those five people would each call another five people so that within thirty minutes, everyone in Lake Eden, and in the surrounding environs, would know exactly what had happened.

There were times when Hannah wished that her mother was not an active member of the Lake Eden Gossip Hotline. It had been established years ago as a community service to spread the word about council meetings, new city parking regulations, concerts and plays at Jordan High School, and emergency events like tornadoes and blizzards. Now that almost everyone had access to cell phones, television, and radio, it was mostly gossip. Hannah had grown up knowing that it was wise to avoid any private conversations with the hotline founders. She knew that if she spoke to certain people and told them personal things, she could end up being the subject of a discussion on the Lake Eden Gossip Hotline.

PINK PEPPERMINT COOKIES

DO NOT preheat the oven. This dough needs to chill before baking.

2 cups melted butter *(4 sticks, 16 ounces, 1 pound)*
2 cups powdered *(confectioners)* sugar
1 cup white *(granulated)* sugar
½ cup heavy *(whipping)* cream
2 beaten eggs *(just whip them up in a glass with a fork)*
1 teaspoon baking soda
1 teaspoon cream of tartar
1 teaspoon salt
½ teaspoon peppermint extract
4 and ¼ cups flour *(don't sift - pack it down in the cup when you measure it)*
3 or 4 drops red food coloring *(enough to make the dough bright pink)*
2 cups *(11- or 12-ounce package)* white chocolate or vanilla baking chips *(I used Nestlé)*

½ cup white *(granulated)* sugar in a small bowl for coating cookie dough balls
Hershey's Candy Cane Kisses *(or any soft, pink peppermint candy)* to decorate

Hannah's 1st Note: If you want to make these cookies extra crunchy, use either white or red decorators sugar when you roll the cookie balls.

Melt the butter in a large microwave-safe bowl. Add the sugars and the cream, and stir thoroughly. Let the mixture cool to room temperature.

Add the beaten eggs, baking soda, cream of tartar, salt, and peppermint extract, stirring after each addition.

Add the flour in one-cup increments, mixing thoroughly after each increment. Add the 3 or 4 drops of red food coloring and stir well.

Add the chips and stir them in.

Cover the bowl with plastic wrap and refrigerate the dough at least 2 hours *(overnight's even better)*.

When you're ready to bake, preheat your oven to 350 degrees F., rack in the middle position.

Roll the chilled dough into walnut-sized balls with your impeccably clean hands. Put ½ cup white sugar in a small bowl and roll the balls in it to coat them. Place them on a greased cookie sheet *(or a cookie sheet you've*

sprayed with Pam or another nonstick cooking spray), 12 dough balls to a standard-sized sheet. Press the dough balls down just a little so they won't roll off on the floor when you put them in the oven. Place a peppermint candy in the center of each dough ball and place the cookie sheet in the oven.

Bake for 10 to 12 minutes at 350 degrees F. The dough balls will flatten out, all by themselves. Let the cookies cool for 2 minutes on the cookie sheet and then move them to a wire rack to finish cooling.

Yield—approximately 7 to 8 dozen cookies, depending on cookie size.

Chapter Three

Breathing a sigh of relief once she was out of sight, Hannah walked down the hall to the lobby. She found Delores and Carrie sitting at a table, sorting through ornaments.

"You're here!" Delores said, spotting Hannah the instant she came through the door. "We haven't put the lights on yet, dear. Will you help us with that?"

"Of course," Hannah said, but inwardly she was groaning. The tree, which was standing tall and proud in the center of the lobby, was at least fourteen feet high. As she'd feared, there would be a ladder involved.

"Freddy Sawyer should be here any minute," Carrie told her. "He's going to climb the ladder and we want you to hand him the strings of lights. Is that all right with you, Hannah?"

"That's just fine with me!" Hannah said immediately, feeling the jolt of trepidation she'd felt when she'd seen the height of the tree disappear completely. "Have you tested the lights yet?"

"Not yet," Delores said. "We were saving that for you. And you got here just in time. Thank you, dear."

"You're welcome."

"Hannah!"

Hannah turned around to see Freddy Sawyer standing by the lobby door. "Your mother said you were coming here."

"Hi, Freddy," Hannah greeted him. "I'm glad you're still working here."

"Me too!" Freddy grinned back at her. "They all like me here, 'specially Doc. I lift things for him almost every day. I'm strong."

"You certainly are!" Delores told him. Then she turned to Hannah. "Freddy carried all the decorations in here for us. We didn't have to lift a thing."

"My mother said ladies shouldn't lift very much. She died."

"I know." Hannah walked over to give him a pat on the shoulder. "Come on, Freddy. Let's plug in all those strings of lights to make sure they work before we put them on the tree."

Freddy nodded. "That's smart. It's the way my mother used to do it. Then she could re . . . re . . . ." He stopped speaking and looked at Hannah for help.

"So she could replace them?"

"That's it! Then she could re . . . place the bulbs that

didn't work. Let's do it, Hannah. I want to make the tree really pretty this year."

"We will," Hannah promised, leading him over to the box that had *LIGHTS* written on the cover.

As Freddy plugged in the strings and tested them, she thought about how much better he was now that he had a job, and Doc and the nurses had taken him under their wing. Freddy was what some people called *slow* several decades ago. When his mother died, Freddy lived in her little house for a while, but everyone knew he needed some help. The people in Lake Eden liked Freddy and he had plenty of what his mother had called *odd jobs* around town, but it was clear that he needed someone to guide him. That was when Doc Knight had stepped in and offered Freddy a job at the hospital three days a week. Freddy loved working at the hospital and everyone there liked him. Freddy had found his niche.

"I did it, Hannah!" Freddy said proudly, once he'd tested all the lights. "Do you think we'll have enough? This tree is fatter than last year's tree."

"There'll be enough, Freddy," Delores answered, overhearing the question. "I bought extra strings of lights, just in case."

"Shall I start from the top or the bottom?" Freddy asked.

"The top," Carrie said.

"The bottom," Delores said at the same time.

"Oh-oh!" Freddy said, almost under his breath as he turned to Hannah. "What do we do now?"

"I'll start from the bottom and you start from the

top," Hannah said quickly, knowing she was bound to receive complaints from both Carrie and her mother.

"You can't do that!" Carrie said immediately.

"Carrie's right." Delores gave a little nod. "You're bound to come out uneven near the middle of the tree, and that's right at eye level."

"Right. People will notice if it's not symmetrical," Carrie added. "Since you're used to starting from the bottom, you had better do it that way. If you're not used to starting from the top and stringing the lights vertically, it might be more difficult."

Freddy exhaled in relief so loudly that all three women heard him. "Okay. That's what we'll do," he said, "but Hannah will have to walk around the tree to hand me the lights."

"I can do that," Hannah agreed. "I'll string the lights as high as I can reach and you can do the rest."

"While you're doing that, we'll set out all the decorations we want to use," Delores told them.

"And we'll tell you where we want you to hang them," Carrie added.

"The breakable things should go on the upper half of the tree just in case Reverend Bob brings Vespers with him when he visits this year."

Delores laughed. "You're right. I almost forgot about Vespers. He came very close to eating an antique gold ball last year."

"Don't blame Vespers. Dogs play with balls," Freddy pointed out. "We'll put those on the top half where Vespers can't reach them. I really like him. He wears a little

Santa hat and all the patients like to pet him and give him treats."

Hannah chuckled. Vespers usually spent nights at the hospital if there were young patients who needed to stay over Christmastime. He slept in the corner of the child's hospital room on a bed that Reverend Bob brought, and the young patients seemed to find comfort in that. There was one drawback though. The children gave Vespers so many little treats that he gained weight over the holidays. Grandma Knudson, Reverend Bob's grandmother and housekeeper, had told Hannah that she needed to put Vespers on a diet after every Christmas season he spent at the hospital.

With all four of them working, the huge Christmas tree was decorated in less than an hour. Freddy went to close the lobby door. They'd all agreed that they didn't want anyone to see the tree fully lighted before the official ceremony.

"Beautiful!" Delores breathed, as Hannah stepped on the foot switch that was attached to the extension cord.

"Yes, it is," Carrie agreed. "I think it's even better than last year."

"Pretty," Freddy said, but his voice sounded a bit hoarse.

Hannah looked at him, realized that he had tears in his eyes, and walked over to slip her arm around his shoulders. "Does the tree make you miss your mother?" she asked.

Freddy didn't say anything. He just nodded, but he gave her a little smile.

"Your mother would be very proud of you, Freddy. The tree looks beautiful."

"Let's do the staff lunchroom next," Delores suggested. "I have a big wreath to hang in there and a little tree for the table where they keep the coffeepot." She turned to Freddy. "Do you think you could hang some big Christmas ornaments from the ceiling the way you did last year?"

Freddy smiled. "Sure. I know how to do it now, and I like to climb ladders."

Delores looked at Freddy gratefully. "Well, I don't and neither does Carrie. We're glad you're helping us, Freddy."

Freddy looked proud as he picked up the boxes that Delores indicated and led the way to the lunchroom. They left Freddy there to finish up and went off to decorate the patients' rooms.

"Let's split up," Carrie suggested. "It'll go faster that way. We're doing each room the same, aren't we, Delores?"

"Yes. We'll do the first one together, so that Hannah can see what to do, and then we'll split up."

Hannah nodded. "That sounds like a plan to me. Where shall we meet up when we're finished?"

"The lobby," Delores told her. "Then all three of us will go to decorate Doc's office."

It took several hours to complete the hospital rooms. By the time she finished, Hannah was tired of stretching and bending. She hurried back to the staff lunchroom to get a rejuvenating cup of coffee and carried it to the lobby to wait for her mother and Carrie.

Christmas music was playing softly over the loud-speakers in the lobby and Hannah leaned back in her chair and closed her eyes. Even though she'd gotten a full night's sleep, she was tired. And although she loved providing sweet treats for her customers, she sometimes wished that she could take a little time off during her favorite holidays. Baking was always a joy for her. The scent of vanilla, chocolate, and spices was practically an addiction, but there were times when she wished that she could take a little time for herself. Today had been one of those days. Helping her mother and Carrie decorate was a welcome break, and Hannah found she was relaxed for the first time since the overwhelming holiday orders had begun to pour into The Cookie Jar.

Listening to the Christmas music brought happy childhood memories. She remembered stretching out under the branches on the Christmas tree and gazing up at the colored lights. It was an early memory, back before Andrea was born. It was so pretty, she had begged to stay there instead of going up to her bedroom to sleep. Her mother had objected, claiming that regular bedtimes were good for children, and that Hannah had already stayed up too long. Luckily for Hannah, her father had overruled Delores. And when she'd finally fallen to sleep, her father had carried her up the stairs and tucked her into bed.

Memories of her father brought tears to Hannah's eyes and she wiped them away with the back of her hand. He had died several years ago while she was in college working on her doctorate, but she still missed him. Lars Swensen had been a loving father, full of fun, and never so busy that he didn't have time for his children. Even though he'd worked a full day in the hardware store he owned, he'd never been too tired to attend a school play, take them on long drives through the countryside to see the fall leaves, or play games in the backyard with them. He had died several years ago, but Hannah missed him as much now as she had back then.

"Frosty the Snowman" played over the loudspeaker and Hannah began to smile as another, happier memory surfaced. It had been a sunny winter afternoon and her father had told her to put on her parka and snow pants because they were going out to play in the snow. Andrea had been very young, so Delores had stayed in the house with her, but Hannah and her father had gone out to build a snowman outside the living room picture window. The snow had been the perfect consistency, sticky enough to roll into large balls that left patches of bare frozen lawn. They'd rolled three balls, one large, one medium-sized, and one, Hannah's ball, small enough for the head. Her father had stacked them up so that Delores and Andrea could see.

Hannah remembered hearing a tapping on the glass of the window and turning to see her mother holding up an old top hat and the broom she used to sweep the back porch.

"Go get the hat and the broom from your mother," her father had instructed, and Hannah had hurried to the front door. Delores had handed over the things she found for their snowman and Hannah had rushed back to give them to her father.

"Will he have a face?" Hannah had asked after her father had perched the hat on top of the smallest snowball.

"Yes. I've got buttons for his eyes right here," he told her, patting his jacket pocket. "Let's go inside and ask your mother if she has something we can use for his nose."

Hannah had rushed back to the door with her father, but before they could open it, Delores stepped out with several vegetables in her hand. "I've got a little cucumber, a mushroom, and a carrot," she told Lars. "Which one do you think will work best for a nose?"

"Hannah?" her father asked, turning to her. "Which one would you like to use?"

"The carrot," Hannah said immediately, remembering the picture of Frosty, the snowman shown on the Christmas paper her mother had used to wrap her presents.

"That's a good choice," her father complimented her, and then he turned to Delores. "Go back inside, honey. It's cold out here."

· Delores handed the carrot to Hannah and stepped back inside. "I'll put on some hot chocolate for you two," she promised before she shut the door.

"Our snowman doesn't have any arms," Hannah reminded her father. "And he doesn't have any legs, either."

"We'll pretend that he's sitting on his legs," Lars explained, "and I'm going to get two branches for his arms."

Hannah watched as her father went to the lilac bush in the corner of the lawn and broke off two long branches. "Will those work?" she asked him.

"I think so. Just watch while I attach them."

Once the branches were in place, Hannah began to smile. "It's perfect," she told her father. "I like our snowman, Dad."

"So do I, but you have to do one more thing before we go back inside."

"What's that?"

"You have to choose his name. We can't have a snowman without a name."

Hannah thought for a moment and then she began to smile. "Chilly," she said.

"You're cold?"

"No, Dad. His name is Chilly."

"That's perfect," Lars had told her, slipping his arm around her shoulders and leading her back to the door. "Let's go see if your mother had time to make that hot chocolate for us."

Memories of hot chocolate with miniature marshmallows floating on top brought a smile to Hannah's face. She shut her eyes, remembering how comforting it had been to sit next to her father and mother at the kitchen table and enjoy the rich chocolate flavor.

"Hannah? Are you awake?" a female voice asked.

Hannah opened her eyes and stared up at the young woman who was standing next to her. "Yes. I'm awake."

"I'm Rachael," the young woman said, sitting down in the chair next to Hannah. "You probably don't remember me. I'm Lisa's cousin."

"Nice to meet you," Hannah said, smiling back. "Did you bring the cupcakes?"

"Yes. Actually . . . I brought two kinds of cupcakes. I brought yours and the ones Lisa let me bake this morning. I wanted you to taste mine to see if you like them."

"I'd love to try one. What kind are they?"

"They're called White Chocolate Eggnog Cupcakes. My college roommate's older sister works at the Kraft test kitchens. She sends us some of their new recipes and we test them for her. How about some fresh coffee to go with it? You take it black, don't you?"

"Yes, I do. How did you know?"

"Lisa mentioned that you'd probably want coffee about now, so the hospital cook put on coffee for us."

Hannah watched as Rachael hurried back to the kitchen to get her coffee and one of the Kraft test kitchen cupcakes. In less time than she'd expected, Rachael was back. She was carrying a tray with three cupcakes, three cups, and a carafe of coffee.

"Here they are," Rachael said, lifting one cupcake onto a napkin and pouring a cup of black coffee for Hannah. "Let me know if you like the cupcake and I'll text my roommate so she can tell her sister."

"Who are the other cupcakes for?" Hannah asked,

reaching for her cupcake so that she could remove the paper.

"Your mother and her friend. I ran into them in the corridor and they said they'd be here in a couple of minutes."

"These cupcakes smell like Christmas," Hannah said, enjoying the scent of eggnog spices. "Do you use real eggnog when you make them?"

"Yes, the commercial kind. There's a cup of it in the batter along with a little extra nutmeg. I really hope you like them, Hannah. My roommate and I made them right after her sister sent us the recipe, and I brought some to Lisa and Herb."

Hannah took a bite of the cupcake and her eyebrows shot up in surprise. "There's whipped cream inside!" she said.

"Actually, it's Cool Whip. And it's mixed with cream cheese, butter, rum extract, and powdered sugar. You have to refrigerate it while the cupcakes are cooling, and then you inject some of it inside each cupcake."

Hannah smiled. "It sure makes the cupcake more interesting."

Rachael looked pleased. "That's exactly what my roommate's sister said!"

"You use the same combination on top for a frosting, don't you?"

Rachael nodded. "That's right, except you sprinkle a little nutmeg on the top after you frost the cupcakes. Lisa thought you could use the recipe in the coffee shop, but there's a little drawback."

"What's that?"

"You have to keep the cupcakes refrigerated because of the Cool Whip."

"Of course you do," Hannah said. "That's not really a drawback, Rachael. We have a walk-in cooler in our kitchen at The Cookie Jar."

"I can help you make them the first time," Rachael offered. "I discovered some shortcuts."

"Shortcuts can be very helpful. Which one saves the most time?"

Rachael thought about that for a moment and then she smiled. "Not having to use a pastry bag."

It took Hannah a moment, but then she understood. "To inject the Cool Whip frosting inside the cupcake?"

"That's right. I'm really not very good at using a pastry bag, so I tried to think of what else I could use. And I discovered another way that I could do it."

"Tell me."

"The cupcakes have to be cool before you inject the Cool Whip in the middle. You need something that'll hold the right amount of Cool Whip and it has to have a hollow point on the end."

Hannah nodded, going through the possibilities. "A large syringe or a turkey baster?"

"Those would work, but there's something that's easier. It's called a Jell-O shot injector."

"What's a Jell-O shot?"

Rachael looked at her in disbelief. "Didn't you ever go to college parties?"

Hannah shook her head, "Not really, I was too busy studying. "

"OK fine, let me explain. A Jell-O shot is Jell-O made with booze instead of water. You pour shots into little plastic shot glasses and refrigerate it. Then you set them out on a tray and everyone parties with them. You can use any flavor Jell-O, but most people prefer to use vodka or tequila because they don't change the color of the Jell-O."

"We're here!" Delores called out, coming in the doorway with Carrie in time to save Hannah from the necessity of making a comment. Jell-O shots didn't sound very appealing to her, but the Jell-O shot injectors were interesting. She'd never been very proficient with a pastry bag, so she would ask Michelle to look for the Jell-O shot injectors online.

"We hurried through the last two rooms," Carrie said, sitting down on the couch by the coffee table.

"Yes we did," Delores added. "We're looking forward to tasting your White Chocolate Eggnog Cupcakes, Rachael."

"Well, here they are," Rachael told them, gesturing toward the tray on the coffee table. "Help yourselves, ladies. I really hope you like them as much as my roommate and I do."

For at least fifteen seconds, no one spoke. They were too busy eating and it was clear that they were enjoying every bite.

"Wonderful!" Carrie was the first to offer her opinion. "They're so light and fluffy, I could eat at least one more."

Delores nodded. "I agree. And the whipped cream in the center is just delicious."

"Hannah?" Rachael looked slightly worried as she turned to Hannah. "What did you think?"

"They're absolutely delicious, Rachael. And I think we're going to sell tons of cupcakes, if you teach me how to use a Jell-O shot injector."

WHITE CHOCOLATE EGGNOG CUPCAKES

Preheat oven to 350 degrees F., rack in the middle position.

Cupcake Ingredients:

1 box white cake mix *(the kind that will make a 9-inch by 13-inch cake or a 2-layer cake)* with or without pudding in the mix *(I used Duncan Hines)*

1 cup eggnog

⅓ cup vegetable oil *(use pure vegetable oil, not canola, or olive oil, or corn oil)*

3 large egg whites

½ teaspoon ground nutmeg *(freshly ground is best, of course)*

1 package *(4 ounces by weight)* Baker's White Chocolate, chopped *(or ½ cup white chocolate or vanilla chips, chopped)*

Frosting Ingredients:

1 package *(8 ounces by weight)* cream cheese, softened *(NOT whipped cream cheese—I used Philadelphia in the silver package)*

¼ cup salted butter *(½ stick, 2 ounces)*, softened

½ teaspoon rum extract *(if you can't find it, substitute vanilla or brandy extract)*

3 cups powdered (confectioners') sugar *(no need to sift unless it has big lumps)*

1 cup original Cool Whip, thawed *(measure this—even a small tub contains more than a cup)*

½ cup additional powdered sugar to use, if needed, to thicken frosting

½ teaspoon ground nutmeg *(freshly ground is best, of course)* to sprinkle on top of each frosted cupcake

Before you begin to make these cupcakes, prepare your cupcake pans by lining them with cupcake papers. (You will need 2 cupcake pans, the kind that will hold 12 regular-size cupcakes). If you use the kind of cupcake papers with foil on the outside, you don't have to use more than one. If you don't, use double cupcake papers so it's easier to peel off the paper before you eat them.

Hannah's 1st Note: Both Lisa and I still call them "cupcake tins" when we bake cupcakes at The Cookie Jar, even though they are no longer made of tin. Lisa's mother used to refer to them that way and so did my Great-Grandmother Elsa.

To Make the Cupcakes:

Hannah's 2ⁿᵈ Note: It's possible to make these cupcakes by hand, but it's a lot easier with an electric mixer!

Open the package of cake mix and dump *(yes, that's a baking term at The Cookie Jar)* it into the bowl of an electric mixer.

Add the cup of eggnog and mix it in on LOW speed.

Add the oil and continue to mix on LOW speed.

Crack the eggs, separate the whites from the yolks, and add the whites to your bowl. (You can put the yolks in an airtight bowl, refrigerate them, and add them to scrambled eggs in the morning.)

Mix in the egg whites on LOW speed.

Add the half-teaspoon of ground nutmeg and mix that in at LOW speed.

Scrape down the sides of the mixing bowl and remove it from the mixer.

Give your cupcake batter a final stir by hand with a wooden spoon or your favorite mixing spoon.

Use the mixing spoon to stir in the chopped white chocolate pieces.

Hannah's 3rd Note: Lisa and I chop the white chocolate in the bowl of a food processor. We chop it in an on-and-off motion with the steel blade until the pieces are the size of coarse gravel.

If you haven't done so already, preheat your oven to 350 degrees F., rack in the middle position.

Transfer the batter to the paper-lined cupcake cups, filling them ¾ full.

Hannah's 4th Note: The easiest way I've found to transfer the cupcake batter to the baking cups is to pour it into a measuring cup with a spout. Then all you have to do is pour and that prevents batter spill in the spaces between the cupcake cups. You can also use a 2-Tablespoon scooper to do this, but you'll have to be careful that it doesn't drip.

Bake your cupcakes at 350 degrees F. for 18 to 20 minutes. To test for doneness, insert a cake tester, thin wooden skewer, or long toothpick in the center of a test cupcake. Pull out the tester and if any sticky dough clings to it, your cupcakes are not yet done. Bake them for an-

other 2 or 3 minutes and then test again, using a different cupcake.

When your cupcakes test as done, remove the cupcake pans from the oven and set them on cold stovetop burners or wire racks.

Begin to make the frosting now. The instructions for the frosting are below:

To Make the Frosting:

Rinse out the bowl of your electric mixer and dry it with paper towels. Do the same with the beater(s).

When everything is back in place, put the softened cream cheese in the bottom of the bowl.

Add the softened, salted butter and the rum extract.

Turn the mixer on LOW and mix until the ingredients are thoroughly blended together.

Beat in powdered sugar at LOW speed, one cup at a time.

Turn off the mixer, move the bowl to the kitchen counter, and stir in the cup of thawed Cool Whip.

Cover the bowl with plastic wrap and place it in the refrigerator for at least 30 minutes.

If you choose to use a pastry bag with a large, round tip, spoon the cold frosting into the pastry bag.

Hannah's 1st Frosting Note: If you'd rather not use a pastry bag, you can use a bulb turkey baster or a cupcake injector (similar to a large syringe without a needle). The cupcake injector is sometimes called a Jell-O shot injector and is available online.

Insert the point of the pastry bag (or cupcake injector) into the center of each cooled cupcake and inject approximately 1 Tablespoon of frosting inside the cupcake.

Hannah's 2nd Frosting Note: Don't worry about the little hole that the pastry bag or the cupcake injector will leave in the top of each cupcake. It will be covered with frosting.

Hannah's 3rd Frosting Note: If the frosting is too thin, this is where you will mix in the additional half-cup of powdered sugar to thicken it.

Spread the tops of your White Chocolate Eggnog Cupcakes with the remaining frosting. *(If you're using the pastry bag, just pipe it on and then spread it out with a frosting knife.)*

Store the frosted cupcakes in the refrigerator until you're ready to serve them, then sprinkle on the extra nutmeg just before you plate them.

Yield: 18 to 22 regular-size cupcakes, depending on how full you fill the cupcake papers. Both adults and children will enjoy these light, tasty, and flavorful treats. Serve with cups of hot chocolate or strong coffee.

Hannah's 4th Frosting Note: Most grocery stores consider eggnog to be a seasonal item, and it is available only over the Thanksgiving and Christmas holidays. I've included my recipe for English Eggnog, just in case you want to make these cupcakes at other times of the year. The recipe follows:

This recipe was exclusively created for Hannah Swensen by

ENGLISH EGGNOG

Ingredients:

3 large eggs
½ cup whipping cream *(heavy cream)*
¼ cup white *(granulated)* sugar
1 cup whole milk
½ cup half-and-half *(light cream)*
2 teaspoons rum extract *(you can substitute brandy extract)*
½ teaspoon ground cinnamon
¼ teaspoon ground cloves
¼ teaspoon ground cardamom

Instructions:

Crack the eggs and separate the whites and the yolks into two bowls.

Beat the egg whites with a whisk or an electric mixer until they form soft peaks.

Hannah's 1st Note: Soft peaks are peaks that droop over a bit when you dip the flat side of a rubber spatula into the mixture and pull it up.

Pour the whipping cream into a bowl and beat it until it forms soft peaks. You can do this with a whisk or with an electric mixer.

Fold the whipping cream into the beaten egg whites and set the bowl aside on the counter.

Beat the egg yolks until they are light colored and fluffy.

Mix the sugar, whole milk, half-and-half, and rum extract into the bowl with the egg yolks.

Fold the contents of the bowl with the egg white and whipping cream mixture into the bowl with the egg yolk mixture.

Carefully, so that you do not flatten this creamy mixture, stir in the ground cinnamon, ground cloves, and ground cardamom.

At this point, the mixture can be refrigerated in a tightly covered container for up to 12 hours.

Hannah's 2nd Note: To use in White Chocolate Eggnog Cupcakes, stir the mixture, measure out one cup, and use it in the cupcake recipe. Use the rest of the eggnog mixture for a refreshing drink.

Hannah's 3rd Note: If you like, you can add rum or brandy to the eggnog mixture to serve as a delicious adult beverage.

Yield: Approximately 3 cups of delicious, refreshing eggnog.

Chapter Four

"You're coming out to the Lake Eden Inn with us, aren't you, Hannah?" Carrie asked as they drove into Lake Eden and turned down Main Street.

"Well . . ." Hannah said, wondering how she could politely refuse. She was tired and all she really wanted to do was go home, get into her warmest pajamas, and go to sleep with Moishe purring beside her.

"Doc Knight specifically invited you, Hannah," Delores reminded her.

"I know, but . . ."

"Carrie and I will take my car and you can drive your cookie truck. Then, if you get really tired, you can excuse yourself right after dinner and drive home."

Hannah sighed. She knew when she had been beaten. Doc Knight wanted her to go, Carrie wanted her to go, and Delores wanted her to go. "All right," she said, doing her best to be cheerful. "Let's drive past Al's office first to see if he's still here. We should stop in and put him on the lookout for an antique storage place for you."

It didn't take long to get to town. Lake Eden Realty was directly across from The Cookie Jar, and when Hannah noticed that the lights were off and her bakery and coffee shop were closed for the evening, she gave a little sigh of disappointment. She'd been hoping to check in with Lisa to make sure that everything had run smoothly. Obviously it had, or Lisa would still be inside, mixing up cookie dough for the next morning.

Hannah hadn't been planning to go into the real estate office with her mother and Carrie, but now she had no excuse. She told herself that it might be for the best, that Al, who had a reputation as a fast talker, might convince them to rent something totally unsuitable for their needs.

"Oh, good. You're going with us," Delores said when Hannah got out of her cookie truck. "Carrie and I were hoping you would since you've seen how many antiques I have in that old shed your father built for me."

Hannah smiled. It was nice to be needed and flattering to know that her mother valued her opinion. She pulled open the door and held it open so that Delores and Carrie could precede her inside.

"Hello, Al," Delores greeted him. "I'm glad you're working late. We have something we need to discuss with you."

"Let me guess," Al said, motioning to the two chairs in front of his desk and pushing a third chair into place for Hannah. "You want to buy three adjacent mansions . . . is that right?"

Delores laughed and so did Carrie. Hannah managed a smile. Al always joked around with potential clients. "Tell Al what you need," Hannah said to Delores.

"It's like this, Al . . ." Delores began. "I have all the antiques I've been buying for the past twenty years stored in an old shed that Lars built for me when we bought our house."

"And I have way too many antiques in my house," Carrie added.

Both women turned to look at Hannah and Hannah knew they wanted her to describe what they needed. "What they really need to rent is a vacant storefront, a large one with a back room to use for refurnishing the antiques and another area to place the antiques that are already in good condition. Of course, it has to be heated and air conditioned, and have excellent lighting, especially in the area where they'll be working. It should definitely have a bathroom, and it would be wonderful if the plumbing would support a large utility sink in the workroom."

"Anything else?" Al asked, and Hannah noticed that he looked amused. This made her slightly nervous, but she went on with her explanation.

"Yes. It would be a nice bonus if it had a small kitchenette where they could make coffee and have lunch. And the door to the workroom should be large enough to bring in big pieces of furniture and handcarts."

"That's it?" Al asked, and Hannah noticed that he looked even more amused.

"Yes, that's it," Hannah replied. "We just wanted to stop in and give you a heads-up so you could keep your eye out for a property like that."

"Got it," Al said, nodding as he pulled out a drawer on his desk. "I think I have the perfect place for you."

"Wonderful!" Delores clapped her hands.

"This is so exciting!" Carrie looked as if she wanted to jump out of her chair and hug Al.

"This property isn't too far away, is it?" Hannah asked him.

"Oh, no. It's very conveniently located."

"Perfect." Delores began to smile. "You're a real magician, Al. When can we see this property?"

Al glanced up at the clock on his wall. "Unfortunately, I can't take you there tonight. My daughter and her husband have invited us over for dinner, and my wife will be in a snit if I don't get home in fifteen minutes or so."

"So Mother and Carrie can see it tomorrow?" Hannah asked him.

"No, they can see it now." Al handed a key ring to Delores. "All three of you can go to look at it. The heat is on and so is the electricity. Take a look around and come back in the morning to tell me if you think it's suitable for you."

"Perfect!" Delores said, taking the key ring.

"Maybe, but we're supposed to meet Doc Knight for

dinner," Hannah reminded her, and then she turned to Al. "How far away is this place?"

"Not far at all. It's right across the street, next to Bertie's Cut 'n Curl."

Hannah's jaw dropped. She snapped it back closed so that she wouldn't resemble a fish on a hook, and blinked several times. "You mean . . . two doors down from me?!"

"Exactly right," Al said, chuckling at the look of shock on Hannah's face. "It's just two doors down from The Cookie Jar. That'll be nice and close to you, Hannah. Go take a look."

"Let's go!" Carrie said, jumping to her feet. "It sounds wonderful!"

"It certainly does!" Delores echoed her excitement. "Come on, dear. Let's go."

Right across the street, Hannah's mind echoed Al's words as she followed Delores and Carrie out the door. *Very convenient. Next door to Bertie's Cut 'n Curl. Just two doors down from The Cookie Jar.* What would her day be like if Delores and Carrie stopped by every morning for coffee? Or even worse, came by to use the restroom because the one in the antique storage building didn't meet their needs? What if . . .

Hannah gave herself a mental shake. She was being silly. They were storing the antiques in the building they wanted to rent. Her mother and Carrie wouldn't be down here every day, refinishing tables or upholstering chairs and davenports. It was silly for her to feel that her "at work privacy," if there was such a thing, was being invaded. She should be glad if the vacant building turned out to be perfect for them.

"Here we are," Delores said, inserting the key in the front door. She attempted to turn it to unlock the door, but nothing happened. "This must be the wrong key," she remarked, and tried the second key on the ring. Again, nothing happened. The key went into the lock, but it wouldn't turn. "We can't get in!" she said, sounding very upset. "Al must have given us the wrong set of keys."

Hannah turned around to look at Al's office. The lights were off and his car was no longer parked in front of the building. She remembered hearing a car start up and drive away when her mother was trying the second key. "Al's gone already," she said.

"Oh, drat!" Delores exclaimed, coming as close to swearing as she ever did. "What are we going to do now?"

"Try the back door?" Hannah suggested. "There are two keys on the ring. Neither one works on the front door, but one of them might work on the back door."

Even in the dim light from the streetlight on the corner, Hannah could see her mother roll her eyes. "Of course," she said, sounding exasperated that she hadn't thought of it herself. "Let's go try the back."

Since the snow wasn't shoveled on the walkway that led around the building, they walked to the corner and went down the alley to the back. Once there, Delores tried the first key again.

"It works!" she said, all smiles. "Let's go see what's inside."

Hannah let her mother lead the way and she followed Carrie inside. "I can't find the light switch."

"Wait a moment, Mother," Hannah said. "I've got the flashlight on my cell phone."

Hannah, who had followed her mother and Carrie into the back room, switched on the light on her cell phone. She shined the light on the left of the back door, but there was no light switch. "Here it is," she said, spotting it to the right. She flicked the switch on, but absolutely nothing happened. "I think the bulb's burned out," Hannah said, beginning to frown.

"Hannah, we'll be all right as long as your light holds out. Did you remember to charge your phone this morning?"

"I think so," Hannah said, hoping she had.

"Then walk beside me and shine the light ahead," Delores suggested. "We'll walk through here and go to the front room to check that out."

Hannah did as her mother requested, hoping that she wouldn't run out of battery power before they'd finished. If that happened, it might be difficult navigating the back room and getting outside again.

"Wait!" Delores grabbed Hannah's arm. "I thought I saw something over there."

"Over where?" Carrie asked her.

"Over by that pile of rags in the corner," Delores said, pointing to the corner of the back room.

Hannah shined her light in that direction and illuminated the rags. They watched carefully for several moments, but there was no movement.

"It must have been your imagination," Carrie said.

"It could have been a rat," Delores said. "This store went out of business at least two years ago. It was a little lunch place that served sandwiches, so there must have been food around."

Carrie drew her breath in quickly, and Hannah knew that her mother had made Carrie nervous again. "I'll go check it out," Hannah promised.

"But . . . you'll have to take your light with you," Delores said, and Hannah noticed that she also sounded a bit nervous.

"Do you have your phone with you, Carrie?" Hannah asked her.

"Why, yes. It's right here in my purse. Shine your flashlight over here and I'll get it out."

With the aid of Hannah's cell phone flashlight, Carrie opened her large purse and located her phone. "It's not as new as yours is," Carrie said, holding it out to Hannah. "If you're thinking about turning on my flashlight, I'm not sure I have one."

"Let's see," Hannah said, turning on Carrie's phone and examining the apps. "You have one," she said, turning on the flashlight and handing it back to Carrie.

"Oh, good. Delores and I will stay right here then."

Hannah was grinning as she walked over to the pile of rags. It was clear that Carrie was still nervous about marauding rodents. As she approached the pile, she realized that the rags were covering something large and bulky. Did the owner leave some piece of equipment behind when they left Lake Eden? "There's something under here," she reported. "Hold on a second and I'll take a look."

"Bu . . . bu . . . but be careful, Hannah," Delores warned, quite unnecessarily. "You don't know what's under there!"

The rags were tucked around something and Hannah managed to pull one corner free. She couldn't loosen it without using both hands, and that meant that she couldn't hold her phone flashlight. "Shine your flashlight over here, Carrie," she instructed. "I'll need both hands to see what's here."

Carrie aimed the light at the pile of rags, Hannah put her cell phone down on the floor, and pulled on the largest piece. It was a remnant of a blanket, and it was tucked around something large. "I got it," she said, pulling the edge loose and flipping it back.

"What is it?" Carrie asked her.

"It's . . ." Hannah stopped speaking and swallowed hard. "It's someone's leg."

"You mean . . . a person?" Carrie asked.

"Yes." Hannah pulled the blanket up higher. "I think so. . . ."

"You mean it's a *body*!?" Delores sounded horrified. "Get away from it, Hannah! We have to call someone."

"Yes," Hannah agreed. And then she spotted something that made her draw in her breath sharply. "It's moving."

"Are you sure?" Carrie asked her.

"Yes, I hear . . ."

"Oh, my!" Carrie sounded very upset. "What should we do?"

"Wait," Hannah said, holding up her hand. "Call Doc! It's the homeless man I saw this morning! And he's still alive!"

Chapter Five

O f course, all three of them had gone to the hospital, hoping that the man would be all right. They had taken seats in the waiting room and Doc had promised to come out there to let them know how his newest patient was doing.

"I hope he's all right," Hannah said, shifting a bit in her chair. "Did I tell you how nice and polite he was this morning?"

Delores nodded. "You told us, dear. This whole thing is very unfortunate."

Carrie glanced at her watch. "He's been in the emergency room for more than forty-five minutes. I hope it's nothing terribly serious."

"So do I," Delores said. "From what Hannah told us, that poor man deserves a break. If he's going to be all right, I might just hire him to tear down that shed when we're finished moving our antiques to a larger space."

"And I need someone to help me get down some

boxes from the shelves in my basement," Carrie agreed. "You have things for him to do, don't you, Hannah?"

"I'm sure I do," Hannah agreed. "And if I don't, I'll think of something. Florence might have work for him at the grocery store. He's tall enough to help her re-arrange things on her top shelves."

They sat there in silence for a moment, thinking about the man they'd found and hoping he'd be all right. They didn't really know him, but Hannah realized that they all wanted to know his story and to find a way to help him. She hadn't been able to give Doc and his staff any real information on the man's background. Since she didn't know the man's name, his identity, where he'd come from, or why he was in Lake Eden, everything about John Doe, the name Doc and his staff had given the man, was a complete mystery.

"I hope they can find out more about him," Delores said, and Hannah suspected all three of them were thinking along the same lines.

"So do I," Carrie agreed. Then she looked over at Hannah. "You're good at solving mysteries, Hannah. Maybe you ought to take him on as your next project."

"What a wonderful idea!" Delores agreed. "Hannah should stop getting involved in murder cases and con-centrate on finding out more about our John Doe."

"Here comes Norman," Carrie said, smiling as she recognized the man who was walking toward them down the hallway. "I called him and asked him to give you a ride home, Hannah."

Hannah sighed. It was true that she needed a ride

back to town since she'd ridden to the hospital with Carrie and Delores, but Carrie had seized this opportunity like a rottweiler with a big, meaty bone. Carrie was always trying to pair her with Norman. Hannah guessed it was a natural reaction because they liked each other and they had been dating, but their relationship wasn't as serious as Carrie hoped it would be. Both Norman and Hannah knew this. They'd even talked about it a couple of times. Both Delores and Carrie wanted them to settle down and give them grandchildren.

Hannah smiled at Norman as he walked into the waiting room. He wasn't what Delores and Carrie would have referred to as a heartthrob, but he was nice looking. And, as far as Hannah was concerned, Norman's personality and sense of humor were delightful. Norman knew how to laugh at himself for his foibles.

"Hi, Norman," Hannah greeted him. "Is it snowing out there?"

"Not yet, but they're predicting another inch or two on KCOW-TV."

Hannah's smile grew wider. She knew exactly what Norman would say next.

"It's the sole job in Lake Eden where you only have to be right thirty percent of the time and they don't fire you!"

"That's not very nice, Norman," Carrie chided him, but Hannah noticed that Carrie was beginning to smile. "Forecasting weather is an unpredictable occupation."

"That's right," Delores agreed. "But I've noticed that Rayne Phillips seems to be wrong more than the weathermen on other channels."

Just then Doc Knight entered the waiting room. He walked straight over to Delores and put his arm around her shoulders. "Don't worry, Lori," he told her. "The man you found is going to be all right."

"Wonderful!" Delores gave him a relieved smile. "We were all worried. Are you going to keep him overnight? I don't think he has anywhere else to go. Hannah said he came around to The Cookie Jar this morning, looking for work."

"I suspected as much," Doc said, giving her a hug before he turned to Hannah. "What did you tell him?"

"I told him to come back tomorrow morning and I might have some work for him. It was really sad, Doc. He was shaking and he was so thin, I gave him a bag of cupcakes and poured him some coffee with cream and sugar." Hannah stopped speaking and gave a little sigh. "He's a nice man, Doc. Very polite. And he called me *ma'am*."

"That's what he called my nurse when she came in to check his vitals. I wonder how he got to Lake Eden and where he came from."

"Did you ask him?" Norman clearly wanted to know. "There may be someone out there we could contact."

Hannah gave Norman a grateful look. He was obviously as concerned about the man as she was.

"We'll try to get more information in the morning," Doc promised. "He's resting now. I want him to keep warm and give him a full night's sleep. He's still in pretty bad shape."

"Malnourished?" Carrie asked.

"Yes. He was only a few steps away from starvation. That cream and sugar and the food you gave him this morning probably staved that off for a few hours. Our mission here is to stabilize him so we can run some tests to find out if there's any permanent damage. I think you ladies found him just in time to prevent his total collapse."

"Oh, thank goodness for that!" Delores exclaimed, giving Doc a big smile. "I don't even want to think of what would have happened if Carrie and I hadn't decided to rent a place to store our antiques!"

Doc reached out to give Delores's shoulder a comforting pat and Hannah noticed that her mother covered Doc's hand with hers. They smiled at each other, and Hannah was grateful that Doc was in their lives. He had been a good friend of her father's and he still was their closest family friend. Doc had delivered all three of the Swensen sisters starting with Hannah, who was the oldest, Andrea, who was the middle Swensen sister, and Michelle, the youngest. He'd been their pediatrician until the three sisters grew up, and he was still their family doctor.

"Can I peek in his room before we go?" Hannah asked Doc. "I promise I won't go in or anything like that. I'd feel better if I just looked in on him. I'm not really sure why."

"It's because you have a good heart, Hannah," Doc told her. "I'll let you peek in, but that's it. What he needs right now is nourishment, rest, and peace of mind. Although I don't really have any way of knowing exactly what happened to him, I think he's been through a trauma or two and his body and mind can both do with a little worry-free time."

"Can we visit him tomorrow?" Delores asked.

"Perhaps. I'll call and let you know in the morning. He's safe tonight. You don't need to worry about him while he's with us. And in the meantime, I think you could use a little rest and relaxation, too. You and your mother and Carrie did a lot to help us out at the hospital today. Everyone enjoyed our tree lighting ceremony and it really looks like Christmas around here."

"I'm so glad you like the decorations," Delores said.

"I want all of you to come with me," Doc said, motioning for them to stand up. "I'll walk you past his room, but I want you to be totally silent. I'm willing to bet that our John Doe hasn't had a good night's sleep in a month of Sundays, and we're going to make sure he gets it tonight. And then I'm going to take you out to dinner the way I'd planned to do." He turned to Norman. "You too, Norman. I'm outnumbered by females here and I need another man to keep me company."

In less than twenty minutes, they were all seated at a table in Lake Eden's only gourmet restaurant, Sally and Dick Laughlin's Lake Eden Inn. Since none of them had eaten anything in hours, they were all hungry.

"I have a new appetizer for you to try tonight," Sally told them.

Since Sally's appetizers were always wonderful, Hannah began to smile. "Please tell us about it," she said.

"Or better yet, just bring it," Doc countered her. "You've never made anything that wasn't great, Sally."

"That's because you didn't know me when Dick and I were first married."

"I don't believe it," Delores said. "I'm sure you were born knowing how to make delicious food."

"Oh, no I wasn't!" Sally said, shaking her head. "The first week after our honeymoon, I tried to make Dick's favorite breakfast, eggs, sausage, and baking powder biscuits. The eggs were fine and the sausage was the precooked kind that I just had to heat up, but the biscuits were a disaster! Instead of buying the ones in the refrigerated section at the grocery store, I decided to make them from scratch."

"That could be difficult," Hannah commiserated, "especially if you'd never made them before."

"It was. They turned out to be just as hard as rocks."

"Dick wasn't angry, was he?" Carrie looked concerned.

"No, not a bit. He moved the kitchen wastebasket across the room, took off the cover, and said he'd take me out to dinner that night if I could make a basket with two of the dozen biscuits I'd baked."

"And you won?" Norman asked.

Sally nodded. "We went out to a fancy French restaurant, and that's where I got the idea for my new Christmas appetizer. It doesn't have a name yet. I'll leave it to you folks to come up with a good name for me."

"Describe it to us," Hannah asked for more information.

"It's Brie with an unusual topping encased in puff pastry. It's really easy to make and you can put it together in advance if you cover and refrigerate it."

"What's the unusual topping?" Hannah asked.

"I won't tell you, but it's one of those tastes that always reminds me of Christmas."

"And you won't tell us what it is?" Delores asked, sounding disappointed.

"No. I'm curious to see if any of you recognize it." Sally took out her order pad and turned to Delores. "I have something special for an entrée tonight and it's not on the menu."

"I love it when you surprise us," Delores said. "What is it?"

"Of course. It's roast goose."

"Oh, I want that!" Carrie said quickly, and then she looked a bit embarrassed. "I'm sorry, Delores. I should have waited until you ordered. It's just that I was so excited to have goose again! I haven't had it since my mother died. We raised geese in our side yard and we used to have roast goose every New Year's Eve."

Delores shuddered slightly. "Did you really kill one of your pet geese?"

"They weren't pets," Carrie explained. "They were mean, nasty birds and they pecked at our feet and legs. They hissed at us and they made a real mess in the side yard. We kids used to have to catch them, put them in the big shed Dad used as a pen, and hose off the yard every day after school. I don't even want to think of the times I slipped and fell in . . ." Carrie stopped in mid-sentence and looked embarrassed again. "Never mind. I shouldn't have brought *that* up. Let's just say that eating roast goose on New Year's Eve was a real payback for us." She turned to look at Sally. "You're not serving Canada geese, are you, Sally?"

"Heavens, no!" Sally shook her head. "The Canada goose is a wild bird and it has to be roasted in an entirely different way."

Hannah was intrigued. "I don't know anything about preparing goose. How are the wild ones different than the domestic ones?"

"There's a lot of fat on domestic geese and you have to drain it off every half hour or so. If you don't, it's almost like deep-frying it. Canada geese are usually very lean and they require larding."

"What's larding?" Doc asked her.

"It's using lard to give wild game birds enough fat to roast well. I generally wrap wild Canada geese in strips of fatty bacon to compensate for the fat they've lost from flying all those miles."

"But don't they taste like bacon then?" Hannah asked her.

"Yes, but most people really like the smoked flavor. Those that don't can use lard. Florence carries pure pig fat at the Red Owl for me. I use it for some cuts of venison when it's too lean and I don't want the smoked taste of bacon for the entrée I'm preparing."

Sally was smiling as she finished taking their orders, told them that she was going in the kitchen to personally start their appetizers, and walked away from the table. Of course they'd all ordered the roast goose. None of them had wanted to miss one of Sally's special entrées.

"This is exciting," Hannah said, smiling. "I've never had roast goose before."

"Neither have I," Norman confessed. "Mother never made it."

"That's because your dad didn't like it," Carrie told him. "And I wasn't sure where you could buy a domestic goose." She turned to Delores. "I don't know anyone around Lake Eden who raises them, do you?"

Delores shook her head. "I don't either. How about you, Doc?"

"No. I've never heard any of my patients mention it. I wonder if Florence could order frozen geese for the store."

"I'll ask her the next time I see her," Hannah promised. "Florence sometimes orders special items for me that she doesn't regularly carry. It can cost a bit extra, since she's not ordering a large quantity, but it's worth it to get what I need right here in Lake Eden."

The conversation flowed, and the subject was mainly the homeless man who was now Doc's patient. They were all concerned about him, but Doc did his best to reassure them.

"He's fairly young, and it looks as though he was in very good shape until recently," Doc told them. "Don't get me wrong. He was in dire straits when you found him, but the three of you rescued him in time."

"Then he'll recover?" Norman asked.

"My guess is yes, but my staff is running non-invasive tests tonight. Then we'll let him rest until morning and reassess his condition."

"Are you ready for your appetizers?" Sally asked, arriving at their table with a waiter who was carrying their beverages. "Doc called ahead to order champagne for you, Delores."

Delores began to smile when she saw the familiar label. "Perrier-Jouët!" she exclaimed. "That's my absolute favorite champagne! How did you know, Doc?"

Doc laughed. "I know everything about you, Lori. Don't forget that I've known you longer than anyone else in this room."

Hannah smiled. She'd heard Doc say that before.

"You'll have a glass, won't you, Carrie?" Delores turned to her friend.

Carrie nodded. "Yes, but just one. I want to do an inventory of my antiques when I get home tonight. Then, if we're serious about finding a place to rent, I'll know how much space my things will take."

"Here's your favorite ginger ale, Norman," Sally said, taking a glass from her busboy's tray and setting it down in front of Norman. "Was I right in guessing what you'd order?"

"You were right," Norman confirmed it. "Thanks, Sally."

"Coffee for you, Doc?" Sally asked, and when he nodded, she gestured to the busboy to pour a cup for him.

"And, Hannah, will you have champagne?"

"Yes, please. It's been a long day and I'd like to relax."

When all the drinks had been delivered, Sally gave a nod to the waiter who was standing behind the busboy, and the waiter stepped forward and placed a covered platter on the table. Sally whisked off the cover, and used the knife to slice the appetizer into pieces.

"It's beautiful, Sally," Hannah said immediately.

"And it smells every bit as good as it looks," Norman added. "What is it?"

"Thank you," Sally said, serving each of them a slice. "Taste it and tell me if you can identify the Christmas topping."

Hannah tasted the appetizer and made a sound of approval. "Good," she managed to say, taking a second bite.

"Can you identify the topping?" Sally asked again.

Hannah shook her head. "I don't recognize it."

"How about you?" Sally turned to Norman, but he shook his head as well. Doc followed suit and so did Carrie.

"It's familiar," Delores said, taking another bite. "I know I've had it before and it was either Thanksgiving or Christmas. And I think it was in a pie that my mother-in-law made."

"You're on the right track," Sally said, sounding pleased as she turned back to Hannah. "Does that give you any ideas, Hannah?"

Hannah thought for a moment, and then a smile spread over her face. "Mincemeat!"

"You're right!" Delores told her. "We went to my husband's mother's house for Thanksgiving when you were barely three years old. She served two pies. One was pumpkin, and the other was mincemeat. She gave us all a half slice of both on the same dessert plate and she called it *Pince Pie*."

"That's cute!" Sally commented. "I wonder if I could somehow incorporate pumpkin in this recipe."

"Don't do it!" Hannah warned her. "Your appetizer is perfect just the way it is. And I think you should call it Christmas Baked Brie."

"Perfect!" Sally gave Hannah a radiant smile. "Now if I could only figure out a second appetizer with sugar plums, I could serve them at the same time. But first I have to figure out what a sugarplum is. Do you know, Hannah?"

Hannah shook her head. "The only thing I know about them is that they're mentioned in the poem ''Twas The Night Before Christmas.'"

"*. . . while visions of sugar-plums danced in their heads,*" Norman quoted.

Sally looked thoughtful. "They must be like candy, or something else that children would like."

"Hold on, and I'll look it up for you," Norman said, taking out his cell phone.

It took several minutes for Norman to research Sally's question between bites of his mincemeat appetizer. He was just swallowing the last bite when he looked up from the screen. "Got it!" he said with a smile. "I'll read it to you, but it's a little vague, Sally."

"That's okay. As long as I have a general idea, Hannah and I can probably come up with something close."

Hannah looked surprised. "How did I get into this?"

"If we can figure it out between us, you can come up with a Sugar Plum Cookie. Everyone in Lake Eden would like that."

Hannah knew she was trapped into helping solve the sugarplum question, but she had to admit that she was intrigued by the problem. "Okay, I'm in," she said. "Read it to us, Norman."

Norman looked down at the screen again. "It's a long article. I'll just tell you the important parts, if that's okay."

"That's perfect," Sally told him quickly.

"It says that the sweets mentioned in the poem were probably coriander with a sugar coating." He turned to Sally. "Do you know what coriander looks like?"

"Just the powdered kind. Actually, the only thing I really know about it is that it's a spice. Do you know anything about it, Hannah?"

"Just a little. I know that the seeds are the spice, but I've never seen them in seed form. I don't use it often, but when I do, I use the powdered kind that Florence sells at the Red Owl. The plant is classified as an herb and the leaves are sometimes called Chinese parsley or cilantro."

"What does the spice taste like?" Doc wanted to know.

"It's . . . spicy. If you've ever had curry, it was probably in there. It's used in a lot of dishes from India."

"And you think you can use it in a cookie?" Delores sounded dubious.

Hannah laughed. "Don't look so worried, Mother. My cookies will have the usual spices like cinnamon and nutmeg. And the sugar plum will be the decoration on top of the frosting."

"Oh, good!" This time Delores sounded relieved. "I love your cookies, dear. When can we taste them?"

"When I figure out how to make a sugar plum."

"I think I might be able to help you with that," Norman said, looking down at his screen again. "It says that nobody seems to know for sure, but some researchers think that sugar plums are called plums, because they have a cylindrical shape like a plum. Other researchers seem to think they're made from dried fruit and nuts. The dried fruit is combined with the nuts and then they're dipped in honey or rolled in sugar. Evidently, that was a way of preserving fruit."

"Oh, my!" Hannah gave a little gasp. "Now I know why she did it!"

"Who?" Sally asked.

"And what?" Carrie added.

"Grandma Inge. She made what she called candy for Christmas, but it wasn't really candy."

"What was it, dear?" Delores asked her.

"Dates. Grandma Inge used to always put them out for a Christmas treat." Hannah turned to Sally. "The ones you buy in the store are dried dates, aren't they?"

"Yes, I think so. I know they're fruit, and they grow on date palm trees. What did she do with the dates?"

"She cut them open, pitted them, and put a quarter of a walnut inside. And then she rolled them in white sugar and arranged them on a plate."

"I remember that!" Delores sounded excited. "They were just like candy and so sweet you could only eat one."

"Got it!" Hannah said, smiling widely.

"Got what?" Doc asked her.

"My Sugar Plum Cookies. I can hardly wait to try to bake them!" She turned to Sally. "If they turn out the way I think they will, I'll drive out here tomorrow with some for you."

"What about me?" Delores asked.

"You and Carrie can come in tomorrow morning to taste them. I'm going to bake early."

"And me?" Norman asked.

"You too."

"How about me?" Doc sounded more than a little deprived.

"That depends. Are you going to sleep at the hospital tonight?"

"I wasn't planning on it. Unless John Doe takes a turn for the worse, I'll be heading back to town."

"Then come over before you go to the hospital in the morning and I'll give you a plate of cookies to take out there for breakfast."

"And you'll drive out here at lunchtime and have lunch with me?" Sally asked her.

"I will. Lisa's got help for the next couple of weeks.

Her cousin Rachael is staying with Jack and Lisa for Christmas."

Sally reached over to refill their champagne glasses, and then she collected their appetizer plates. "I'm off to get the rest of your meal," she told them. "I'll see you at lunch tomorrow, Hannah. And don't forget to bring those cookies, even if they don't turn out exactly the way you want them to."

CHRISTMAS BAKED BRIE

Preheat oven to 425 degrees F., rack in the center position.

Ingredients:

- 1 Tablespoon all-purpose flour
- 1 package frozen puff pastry *(I used Pepperidge Farm, which contains 2 sheets)*
- 1 wheel of Brie or Camembert cheese *(7 to 10 ounces by weight)*
- 1 small jar of mincemeat *(you will use ¼ to ½ cup)*

Prepare your baking pan by spraying a cookie sheet with Pam or another nonstick cooking spray. Alternatively, you can line it with parchment paper and spray that with Pam or another nonstick cooking spray.

Hannah's 1st Note: If your grocery store doesn't carry jars of mincemeat, you can usually order it from Wal-Mart, Sam's Club, or Amazon. If you're in a hurry and don't want to wait for your order to come, you can substitute your favorite kind of chutney or use whole berry cranberry sauce.

Place a bread board *(if you have one)* or a large square of wax paper on your kitchen counter. Sprinkle

the Tablespoon of flour on it and spread it around a bit with your impeccably clean palms to form a light coating.

Unwrap one sheet of puff pastry *(it usually comes with 2 sheets to a package)* and leave the second one in the freezer.

Place the sheet of frozen puff pastry in the center of the space you've floured and thaw it according to package directions.

When your puff pastry has thawed, spread a little flour on your rolling pin and roll the puff pastry out into a square that's large enough to wrap around your cheese.

Transfer the puff pastry square to the center of the baking sheet you've prepared.

Move your wheel of Brie or Camembert cheese to the counter and place it in the center of your puff pastry square. Make sure there's enough pastry dough to bring it up the sides of the cheese and ALMOST cover the top. *(You'll want to leave a little bit of your mincemeat topping showing in the very center of the cheese.)*

Open your jar of mincemeat and use a spoon to spread from a quarter-cup to a half-cup of mincemeat on the top of your cheese.

Using both hands, wrap the puff pastry up over the sides of the cheese, patting it in place. Then bring it over the top of the cheese wheel, leaving a little room so that the mincemeat can bubble up in the center when it bakes.

Hannah's 2nd Note: You may have to fold some of the edges so that your guests can see the mincemeat topping inside.

Bake your Christmas Baked Brie at 425 degrees F. for 12 to 16 minutes or until the top of the puff pastry is a lovely golden brown.

Take the cookie sheet out of the oven and let your Christmas Baked Brie cool on a cold stovetop burner or a wire rack for 15 minutes.

Use a wide metal spatula to transfer your creation to a wooden cutting board and carry it to the table.

Cut your Christmas Baked Brie into wedges with a long, sharp knife. *(A chef's knife would be perfect.)* Do

this by first cutting it in half and then turning the cutting board so that you can cut it in half again. This will give you 4 pieces.

Continue by cutting the 4 pieces in half to make 8 pieces.

Hannah's 3rd Note: This is easier to do than to describe. It's like cutting a pie into 8 pieces.

To make this easier for your guests to transfer to appetizer plates, insert a food pick in the center of each piece so that they can pick them up.

To serve, present the cutting board to each guest so that he or she can choose their own slice of Christmas Baked Brie. Be sure to serve this tasty appetizer while it is still warm. This is especially wonderful when it's served with wine or champagne.

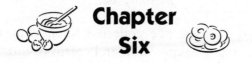

Chapter Six

Hannah stepped back and looked at her work. She had been busy this morning, baking the cookie dough that Lisa and Rachael had stored in the walk-in cooler. Once she'd finished that, she found her favorite sugar cookie recipe and modified it to suit her parameters for Sugar Plum Cookies.

As she mixed up a trial batch, she glanced at the clock. She would just have time to bake a test batch of cookies before Lisa came in to work.

The first order of business was to gather her ingredients. Hannah went to the pantry, and got out the dates she'd bought for the Christmas Date Cupcakes she planned to make this week, and reminded herself to walk down to the Red Owl later to pick up another package.

A smile crossed Hannah's face as she realized that Florence had ordered pitted dates. That would save her time when she made the sugar plums to put on top of the frosted cookies. She collected flour, white sugar, powdered sugar, baking soda and cream of tartar, salt, and spices. Once she'd arranged those on the stainless steel work surface, she went into the walk-in cooler to get salted butter and eggs.

Hannah placed the white sugar in the bowl of her electric stand mixer and went to the microwave to soften the sticks of butter. She unwrapped each one and put them, individually, in the microwave for five seconds, turning them to give all four sides the same amount of time, and added the softened butter to her mixing bowl. As she worked, adding ingredient after ingredient and mixing everything together to form cookie dough, she thought about John Doe, the homeless man they'd found. If Doc Knight let him have visitors today, she'd take him some of her new Sugar Plum Cookies, too.

It didn't take long for Hannah to mix up the cookie dough. Once it was done, she removed it from the mixer and, since a whole batch made approximately eight dozen cookies, she rounded it up in a ball, cut it in half, and put half of it in a ziplock bag that she carried to her walk-in cooler. That way, if her test batch of Sugar Plum Cookies didn't please her, she could always use the second half of the dough to bake Grandma Knudson's Cinful Sugar Cookies.

As she worked with the Sugar Plum Cookie dough, Hannah thought about Grandma Knudson, who took her duties as the unofficial head of the Holy Redeemer Lutheran Church seriously. *Grandma*, the name both parishioners and non-parishioners called her, often traveled out to Doc Knight's hospital with her grandson and made her own rounds by visiting the patients. If Doc Knight said that John Doe could have visitors today, she'd call Grandma Knudson and ask her to include him on her visiting list.

Hannah worked non-stop, rolling dough balls, flattening them, and placing them on cookie sheets. Just as soon as she had enough unbaked cookies to fill all the racks in her revolving industrial oven, she checked to see that she'd preheated it to the proper temperature and slipped the cookie sheets inside.

It took almost an hour to bake and cool the cookies she'd made, frost them, and place one of her walnut-filled, sugar-coated dates on top. The next time she baked them it would be faster, now that she knew exactly how to do it. The cookies were more work than most because there were three separate steps to completing them, but they would be a novelty for The Cookie Jar clientele.

It was time for a coffee break, and Hannah had just poured herself a cup from the kitchen coffeepot when there was a knock at the back kitchen door. She began to smile as she recognized the knock, and went to let Norman in.

"Hi, Hannah," Norman greeted her. "Do you have time for coffee with me?"

"Yes. I was about to sit down for a coffee break. Hang up your parka and I'll get you a cup."

"What smells so good in here?" Norman asked, as she carried his coffee to the stainless steel work station.

"I baked a lot of cookies this morning, but I hope you're smelling my new Sugar Plum Cookies. Would you like to taste one?"

"Do you have to even ask?"

Hannah laughed. "I'll get a plateful for us. I haven't tasted them yet either."

Norman watched Hannah plate the cookies, and when she set them down at the work station, he said, "They look wonderful, Hannah! Very pretty and definitely appealing."

"Good. Let's taste them and see if they taste as good as they look." Hannah waited until Norman had bitten into a cookie and made a sound of approval. "What do you think?"

"They're great, Hannah! I'm about to taste the sugar plum." Norman took another bite and looked surprised. "It's good. No wonder the kids in the poem were dreaming about visions of sugar-plums dancing in their heads!"

"They didn't have this kind of sugar plum, Norman."

"True, but if they had, they would have dreamed about it. It's really sweet, Hannah. Almost too sweet, but maybe you'd better make a few dozen for me to give out at my dental clinic."

"Because they're loaded with sugar?"

Norman smiled. "You got it." Then he reached across the table and patted her hand. "You did it, Hannah. You made a delicious Sugar Plum Cookie."

"Thank you, Norman. I like them, too. I think I'll have Lisa bake some more and we'll try them out on our customers at the coffee . . ." She stopped speaking as she heard a knock at the door. It was a knock she didn't recognize and she got up to answer it.

"Doc!" Hannah greeted him. "Come in. You look cold."

"I am. I left my parka at the hospital and all I had to wear this morning was this jacket." He shrugged out of the jacket and hung it on one of the hooks by the door. "Do you have time for coffee? I have some news about John Doe."

"Come sit at the stool at the work station and I'll pour you a cup. I want you to taste my Sugar Plum Cookies anyway and this saves me from having to drive out with a dozen."

"Hello, Norman," Doc said, spotting him at the work station. "Did you try one of Hannah's new cookies?"

"I did. They're great, Doc. Did I hear you say you had news about John Doe?"

"Yes. I'll just wait until Hannah joins . . ." Doc stopped as Hannah delivered his coffee and sat down across from him. "Thanks, Hannah. Do you want me to taste the cookies first? Or would you rather I tell you about Joe Smith right away?"

"You found out his name?" Norman asked.

Doc shook his head. "Not really. We had him listed as John Doe, but he saw it on his chart and asked if he could change the name. He said John Doe sounded too common. His nurse suggested Jake Doe, but he became very agitated and said he hated that name. Then he asked her if she could change it to Joe. He told my nurse that Joe just sounded more familiar to him. And then he gave a little laugh and said he guessed he'd have to change the last name, too, since Joe Doe was too ridiculous."

"So now he's Joe Smith?" Hannah asked with a smile.

"That's right."

"I wonder if his name really is Joe," Norman said, looking thoughtful. "If it is, it might seem more familiar than any other name."

Doc shrugged. "There's no way to be sure unless he regains his memory. Joe could sound familiar if it were his father's name, or a brother, or even a best friend."

Hannah gave a little nod. "You're right, Doc. Please tell us how he's doing. I've been worried about him."

"It's rather complicated," Doc began, taking a sip of his coffee. "Physically, he's recovering nicely. He's able to sit up in bed and he smiled at one of my nurses, but the memory loss concerns me. That's why I'm going out there so early this morning, to check for possible TBI."

"Traumatic brain injury?" Norman asked him.

"Yes. Very good, Norman. I wasn't sure you and Hannah would know what that was."

"I didn't know," Hannah admitted.

"Does your Joe Smith have any signs of TBI?" Norman asked.

"That's what I'm going to find out. I told my staff to hold off and let him sleep as late as he could. And then to feed him a nourishing breakfast and wait until I got there."

Hannah glanced at the clock on the wall. "It's only six o'clock, Doc. Do you think he's awake yet?"

"He could be, but I doubt it."

"Did Joe Smith ask the nurse any questions, like where he was and why he was there?"

"Yes. She told him exactly what I said to say, that he was suffering from malnutrition and he'd collapsed. The people who'd found him had called my paramedics and we'd taken him to the hospital to help him."

Norman nodded. "And did that answer satisfy him?"

"It seemed to until she asked the follow-up question that I left with the nurses."

"Which was . . . ?" Hannah asked.

"His name. They told me that the patient paused for a moment and then he said he wasn't sure. Then he closed his eyes and went back to sleep again."

"Because he didn't want to answer any more of your nurse's questions?" Hannah asked.

"Perhaps. It could have been for a myriad of reasons."

"Simple paranoia?" Norman suggested. "He might have been afraid he could say something that would kick him back out on the streets again?"

"That's certainly possible," Doc agreed.

"Or maybe he's running away from someone or something, and he's afraid that if he gives his name, whoever it is will find him and do whatever he fears," Hannah suggested.

"That's possible, too," Doc told her. "I won't know any of these things until I drive out there and examine him myself. When I called to check on him, he'd gone back to sleep and he hadn't awakened again."

Hannah sighed deeply. "He probably hasn't had a good night's sleep in months. Or a good meal either. How long do you think he's been out there, Doc?"

"It's hard to tell, Hannah. That's a question that only he can answer . . . if he remembers enough to answer it, that is."

Norman frowned slightly. "You sound a little dubious about that, Doc."

"That's because there's no way of telling with TBI . . . if it truly is TBI."

"And how will you know that?" Hannah asked, even though she suspected that she already knew the answer to her question.

"I can check to see if he suffered any apparent head injuries, and if he did, whether it's recently healed. And there's always the possibility that Joe Smith is simply too exhausted to answer our questions right now. When he regains strength, he may be able to tell us what we need to know."

"What are the chances of that happening?" Hannah asked.

Doc shrugged. "I wouldn't even hazard a guess. Amnesia is a tricky thing, Hannah. We'll just have to wait. It could be when he wakes up today, and it could be we'll never know. All I can say is I'm glad your mother, Carrie, and you found Joe when you did. Another day or two, and it might have been too late to save him."

Hannah shuddered slightly. "I'm glad we found him,

too. Really, Doc . . . I think he's a very nice man. And I wish I knew his story."

"Perhaps we will, Hannah. At least we can help him now with the physical problems he has. There's no doubt in my mind that he'll recover from those."

Once Doc had tasted the Sugar Plum Cookies and given his seal of approval, Hannah filled one of her distinctive bags with the sweet treats and sent them to the hospital with him. She promised him that she'd check with him later, and then she sat down at the work station again. She gave a sigh that seemed to come from the very bottoms of her feet and faced Norman.

"It's a real mystery," he said.

"Yes. I just wish I knew what to do about Joe. I'd like to help him, but I really don't know how."

Norman reached across the table to take her hand. "Let Doc and his staff deal with it for now. And when Doc says that you can see Joe, talk to him. You can draw him out, Hannah. You're good at that. If he really doesn't remember who he is and what happened to him, start jotting down everything he tells you that might be relevant to his background. He may give you clues about things that he does remember."

"Like what?"

"Like, living near a lake and going fishing when he was young. Or going out to bring the cows in. He might even remember a teacher he had in school, or what he did for his first job. Just talk with him about anything and everything and see what he says in return."

Hannah gave a grateful smile. "Those are great ideas,

Norman. What you're really telling me is to simply visit with him, is that right?"

"Exactly right. Tell him some things about you and see if he reciprocates. Then you can start putting the puzzle of his life together."

"Yes. I can do that, Norman. If he remembers me at all, he knows I'm not a threat. I gave him coffee, and cupcakes, and . . ."

"What is it?" Norman asked when Hannah suddenly stopped speaking.

"I just remembered something he said when he came into my kitchen yesterday morning."

"What was it?"

"I gave him coffee, but I also gave him a German Chocolate Cupcake."

"That was really nice of you, Hannah. Was he grateful?"

"He was very grateful. I apologized because I hadn't frosted the cupcake yet, but he didn't seem to mind. And then he told me that his mother used to bake German chocolate cake and she made one every year for his birthday."

"Go get a murder book, Hannah."

"But . . . why? Nobody's been murdered."

"I know, but you always use them for important notes and I have the feeling that this is going to turn into a case."

"You mean . . . you think he's going to *die*?"

"No, I just know you like to use those notebooks. And your steno pads are easy to carry around."

Hannah thought about that for a second or two. "You're right. I'll start keeping my Joe Smith notes in there." She got up, went to the drawer where she kept her blank steno pads, and brought one back with her. "Just give me a second and I'll write down what Joe said about his mother."

Norman watched while Hannah jotted down what she remembered about her early morning conversation with Joe. "Got it?" he asked when she closed the book.

"I've got it. I thought of something else while I was writing it down, Norman."

"What's that?"

"I think we should give Mike a heads-up about this. I know there's no crime unless Joe's TBI turns out to be deliberately caused, but Mike's a detective and he knows how to investigate people's backgrounds. That's part of what he does for a living."

Norman thought about that for a moment. "You're right, Hannah. We probably should alert Mike. Why don't you call him and ask him to join us for coffee and some of your new cookies."

"All right," Hannah agreed, "if you're sure it's all right with you."

"Of course it's all right with me. Mike and I are friends. Call him, Hannah. Maybe, between the three of us, we can figure out some way to help Joe Smith."

SUGAR PLUM COOKIES

Preheat oven to 325 degrees F., rack in the middle position.

Hannah's 1st Note: If you plan to make these cookies in the morning, get out 4 sticks of butter on the night before, unwrap them, and put them in a bowl covered with plastic wrap. That way the butter will be soft enough to use in the morning.

Cookie Ingredients:

- 2 cups powdered *(confectioners)* sugar *(don't sift unless it's got big lumps and pack it down when you measure it)*
- 2 cups softened, salted butter *(4 sticks, 16 ounces, 1 pound)*
- 1 cup white *(granulated)* sugar
- 2 large eggs
- 2 teaspoons vanilla extract
- 1 teaspoon baking soda
- 1 teaspoon cream of tartar
- 1 teaspoon ground cinnamon
- ½ teaspoon ground nutmeg *(freshly grated is best, of course)*
- 1 teaspoon salt

4 and ¼ cups flour *(pack it down in the cup when you measure it)*

Directions:

Prepare your cookie sheets by spraying them with Pam or another nonstick baking spray or lining them with parchment paper.

Hannah's 2ⁿᵈ Note: These cookies are easy to mix up if you use an electric mixer like the one Lisa and I have at The Cookie Jar. You can mix them by hand, but it will take more time and more muscle.

Measure out the powdered sugar and put it in the bowl of an electric mixer.

Arrange the 4 sticks of softened butter on top of the powdered sugar.

Sprinkle the cup of white *(granulated)* sugar on top of the butter.

Turn the mixer on to LOW speed and mix the sugars and butter together. Continue mixing on LOW speed until everything is thoroughly combined and the mixture is a uniform color.

Mix in the eggs at LOW speed, one at a time, mixing after each egg is added.

With the mixer still running at LOW speed, mix in the vanilla extract.

Add the baking soda and mix it in thoroughly.

Again, at LOW speed, mix in the cream of tartar. Mix thoroughly.

Hannah's 3rd Note: In case you're wondering, the addition of cream of tartar makes your cookies smoother *(at least that's what Great-Grandma Elsa told me when I asked.)*

Add the ground cinnamon, ground nutmeg, and salt. Mix them in thoroughly.

Add the flour in one-cup increments, mixing after each addition. You can add the quarter cup of flour with the last full cup.

Hannah's 4th Note: Whatever you do, don't try to add all the flour at once. If you do that, when you start the mixer it will fly out of the bowl and all over your kitchen counter and floor. *(And please don't ask me how I know this.)*

Turn off the mixer, scrape down the sides of the bowl, and take the mixing bowl out of the mixer.

Give your cookie dough a final stir by hand with a mixing spoon.

Hannah's 5th Note: This recipe makes from 8 to 10 dozen cookies. If you don't want to make that many Sugar Plum Cookies, round your cookie dough into a ball and cut it in half. Place one half in a freezer bag and stick it in the refrigerator to bake in a week or so, or in the freezer to bake in a month or so. You can use the saved half of the cookie dough to bake more Sugar Plum Cookies or you can roll cookie dough balls and make Grandma Knudson's Cinful Sugar Cookies. The recipe for Cinful Sugar Cookies is given on page 116.

Use your impeccably clean hands to roll the first half of the cookie dough into balls that are approximately one inch in diameter.

Place the dough balls on the cookie sheets you've prepared, 12 cookies on each standard-sized cookie sheet.

Flatten the dough balls with the back of a metal spatula or the palm of your impeccably clean hand.

Hannah's 6th Note: The flatter your cookie dough balls are, the bigger and crispier your cookies will be. Since you will be frosting these cookies, I'd suggest that you DO NOT completely flatten the balls or they might break when you frost them.

Bake at 325 degrees F. for 10 to 15 minutes. *(The cookies should have a tinge of gold on the top.)*

When your cookies have baked, take them out of the oven and set them on a cold stovetop burner or a wire rack.

Cool your Sugar Plum Cookies on the cookie sheet for 2 minutes, then remove them from the cookie sheet and put them on a wire rack to finish cooling completely.

Sugar Plum Ingredients:

4 dozen pitted dates
2 dozen walnut halves
½ cup white *(granulated)* sugar

Directions:

Open the dates. They should be almost cut in half so that you can spread the 2 halves apart.

Break or cut the walnut halves into 2 equal parts lengthwise.

Place the walnut quarter inside the date and close it up again.

Hannah's 1st Note: Dates are very sticky. The two halves of the date will stick together with the walnut quarter inside.

Pour the half-cup of white sugar into a shallow bowl.

Roll the date in the white sugar, coating it completely. Then take it out and place it on a piece of wax paper on the kitchen counter.

Repeat until all the dates have been sugared and are on the wax paper.

Frosting Ingredients:

½ cup *(1 stick, 4 ounces)* softened, salted butter
8-ounce package softened cream cheese *(the brick kind, NOT whipped)*
1 teaspoon vanilla extract
4 cups confectioners *(powdered)* sugar

Mix the softened butter with the softened cream cheese and the vanilla extract until the mixture is smooth.

Hannah's 1st Note: If you heated the cream cheese or the butter to soften it, make sure it's cooled down to room temperature before you mix them together.

Add the confectioners sugar in half-cup increments until the frosting is of proper spreading consistency. *(You'll use all, or almost all, of the sugar.)*

With a frosting knife *(or rubber spatula if you prefer)*, drop a dollop of frosting in the center of a cookie.

Spread the dollop out to cover almost all of the cookie, but don't go all the way to the edge.

Hannah's 2nd Note: If you spread the frosting out all the way, it makes the cookies more difficult to pick up from a platter.

Once the first cookie has been frosted, put a sugar-plum *(the sugared date with walnut inside)* in the center. Since the frosting has not yet hardened, the sugarplum will stay in place.

Yield: Approximately 4 dozen buttery, sugary cookies.

CINFUL SUGAR COOKIES

Preheat oven to 325 degrees F., rack in the middle position.

Hannah's 1st Note: This is an excellent way to make a second batch of cookies from your original Sugar Plum Cookie dough. If you want to make these from scratch, simply reduce the ingredients for Sugar Plum Cookies by half.

Ingredients:

½ of the Sugar Plum Cookie dough
½ cup white *(granulated)* sugar
1 teaspoon ground cinnamon
½ teaspoon ground nutmeg
⅛ teaspoon ground cardamom *(if you don't have it, you can substitute more cinnamon)*

Directions:

Prepare your cookie sheets by spraying them with Pam or another baking spray or lining them with parchment paper.

Place the sugar, cinnamon, nutmeg, and cardamom in a ziplock plastic bag.

Shake the bag until all the ingredients are mixed together thoroughly.

Place the contents of the bag in a shallow bowl.

Use your impeccably clean hands to roll the cookie dough into balls that are approximately one inch in diameter. Roll them in the bowl to coat them with sugar, cinnamon, nutmeg, and cardamom mixture.

Place the dough balls on the cookie sheets you've prepared, 12 cookies on each standard-sized cookie sheet.

Flatten the dough balls with the back of a metal spatula or the palm of your impeccably clean hand.

Hannah's 2nd Note: The flatter your cookie dough balls are, the bigger and crispier your cookies will be. They will spread out some in the oven, so try to make them about a quarter-inch thick. If you flatten them more than that, they may fall apart when someone bites into them.

Bake at 325 degrees F. for 10 to 15 minutes. *(The cookies should have a tinge of gold on the top.)*

When your cookies have baked, take them out of the oven and set them on a cold stovetop burner or a wire rack.

Cool your Cinful Sugar Cookies on the cookie sheet for 2 minutes, then remove them from the cookie sheet and place them on a wire rack to finish cooling completely.

Yield: Approximately 4 dozen sinfully rich and tasty cookies that everyone will love to eat. *(Grandma Knudson, the grandmother of Reverend Bob Knudson, asked me to describe them that way.)*

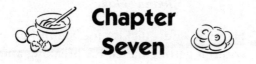

Chapter
Seven

Hannah's breath caught in her throat as Mike Kingston, the chief detective of the Winnetka County Sheriff's Department, walked in. Mike was one of the most handsome men she'd ever seen, worthy of having the lead in a movie, or posing for super-expensive men's advertisements.

"Hi, Hannah," he said, hanging his parka on one of the hooks by the door. "Hello, Norman. What brings you here?"

"Joe Smith," Norman replied immediately.

"Who?" Mike asked, walking over to the work station, taking a stool, and accepting the coffee that Hannah had brought for him.

"The homeless man that Hannah's mother, my mother, and Hannah found in the property that our mothers were looking to rent."

"This is the first I've heard of it," Mike said, taking a cookie from the platter. "Did he break in?"

"No," Hannah said quickly. Joe Smith had enough problems without getting nailed for breaking and entering. "He was living there, Mike. And he was on the verge of starvation."

Mike reached for another cookie. "Good thing you found him then. How's he doing?"

"Doc Knight was just here and he's going to the hospital right now to check on his condition," Norman told him. "He thinks it's a possible case of TBI."

"Traumatic brain injury. That's too bad," Mike said, taking a bite of his cookie. "These are really good, Hannah."

"Thanks," Hannah said. "Doc thinks he's going to be all right physically, but he doesn't remember who he is, or where he came from."

"There's a lot of that going around," Mike said. "Sometimes drugs are involved. Did Doc test him for that?"

"I'm sure he did," Norman answered quickly. "Hannah said the man was perfectly coherent when he came to The Cookie Jar looking for work yesterday morning."

"True?" Mike turned to Hannah.

"True. I don't know anything about him except that he was very polite and really grateful for the work I gave him."

"And that was . . . ?" Mike asked her.

"I had him scrape my windshield and brush the snow off my cookie truck."

"How much did you pay him?" Mike asked.

"Five dollars. I know that's a lot for what he did, but he was cold and he was still willing to do anything I asked, even if it was outside. I gave him coffee and a bag of cupcakes. And then I told him to come back in the morning, because I'd have some other work for him. He didn't have a chance to do that because he collapsed that night."

"Must have been your cupcakes," Mike said, but when he saw the horrified expression on Hannah's face, he reached out to take her hand. "Just kidding," he said quickly. "Cop humor and all that. Sometimes this stuff gets to us and we have to joke about it, you know?"

"I know," Norman said. "Your work is about as funny as gum disease."

"Now, that is funny!" Mike grinned at him and then he turned back to Hannah. "Sorry, Hannah. I didn't mean to make light of it. And I do feel for the poor guy."

"Then you'll help us? We have to find out where he came from and why he's here in Lake Eden."

"Right. Someone has to do that. Unfortunately, it can't be me."

"Why not?" Norman asked him. "You take missing person cases, don't you?"

"Yes, but this isn't a missing person case. I'll check, but if no one has reported him missing, I have no authority to try to find out his particulars. I can ask Sheriff Grant, but I'm pretty sure he won't let me work on the guy's case." Mike stopped and frowned. "Unless, of course, he's a victim of a crime. Then I'm authorized to investigate it."

It took a moment to sink in and then Hannah gave a frustrated sigh. "You mean you can't do anything for us?"

Mike shook his head. "Not officially, no. But if you ask me a specific question, I can research it. I just can't enter it as a case on the books and devote any official time to it."

"But you could help if it's not an official investigation?" Norman asked.

Mike winced slightly. "According to the rules, I should say no. But I'll help you all I can. I just have to be careful that I don't break any rules. Sheriff Grant is a stickler for that."

Hannah gave a brief nod. "I know. Everything by the book. He's that kind of guy."

Mike bit into yet another cookie he'd taken from the plate and began to smile. "These are great! What are they?"

"Sugar Plum Cookies," Hannah told him.

"Yes, but what are sugar plums?"

It was Norman's turn to answer. "No one seems to know, but Hannah came as close as she could."

"Well, these are winners as far as I'm concerned." Mike reached out to the last cookie on the platter. "I like the dates, Hannah. My mother used to make things with dates and nobody does that much anymore."

"That's true," Hannah said, remembering the sheet cake that her Great-Grandma Elsa used to make. She'd called it Christmas Date Cake and Hannah had loved it. Right then and there, she decided to try to make it as

Christmas cupcakes. There was no reason in the world why it wouldn't work, and everyone who came into The Cookie Jar would love to taste cupcakes with dates, sugar, nuts, and chocolate chips.

"You just thought of something, didn't you," Norman asked, and it wasn't really a question. He'd seen Hannah's thoughtful expression.

"I did. I'll have a new cupcake by this afternoon. Would you two like to come by around two to taste one?"

Norman looked at Mike and both of them burst into laughter. "Of course we would," Mike replied.

"We'll be here," Norman agreed, standing up and heading for the door. "Come on, Mike. Let's go to work and let Hannah get started on those cupcakes."

"Not without taking some of these . . ." Mike said, looking perplexed as he realized that the platter was now empty. "Hannah, are there more?"

Hannah laughed. "Sure, Mike. I see those have evaporated, but I'll get you a bag to go!"

As they went out the back kitchen door, Hannah was smiling. Her Sugar Plum Cookies were a success and she had a new cupcake to try. Life was good, especially if she could solve the mystery of Joe Smith's identity.

"Hello, Hannah," Vonnie Blair, Doc Knight's secretary, greeted her as she came into his office. "Is Doc expecting you?"

"No," Hannah said truthfully. "I just thought I'd drop by with some cookies for both of you."

"Really?" Vonnie said, accepting the cookies with a

smile that told Hannah that she hadn't accepted that excuse for a second. "You came out to see Joe, right?"

"Right," Hannah admitted. "How's he doing, Vonnie?"

"Better than he was last night. Now that he's all cleaned up, he's a pretty good-looking guy. If I wasn't married, I might be interested. Just wait until you see him."

"Do you think Doc will let me?"

"Probably, since you're the only one of us who's met him before. But, you can ask him yourself. He should be here in a minute or . . ." Vonnie stopped speaking mid-sentence and gestured toward the door. "Hello, Doc. Hannah's here to see you and she brought us cookies." She looked down at the plate on her desk. "Cinful Sugar Cookies?"

"That's right," Hannah said, smiling at Doc. "That's what I made with the other half of the Sugar Plum Cookie dough."

"Let's go take some to Joe," Doc said, taking a step toward Vonnie's desk.

"I have more with me," Hannah said quickly, noting Vonnie's panicked expression. It was clear that Vonnie didn't want to give up the plate that Hannah had given to her.

As she went out the door with Doc, Hannah heard the relieved whoosh of breath that Vonnie gave. "Your half of those cookies might be gone by the time you get back to your office, Doc."

"I know they will be. Vonnie loves your cookies. But you say you have more?"

Hannah held out the bag she was carrying.

"That should be about enough. We'll call for coffee and enjoy them with Joe."

"Did you find out any more about him?" Hannah hurried to keep up with Doc's long strides.

"Some. He suffered a blunt force head injury."

"Does that mean somebody hit him on the head?"

"Not necessarily, but the placement of the impact lends itself to that scenario. Something fairly round hit him in the back of the head. It could have been an object like the butt of a revolver, a nightstick, or a round, smooth rock."

"Then you think it was intentional?"

"Either that, or it was accidental. It's possible that he fell on something matching that description."

"Did you learn anything that might help us find out something about his background?"

"Not really. He did say one thing I found curious, though."

"What was that?"

"One of the nurses wheeled him past the charge nurse's desk on his way to the X-ray department. He noticed that there was a large scratch on the surface of her desk and he asked her how it happened. She said she didn't know because it had been there longer than she had. Then he asked if he could take a closer look, and she said he could."

"So he looked at the scratch?" Hannah asked.

"Yes. He told her that he could fix the scratch, that all he needed was a couple of things from the hardware store. He told her what they were and she wrote them down and gave the paper to me."

"What are you going to do with it?"

"I'm going to call Cliff and ask him if I can send someone to pick up the things on the list this afternoon. And then I'm going to let Joe try to fix the scratch."

"Do you think he can?"

"I don't know. I asked him and he said it was child's play, that he'd fixed worse scratches than that. His only concern was that he might not be able to stand on his feet for that long, but we'll figure a way around that."

Hannah's mind went through the possibilities. "Do you think he could have worked in a furniture shop?"

"I asked him that. He thought about it for a minute and he said he didn't remember, but he was pretty sure he knew how to do it."

Hannah began to smile. "And you're going to let him try."

"Why not? I was planning to buy a new desk, but if Joe can fix it, I won't have to."

"And we'll know that he must have worked on wood some time in his life."

"That's right." Doc stopped by a doorway. "This is his room. Wait here, Hannah. I'll make sure he's ready to have visitors."

Hannah waited while Doc went into the room. She heard him talking for a moment and then she heard Joe answer, but she couldn't quite make out what they were saying. A moment later, Doc came back out into the hall.

"Come on, Hannah," Doc beckoned to her. "Joe says he wants to see you."

"Hello, Joe," Hannah greeted the man in the bed. He was propped up on pillows and he smiled at her. "I'm sorry I didn't come to see you this morning."

"That's okay, ma'am. I had an interview with an MRI machine anyway."

Hannah had all she could do not to laugh. An interview with an MRI machine? She really hoped he was being intentionally funny, but she didn't want to ask.

"I'll go tell the nurse we need coffee," Doc said, heading for the door. "You two go ahead and get reacquainted."

"You look a lot better than you did the last time I saw you," Hannah told him. There was a bit of color in his face and he wasn't shaking the way he'd been the previous morning.

"I feel a lot better. They're taking good care of me, Miss Swensen."

Hannah was surprised. "Did Doc tell you my name?"

"No, I saw it on the front window of your coffee shop yesterday, and I remembered it. Doc said you were one of the ladies who found me. Thank you for that. I was just so cold I couldn't seem to get warm."

Doc came back, just in time to hear Joe's comment.

"That's because you were malnourished and you were coming down with a bacterial infection. It's the reason they're giving you antibiotics."

"And that's why I have this needle in my arm?" Joe gestured toward his left arm.

"That's right. You also needed to be hydrated. Is the IV bothering you?"

Joe nodded. "Yes. I'm used to using my hands, and I'm feeling a little confined."

"Let me check your vitals right now. If you're anywhere close enough to normal, I'll remove it."

"That would be great! Thank you so much. It'll make it a lot easier when I fix that desktop for you."

"Do you want me to leave?" Hannah asked Doc.

"No, not unless Joe minds. I'm just going to take his blood pressure, listen to his heart, and take his temperature." Doc turned to Joe. "Would you be more comfortable if Hannah left, Joe?"

Joe shook his head. "No, that's okay. She can stay."

Joe trusts you, Hannah's rational mind told her.

Not necessarily, the suspicious part of her argued. *Joe could be an exhibitionist, or something like that.*

But it's not like Doc's going to ask him to take off his hospital gown, the rational part of her mind argued. *I'm sure Joe trusts her. After all, she found him and called for the paramedics.*

Wrong, the rational part of her mind insisted. *Hannah's mother was the one who called for the paramedics.*

Oh, don't be so literal! her suspicious mind chided.

I can't help it, I'm rational and you're not!

Hannah made a conscious effort to stop listening to the internal argument. Instead, she concentrated on Doc, who had just finished taking Joe's temperature.

"Do I still have a fever?" Joe asked.

Doc shook his head. "It's normal now. We've been pumping you full of antibiotics ever since we got the results of your blood panel."

Doc took out his stethoscope and listened to Joe's heart. He gave a nod and patted Joe on the shoulder. "Everything's fine," he said. "If you'll agree to take the antibiotics by mouth, we can take out our IV now."

"You betcha!" Joe agreed, and Hannah made a mental note to jot down that he'd used a common, regional midwestern term. That didn't necessarily mean that Joe had come from the Midwest, but she'd jot it down in her steno book.

Doc turned a valve on the bag that was hanging on a stand by the side of Joe's bed, and made short work of removing Joe's IV. He replaced the bandage he'd taken off with a smaller one and stepped back. "All done," he said.

"Thank you, Doc." Joe looked a bit worried. "Do you mind if I call you Doc? That's the name most of the nurses here use for you and I don't know your last name."

"It's Knight, but you can call me Doc. That's what everyone in Lake Eden calls me."

"What a wonderful name!" Joe exclaimed.

"Knight?" Hannah asked.

"No, but that's a nice name, too. I was talking about Lake Eden. It's like the Garden of Eden, and the Bible tells us that it was beautiful."

"Are you a religious man, Joe?" Doc asked him.

Joe looked slightly puzzled. "I . . . I don't remember, but I guess I must be. Or at least, I must have been in the past. I'm sorry, but I don't really remember." He looked even more worried and he gave a little sigh. "Do you think I'll ever remember, Doc?"

"I wish I could say yes, but I really don't know, Joe. Memory is a nebulous thing."

"I know exactly what you mean. It's intangible. Sometimes memories pop into my head and before I can grasp them, they're gone again."

"That must be horribly frustrating, Joe," Hannah sympathized.

"It is. It's almost like dreaming and then waking up. You tell yourself that you're going to remember the details, but when you wake up again in the morning, you don't. You're just left with a feeling."

Hannah exchanged glances with Doc. Joe was not an uneducated man. Perhaps he'd not been formally schooled, but he was what the ancient philosophers would have called a thinker.

"Are you ready for your coffee?" one of Doc's nurses asked, appearing in the doorway with a tray, a coffeepot, and cups.

"We are," Doc told her. "Just set it on Joe's bedside table, Molly, and we'll pour it ourselves."

"Of course." Molly walked over to the far side of Joe's bed and set the tray on his bedside table. Then she stared at his arm in shock. "Did you pull out your IV, Joe?"

"Joe decided he didn't need it anymore," Doc said, winking at Joe.

"You did?" Molly looked at Joe in surprise. "But . . ."

"Relax, Molly," Doc told her. "I removed it. You're going to have to add to your duties this afternoon. Joe is going to take his antibiotics by mouth from now on."

"But we were giving him hydration, and . . ."

"I know," Doc interrupted her. "I don't think that'll be a problem, Molly. Just make sure that Joe has a full pitcher of water and that you bring him food whenever he's hungry. Keep a record of what he ingests for me, will you, please?"

"Of course I will, Doc."

"And, Joe . . . I want you to ring Molly for food every time you think you can eat something. Fruit juice will be good, too. We have to keep up your caloric intake . . . isn't that right, Molly."

"Yes, it is, Doc." She reached out to pat Joe gently on the shoulder. "Good for you, Joe. Doc wouldn't have removed your IV unless you were getting better."

"That's right," Doc agreed, giving her an approving smile.

"I'd better go see what the kitchen has to go with your coffee," Molly said, and then she caught sight of the distinctive cookie bag on Joe's bedside table. "Are those more of your cupcakes, Hannah?"

"Not this time. I brought three dozen of Grandma Knudson's Cinful Sugar Cookies."

"I love those cinnamon cookies!" Molly said quickly. And then she looked slightly embarrassed. "Now you're all going to think I was asking for one of Joe's cookies."

"You were, and you might as well admit it," Doc told her, smiling to show that what Molly had said was perfectly all right. Then he turned to Hannah. "You said there were three dozen in there?"

Hannah nodded. "Three dozen, but they're *baker's* dozen."

"Three extra, one for each dozen?" Joe asked her.

"That's right!" Hannah said, smiling at him. "How do you know about a baker's dozen, Joe?"

"I . . . I don't know, but I do. Someone must have told me about it, but I have no idea who."

"You may remember later," Hannah said quickly, noticing that Joe looked a bit sad that he couldn't come up with a name.

"Maybe," Joe replied, and then he turned to Molly. "Take a dozen cookies with you and give them to my other nurses."

"Are you sure?" Molly asked.

"I'm sure. That'll still leave us with twenty-seven cookies and that's nine apiece." He stopped speaking and turned to Doc and Hannah. "That's all right with you two, isn't it?"

"It's fine with me," Hannah told him. "I had a couple this morning when I was baking them."

"And I have to watch my waistline," Doc said.

"Thanks, Joe!" Molly said, taking a napkin from the bag and filling it with cookies. "You're a sweet guy,

Joe. If I were ten years younger . . ." She stopped speaking and gave a little laugh. "Well, I'm not." She picked up the cookies and headed for the door. "I'll see you later, Joe."

Hannah made another mental note. Joe knew what a baker's dozen meant. She had to hurry and write down all of these clues before she forgot.

"Would you two excuse me for a minute?" Hannah asked. "I have to make a quick phone call."

"No problem," Doc said. "While you're gone, I'll pour us all some coffee."

Hannah stepped outside the door, walked down the hall a few feet, and removed her cell phone from her pocket. Thank goodness Lisa had reminded her to charge it at The Cookie Jar this morning! She punched in her own number at her condo, listed the new facts she'd learned about Joe, and hurried back to Joe's room. "Did I miss anything?" she asked.

"Just two rounds of cookies," Joe told her.

"That's okay. I had more than that before I got here." Hannah took a sip of her coffee. Surprisingly, it was good. Doc insisted on that. He'd told the cooks in the hospital kitchen that he'd had enough bad coffee when he was an intern and he wanted his hospital to be different.

"Could I please ask you a question, Miss Swensen?"

"Of course, but only if you call me Hannah. What is it?"

"Please tell me, Hannah . . . who are the other two ladies who found me?"

"One is my mother, Delores Swensen. And the other is her best friend, Carrie Rhodes."

"Rhodes," Joe repeated. "Is Carrie Rhodes any relation to the dentist who works in the Rhodes Clinic?"

"Carrie is the dentist's mother," Doc explained. "The dentist's name is Norman."

"Yes. That's what he said to call him, when I shoveled his sidewalk last week. He was a nice man, Hannah. He paid me more than I asked and then he took me over to the café for breakfast."

Hannah began to smile. "Norman bought breakfast for you?"

"Yes. He told the lady to give me eggs, buttered toast, coffee, and bacon. And then he handed her some money and said he had to get back to the clinic."

"That sounds like Norman," Doc commented.

"Yes, it does," Hannah agreed.

Doc took the last sip of his coffee, got out of his chair, and walked over to the side of Joe's bed. "You're tired, aren't you, Joe?"

"Yes, but I slept. I haven't slept that much since . . . I don't know when."

"Take another little nap now," Doc told him. "It'll be good for you. And when you wake up, you can have some more of Hannah's cookies."

"Then I can stay here?" Joe looked anxious as he asked the question.

"Yes. I want you to stay for a week or so. You need to build up your strength, Joe."

Joe gave a tired smile. "I'm glad you call me Joe," he

said. "It just sounds right to me. Do you think that maybe my name really was Joe?"

"It could have been. We'll know when you remember more, but I'm glad you like to be called Joe for now."

"Thank you for coming and for the cookies, Miss Hannah," Joe said, closing his eyes.

Hannah waited until Doc stepped away from Joe's bedside and then she stood up and followed him out the door. She blinked away tears as she saw how grateful Joe had been when Doc told him that he could stay.

"Would you let Mother and Carrie come with me the next time I visit Joe?" she asked.

"I'll ask him, but I'm sure he'll say yes. He was curious about who he should thank for saving his life."

Hannah shivered slightly even though the hospital corridor was warm. She'd only seen Joe twice, but she already liked him and she didn't want to think about what might have happened to him if they hadn't found him. "How about Norman? Could he visit Joe?"

"Yes. Joe seemed grateful to him, and Norman is good with people."

"Can Grandma Knudson include Joe on her rounds the next time she comes out to the hospital with Reverend Bob?"

"Hold on a second, Hannah. How many people does that make?"

"It's five, Doc. There's Mother, Carrie, Norman, Grandma Knudson, and me."

"All right, but no more than three in one day. I don't want to exhaust him just when he's regaining his strength. And you have to limit yourselves to ten minutes."

"Ten minutes for each of us?" Hannah asked, and Doc laughed.

"I should have known you'd try to increase it," he said. "Ten minutes for just one of you, fifteen minutes if you come with your mother and Carrie. The same fifteen limit if you come with Norman."

"But Norman and I are only two people. Why do we get the same time as Mother, Carrie, and me?"

"Because three women together are more exhausting than a man and a woman."

Hannah smiled a teasing smile. "Isn't that a bit sexist of you, Doc?"

"It's not sexist, it's common sense." Doc opened the door to his office and stepped in. "I'll see you tomorrow, Hannah."

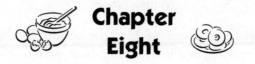

Chapter Eight

"What are you baking, Hannah?" Rachael came into the kitchen a few minutes before time to close for the day. "It smells like garlic."

"And why do you have all those empty cereal boxes on the work station?" Lisa came in behind her cousin.

"I'm making my Cocktail Munchie Mix."

"I've never heard of a mix for drinks that you make in the oven," Rachael said.

"It's not a mix *for* cocktails. It's a mix you have *with* cocktails. Mother invited Carrie over for dinner tonight, and because they always have drinks in the living room first, I thought they'd enjoy it."

Rachael walked over to the industrial oven and peeked through the window on the door. "You only have one big pan in there."

"I know. It's the pan I use for roasting turkey. This oven isn't made for making something like this, but I didn't feel like driving back to the condo, baking it in my regular oven, and then driving back here to Mother's house."

"Your mother invited you for dinner?" Lisa asked, looking surprised. "I thought she always took you out to the Lake Eden Inn."

"Not always, and this is a command appearance. The whole family goes to Mother's house for dinner once a week."

"The whole family?"

Rachael looked a bit shocked and Hannah laughed. "Our whole family isn't as big as your family."

"So who will be there?" Lisa asked.

"Andrea and Bill, Mother and Carrie of course, Norman, Mike, and me."

Lisa asked, "Is your mother still hoping that something might happen between you and Norman?"

"Yes," Hannah sighed.

"But does she think that Mike is a contender, too?" Rachael asked.

Hannah laughed at her wording. "Yeah. I don't think it makes much difference to Mother. She just wants to marry me off before my biological clock stops ticking."

Both Rachael and Lisa laughed. "Because she wants grandchildren?" Rachael asked.

"You got it!" Hannah walked over to the oven, shut off the revolving rack feature, and opened the door. "Pour yourselves a cup of coffee and get one for me, too. I just have to stir this again."

While Hannah stirred the roaster that contained her

Cocktail Munchie Mix, the two younger women filled coffee cups and brought in jars of unsold cookies from the coffee shop. There weren't many left. They'd had a morning rush, a good lunch crowd, and even more customers in the afternoon.

"I hope you weren't planning on taking cookies to your mother's dinner party," Lisa commented.

"I wasn't. I made a batch of Christmas Date Cupcakes, and I'm taking those. They'll be perfect with the ice cream that Mother always gives us as dessert."

"What is your mother serving for dinner?" Rachael wanted to know.

"One of three things," Hannah replied.

"Hannah's mother only makes three entrées," Lisa explained.

"That's right. It'll be Hawaiian Pot Roast, EZ Lasagne, or the roasted chicken that she buys at the Red Owl."

"And you're hoping for the roasted chicken, right?" Lisa asked with a smile.

"I *always* hope for the roasted chicken. Mother's recipe for Hawaiian Pot Roast is a good one, but she always overcooks it. And she doesn't use enough cheese in her lasagna. There's no way she can mess up Florence's roast chicken."

Rachael laughed. "What does she have besides the roast chicken?"

"A green salad and Florence's cheese bread that she warms up in the oven. It's not a bad meal . . . really. I just hope I won't have to feel like peanut butter again."

Lisa laughed, but Rachael looked puzzled. "Why would you feel like peanut butter?"

"Because Mother uses place cards. She likes to arrange the seating for her dinners. And she always sandwiches me in between Mike and Norman. . . ."

"And that makes you feel like a peanut butter sandwich," Rachael said, giving a little groan. "Those family dinners must be horrible!"

"They are, but it makes Mother happy. And we do it every week. When Michelle comes home from college, she's there. And Mother usually invites a couple of other people."

"Tell us about your trip to the hospital," Lisa said. "We've been wondering how that went. I told Rachael about the homeless man and how you, your mother, and Carrie rescued him."

"Doc says he's recovering very well, except that he's lost his memory. They gave him the name Joe Smith on the admittance form."

"Does Doc Knight think his memory will come back?" Lisa wanted to know.

"He's not sure. He told me that memory is a tricky thing, but Joe told us something during our visit with him that was really good."

"What was it?" Rachael asked.

"He said that he liked being called Joe and it just seemed right to him, that he wondered if it might possibly be his real name."

Rachael gave a little nod. "That's encouraging, Hannah. Maybe he's right and it *is* his real name. You might find out and you might not."

"That's what Doc said this afternoon."

"Are you trying to find out who Joe really is, and where he came from?" Lisa asked her.

"Yes. I've been keeping notes on anything he says that might be a clue to his identity."

"If you get enough information, maybe you can find out if there's anyone out there who's looking for him," Lisa suggested.

"Mike's going to check the missing person reports from Wisconsin, Minnesota, Iowa, and the Dakotas," Hannah told them.

"Good!" Lisa sounded relieved. "I'm glad Mike's going to investigate."

"Mike isn't going to *investigate*. He can't, not officially."

"Why not?" Rachael wanted to know. "It's a missing person case, isn't it?"

"Not really. Joe's not officially a missing person. He's right here in Lake Eden. And as far as we know, there's been no crime committed, even though Doc says he's suffering from TBI."

Lisa was clearly puzzled. "What's TBI?"

"What's TBI?" Rachael chimed in, too.

"Traumatic brain injury. Doc says there's evidence of a blow to Joe's head that could have caused his amnesia. But there's no way of knowing if the blow was caused by an accident like a car crash, or whether someone deliberately hit him with something."

"One is a crime, and the other one isn't," Lisa said, understanding the problem immediately.

"That's right. And unless we know that someone deliberately hit Joe, Mike can't officially open a case to find out."

"That's a real problem," Rachael commented.

"I know. Mike promised me he'd ask Sheriff Grant if he can work on Joe's case, but he doesn't hold out much hope since Sheriff Grant's such a stickler for the rules."

"Can he help you unofficially?" Rachael asked.

"He said he would, but he can't devote much time to it."

"Then it's up to you," Lisa said with a sigh.

"And Norman. He promised to help me if he can."

"How about us?" Rachael asked. "Can we do anything to help you find out about Joe?"

"I'm not sure. Let's get a cup of coffee and I'll tell you what I know so far. I do have some clues, but I'm not sure how productive they'll be. But don't you two have to get home to make supper for Jack?"

"Not tonight," Lisa said. "Dad's going to my oldest sister's house for dinner. Her husband is picking him up. Rachael and I have nothing we need to do, except . . ." She stopped speaking and glanced at Rachael. Rachael gave a little nod and Lisa went on. "Herb lined Rachael up with a friend of his and we're all going out tonight. But they're not picking us up until seven-thirty." She stopped and glanced at the clock. "We've got at least an hour before we have to leave to get ready."

"We're going out to the Rock Tavern for burgers and then we're going to stay for the live music," Rachael told her. "It's a country-western band and the Rock Tavern's got a dance floor. Herb's friend promised to teach me the Texas two-step."

"It sounds like a fun evening," Hannah said, delighted to learn that Lisa was still dating Herb Beeseman. Even though she shied away from playing matchmaker, she'd arranged for Herb to take Lisa to one of the traditional Christmas parties that were given in Lake Eden last year. It had been an extravagant affair, and Lisa and Herb had enjoyed themselves and definitely enjoyed being together. Everyone, including Lisa's father, Jack, thought they were a cute couple, and Lisa, after dealing with the death of her mother from cancer and the gradual decline of her father from the onset of Alzheimer's disease, deserved a little joy in her life.

"I'll get more coffee," Rachael offered, heading for the kitchen coffeepot.

"And I'll get a couple of my Christmas Date Cupcakes for you to taste just as soon as I stir my Cocktail Mix and take it out of the oven," Hannah promised.

In a matter of minutes, the three of them were sitting at the work station, drinking coffee and biting into Hannah's cupcakes.

"These are good!" Rachel said, her words somewhat muffled by the bite of cupcake she was chewing.

"Yes, they are," Lisa agreed. "They remind me of your grandma's date cake."

"That's because they are my grandmother's date cake," Hannah told her. "I just rewrote the recipe as a cupcake."

"I really like the sugar and chocolate chips on the top," Rachael commented. "The sugar crunches and the chocolate is smooth. The difference in textures adds interest to the top."

"And you don't have to frost them," Hannah told them. "You put on the topping *before* you put the cupcake batter in the oven."

"They're really good, Hannah." Rachael was clearly impressed. "Can I have a copy of the recipe so I can make them for my college roommate?"

Hannah turned to Lisa. "It's in our recipe binder. Will you run a copy and give it to Rachael when you come in tomorrow?"

"Sure, and I'll run one for me, too. I want to make these for Herb and his mom the next time they come over to have dinner with us."

Once Lisa and Rachael had finished their coffee, they left for the night. Hannah removed her Cocktail Munchie Mix from the oven, stirred it, and added the mixed nuts that were the last ingredient in the recipe. The nuts did not have to be heated since the ingredients called for roasted mixed nuts. The recipe was very clear about that. But Hannah did remove the hazelnuts and the Brazil nuts before she added the rest of the nuts. The recipe she had advised that, and there was an additional note written in her grandmother's perfect Palmer penmanship. It said, *Do this for Uncle Harry – false teeth.*

Hannah had just finished mixing up yet another batch of cookies for the next day's baking when there was a knock at the back kitchen door. It was a very polite but insistent knock and Hannah knew that it belonged to her sister, Andrea.

"Hi, Andrea," she greeted as her sister came in the door. "You're going to dinner at Mother's house tonight, aren't you?"

"Yes, and Bill got the night off work so both of us are going."

"How about Tracey?" Hannah asked, hoping to see her young niece.

Andrea shook her head. "She's staying home with Grandma McCann, our nanny. She's got a little cold and I don't want to take her out at night when it's this cold." She spotted the roaster on the kitchen counter and asked, "What's in there?"

"Cocktail Munchie Mix. Mother's bound to serve drinks, and I thought we'd munch on that before dinner."

"Good idea. Are you bringing something to have with the ice cream Mother always serves for dessert?"

"Yes." Hannah gestured toward the rolling baker's rack that sat next to the oven. "I made Christmas Date Cupcakes and I thought I'd take some of those along."

"Good idea! Be sure to put a birthday candle in the one for Carrie."

Hannah was surprised. "It's Carrie's birthday?"

"No, but I saw Norman at Hal and Rose's Café at noon, and he told me that Carrie's birthday is December twenty-third."

"I wonder if Mother knows that."

"I don't think so. Norman said that his mother never really celebrated her birthday because everyone's so busy with Christmas parties, and most of her friends went away to visit their relatives. She said she'd never had a birthday party, and her own relatives brought her just one present that they said was for her birthday and Christmas combined."

"That's sad," Hannah said. "She really never had a birthday party?"

"No. That's why I just went out to the mall and got Carrie a birthday present from us."

"Thanks! What do I owe you, Andrea?"

"Only ten dollars. I got her a cashmere sweater."

"Cashmere? That must have been expensive!"

Andrea shook her head. "No, it was on sale because it had a little snag down by the hem. The saleslady told me that it would be easy to fix if you knew how to knit."

"But you don't know how to knit, do you?"

"Not me, but Grandma McCann does and she fixed it in about twenty seconds. I gift wrapped it and it's all ready to go."

"Perfect!" Hannah grabbed her saddlebag-sized purse and took out a ten-dollar bill. "Are you sure that this is enough?"

"It's fine."

Hannah just shook her head in amazement. "You're the best shopper I know, Andrea. I should make you my personal shopper when it comes to things like birthdays and Christmas presents."

"Good idea!" Andrea gave a little laugh. "Then I'll be sure to like what I get from you on my birthday and for Christmas."

"You mean you don't like what I buy for you?" Hannah asked.

"Oh!" Andrea looked a bit embarrassed. "No, that's not what I meant at all. I was just joking. You've seen me carrying that tapestry purse you gave me last year, haven't you?"

"I think so. Then you like it?"

"It's very . . . colorful," Andrea said. "You haven't seen me carry it very often because . . . I'm saving it for special occasions."

"Oh, that's nice," Hannah said, smiling back. Andrea was making up an excuse for the tapestry purse, but at least she cared enough to do that.

"Are you bringing anything else to Mother's house?" Andrea asked, and Hannah knew she was trying to change the subject.

"Nope, that's it," Hannah said, grateful that they were off the subjects of purses and Christmas presents.

"I'd better go," Andrea said, heading for the door again. "I have to pick up Bill at the sheriff's station."

"He didn't drive his own car?"

"He did. And that's the problem. It broke down again, and he can't find the time to fix it until the weekend. Until then, I'm taking him to work every morning and picking him up every night."

Once Andrea had left, Hannah went back to work, mixing up two more batches of cookie dough, covering them with plastic wrap, and carrying them to a shelf in her walk-in cooler. She packed up the cupcakes she was taking to her mother's house along with a birthday candle for Carrie, picked up the package of Cocktail Munchie Mix, got into her warm parka and boots, and went out the door. She had to make a lightning fast trip to her condo to feed Moishe, and change her clothes to something more appropriate than jeans and a sweatshirt for Carrie's birthday party.

COCKTAIL MUNCHIE MIX

To preheat oven, see Hannah's 1st Note.

1 box Rice Chex cereal *(12 ounces net weight)*
1 pound *(4 sticks, 16 ounces)* salted butter
5 drops hot sauce *(I used Slap Ya Mama hot sauce)*
1 teaspoon garlic salt
1 box Wheat Chex *(15 ounces net weight)*
1 box Corn Chex *(12 ounces net weight)*
½ box original Cheerios *(18 ounces net weight)*
1 bag *(8 ounces net weight)* Goldfish crackers
1 can *(15 to 20 ounces net weight)* salted, mixed
 nuts without peanuts *(I used Planters)*
1 bag or box *(6 to 10 ounces net weight)* thin pret-
 zel sticks *(I used Snyder's)*

Hannah's 1st Note: You will need a large roaster to make this cocktail mix. BEFORE you preheat your oven, try your roaster in the oven to see which position the rack should be in. Try to center the roaster in the oven, if possible. This will provide even heat for your Cocktail Munchie Mix.

Preheat your oven to 250 degrees F. *(Not a misprint. That's two hundred and fifty degrees.)*

Spray the inside of your roaster with Pam or another nonstick cooking spray.

Place the Rice Chex cereal in the bottom of the roaster.

Melt the butter for 2 minutes on HIGH. Let it sit in the microwave for a minute and stir it with a heat-resistant spatula to make sure that it's melted.

Stir in 5 drops of hot sauce.

Stir in the teaspoon of garlic salt.

Drizzle approximately one-quarter *(about ½ cup)* of the butter mixture on top of the Rice Chex.

Hannah's 2nd Note: This is one of the reasons I like to use a Pyrex measuring cup with a spout to melt the butter.

Place the Wheat Chex cereal on top of the Rice Chex cereal.

Drizzle another half-cup of the butter mixture on top of the Wheat Chex cereal.

Place the Corn Chex cereal on top of the Wheat Chex cereal.

Drizzle another half-cup of the butter mixture on top of the Corn Chex cereal.

Place HALF the box of Cheerios cereal on top of the Corn Chex cereal.

Drizzle the remainder of the butter mixture over the top of the Cheerios cereal.

Sprinkle the bag of Goldfish crackers over the top.

DO NOT add the mixed nuts or the stick pretzels yet! They will be added later.

Wash your hands. You're going to use them as a kitchen tool. Dry your hands and mix the contents of the roaster together with your impeccably clean fingers.

Hannah's 3rd Note: If you've worked rapidly, the cereal, butter, and Goldfish layers might be a bit too hot to mix with your fingers. If so, take a coffee break for 5 minutes or so and then try again.

Once your cereal, butter, and Goldfish layers have been mixed together, bake them, *uncovered*, at 250 degrees F.

Set your oven timer for 15 *(fifteen)* minutes.

You will bake your Cocktail Munchie Mix for a total of 1 and ½ *(one and one-half)* hours, not counting mixing times.

Hannah's 4th Note: Unfortunately, you can't just walk off and leave your Cocktail Munchie Mix for one and a half hours. You do have to stir it every 15 minutes or so, but it's worth staying home for. I have a separate timer at home that I use when I make this. I set the regular timer on the oven for an hour and a half, and my separate timer for 15 minutes after each time I stir it.

When one hour has passed *(that consists of four 15-minute segments)*, open the can of mixed nuts and sprinkle them over the top of your Cocktail Mix.

Hannah's 5th Note: When my grandmother made this recipe she always picked out the hazelnuts and Brazil nuts and set them aside. She made a note on the recipe that reads, "Do this for Uncle Harry – false teeth."

The contents of the roaster will be hot, so use your large mixing spoon to mix in the nuts.

Open the bag of stick pretzels and mix those in. Mix carefully so that they don't break up into little pieces.

Put the roaster back into the oven and bake at 250 degrees F. for an additional ½ *(half)* hour.

Take the roaster out of the oven, give the mixture a final stir, and let it cool.

To store: Keep in a tightly sealed bag in the kitchen cupboard for no more than a week or two. DO NOT keep in the refrigerator or it will get soggy.

Hannah's 5th Note: If you make the mistake of refrigerating these marvelous munchies, all is not lost. Simply place the mixture in a roaster and heat it in the oven, preheated to 250 degrees F. for 15 minutes. Check the cereal to see if it has crisped up again. If it hasn't, stir it and heat it again in 15-minute intervals until the cereal is crisp.

Yield: At least 20 cups of Cocktail Munchie Mix that everyone who tastes it will love to munch.

To Serve: Place the Cocktail Munchie Mix in a large bowl with a scoop in it. Surround the large bowl with disposable plastic bowls or cups. Invite your guests to help themselves to the yummy snack you made.

Chapter Nine

"**I**'m here, Mother," Hannah said when her mother answered the door. "I brought some things for you."

"Wonderful!" Delores said, smiling. "No one's here yet, dear, so you're right on time to help me set the table and get everything ready." She spotted the packages that Hannah was carrying and looked surprised. "What did you bring, dear?"

"Christmas Date Cupcakes for dessert, and a candle to stick in Carrie's. Andrea dropped by The Cookie Jar and told me about her birthday."

"That's nice, dear, although it's actually not her birthday."

"I know. Andrea talked to Norman and he said it was the day before Christmas Eve. But she also said that Carrie never had a birthday party. I was planning on bringing Christmas Date Cupcakes for dessert anyway, and I thought I'd put a candle in hers, and we could say it's her birthday party."

"That's very sweet of you, dear! I have a birthday present for her, and I could give it to her early."

"Andrea and I have one for her, too."

Delores stopped speaking and began to frown. "There's only one problem, dear. I don't think we'd better call it her birthday party. Carrie isn't all that happy about turning sixty-four this year. As a matter of fact, she asked me not to mention it to any of our friends."

Hannah gave a little shrug. "Turning sixty-four is better than the alternative, isn't it?"

"Of course it is, but it's one of those milestone birthdays for Carrie, and she made me promise not to tell anyone how old she is."

Hannah knew she had to tread carefully. Some people were very sensitive about their age and one of those people happened to be her own mother. "I didn't know sixty-four was a milestone birthday. I always thought the real milestone was sixty-five."

"Oh, it is. If you're still working, it means that you can retire with full benefits. But Carrie's not working, and she's one year short of qualifying for Medicare. Actually, dear . . . I suspect she's thinking of that Beatles song. You know the one, don't you?"

"I know it," Hannah said quickly, hoping that her mother wouldn't attempt to break into song and she'd be forced to join in. Hannah had learned early on that she couldn't carry a tune. She'd discovered this in third grade when their class was going to sing a song for a school program and their teacher had pulled Hannah aside and asked her to *please, just mouth the words.*

"So you won't call it a birthday party?" Delores asked.

"No, I won't. Now that I understand how Carrie feels, I'll think of something else to call it."

"But it'll have to be something that calls for presents," Delores reminded her.

"Right. A non-birthday party, but don't call it that. Is that right?"

"That's exactly it, dear. Thank you, Hannah." Delores looked very relieved. And then she noticed the large bag that Hannah was carrying. "I hope you didn't bring the whole dinner. It's my turn, you know. I brought Florence's wonderful roast chicken for us."

"I was hoping you'd serve chicken," Hannah said quickly. "I just brought the cupcakes and . . . I guess you could call it an appetizer, because it's served with drinks. Do you remember Grandma Ingrid's Cocktail Munchie Mix?"

"Of course I do!" Delores looked absolutely delighted. "It was so tasty! I just loved it. I must have asked her for the recipe a half-dozen times, but she wouldn't give it to . . ." She stopped speaking and began to frown. "She gave it to *you*?!"

"Not exactly. I found it in her old recipe file. It was in her kitchen, and I saved it when we got the house ready to sell."

"Oh!" Delores began to smile again. "Well . . . good for you, dear! I still have several boxes of your grandmother's things in the garage. We'll have to go through them sometime, and see if there are any other recipes that you can use."

"That sounds like fun," Hannah replied, and she had to admit that it did. Grandma Ingrid had been a wonderful cook and baker, just like her mother, Great-Grandma Elsa.

"Is there anything in there that we should refrigerate?" Delores asked, looking down at the large box again.

"Just a green salad that I thought I'd throw together at the last minute. You have a large salad bowl, don't you, Mother?"

"I have the one you bought me on the stand. Would you like to use that?"

"Yes, when I make the salad. For right now, I think I'll just put the ingredients in the refrigerator. The bowl's really too large to fit in there easily."

"That's true," Delores agreed. "I have two bottles of champagne, a six-pack of Cold Spring Export for Mike, and white wine for Andrea and Carrie. You'd have to move quite a few things to fit that big salad bowl in there."

Hannah heard the doorbell ring and she escaped to the kitchen to put away her salad ingredients. Delores had a habit of going grocery shopping when she was hungry, and she often bought things that struck her fancy at the time. Then she never got around to eating them and they sat in the refrigerator until, occasionally, they no longer resembled what she'd purchased. Hannah had been meaning to come over to check out her mother's refrigerator for weeks now to identify any out-of-date items and throw them away. Vowing to put that on the top of her mental to-do list, she stashed her salad ingredients inside and closed the refrigerator door.

"Hello, Hannah." Norman came into the kitchen. "Your mother said you were in here. Is there anything I can do to help you?"

"That depends. Is your mother here yet?"

"Yes. She's in the living room talking to your mother."

"Good. Then you can open a bottle of champagne, while I get an ice bucket and glasses so we can take it in to them. And you can tell me what you want to drink."

"Ginger ale, if your mother has it. If not, I'll take any soft drink she has."

"I saw some Vernors Ginger Ale in the refrigerator," Hannah told him. "I think it was behind two cartons of cottage cheese and an elderly tomato."

While Hannah opened several cupboards, looking for her mother's silver ice bucket, Norman took one bottle of champagne out of the refrigerator and put it on the kitchen counter. "You're right about the tomato, Hannah," he remarked. "It looks like some kind of science experiment gone wrong."

Hannah laughed. "Dump it in the trash, Norman. Is the champagne cold?"

"Yes." Norman took the kitchen towel that Hannah handed him, removed the foil and the little cage over the cork from the top of the bottle, and extracted the cork with an ease that Hannah envied. "You did that so well!" she complimented him.

"Thanks. Shall I take the ice bucket and champagne to your mother?"

"Yes. She likes to pour. I'll bring the glasses and a mug for your ginger ale."

Once Hannah had delivered the glassware, she hurried back to the kitchen and put the Cocktail Munchie Mix she'd made in a bowl. She found cute paper cocktail napkins in a drawer, along with her mother's monogrammed coasters, and hurried out to the living room to join the mothers and Norman. They were just sitting down in chairs arranged around her mother's round coffee table when the doorbell rang.

"I'll get it," Norman said, jumping to his feet. "You ladies just sit here and enjoy your drinks."

"He's so thoughtful," Delores commented to Carrie.

"Yes, he is," Hannah agreed. "Norman opened the champagne and he didn't spill a drop."

"I taught him how to do that," Carrie said proudly. "When Norman's father came home from the dental clinic on Saturday nights, he liked to have champagne before dinner."

"Hello, everyone." Andrea came into the room. She was wearing a lavender silk suit, and with her light blond hair arranged in a sleek chignon, she looked like a fashion model.

"What a lovely suit!" Carrie complimented her, and then she turned to Andrea's husband, Bill Todd. "How are you, Bill?"

"Good," Bill said, sitting down next to Delores. "I'm sorry we're a little late. Grandma McCann was just putting Tracey to bed, and we wanted to tuck her in and kiss her good night."

"Of course you did," Delores said with a smile. "I used to do the same thing when I had to leave for one of my clubs and Lars was babysitting with the girls." She turned to Hannah. "Do you remember that?"

"Yes, I do," Hannah said, hoping that her father had never told Delores how the minute she drove off in her car, he let Hannah and her younger sisters get back up from bed again, and watch television with him until they fell asleep on the couch.

"Red wine?" Norman asked Bill, as Delores poured a glass of champagne for Andrea.

"Yes, please."

Andrea smiled. "Bill's not on call tonight. He's actually got the night off and it's the first time this week."

The doorbell rang again, but this time Hannah got up. "It's probably Mike," she said, "since he's the only one not here. I'll get it."

"And I'll get Bill's wine," Norman offered quickly. "I saw the bottle on the kitchen counter."

As soon as everyone had the beverage they wanted, the conversation began to flow. Hannah told them all about her visit with Joe at the hospital, and then she turned to Mike. "Will Sheriff Grant let you help us find out more about Joe and where he came from?"

Mike shook his head. "Sorry, Hannah. I asked, but he said exactly what I thought he'd say, that since Joe's case didn't include a crime, he wouldn't let me work on it."

"I was there when he said that," Bill told them. "Both of us tried to get Sheriff Grant to budge, but he wouldn't give an inch."

"Then we'll just have to solve the mystery of Joe's identity ourselves," Delores said, turning to Hannah. "That's right, isn't it, dear?"

"That's right," Hannah agreed, finishing her glass of champagne and standing up. "I'm going to go make the salad." She turned to Delores. "Would you like me to heat the chicken?"

"Yes, dear. It's already in the oven. All you have to do is turn it on."

"I'll get the table," Andrea offered, rising from her chair. "Do you want the china, Mother?"

"Of course, since it's a celebration. Isn't that right, Hannah?"

"That's right," Hannah confirmed it, glad that she'd figured out a way to refer to their party tonight. "We're all going to celebrate Carrie's anniversary."

Carrie looked thoroughly puzzled. "My anniversary?! What do you mean, Hannah? My anniversary of *what*?"

"You mean you don't know?" Hannah asked her.

"No! I have no idea what you're talking about!"

"Then I'd better tell you. I know that today isn't the actual date, but since we're all together tonight, I thought it was a good time to celebrate the thirty-fourth anniversary of your twentieth birthday!"

"Hannah!" Delores looked completely horrified for a moment. Then her expression changed and she began to smile. This told Hannah that her mother had done the mental math, and all was well.

"My thirty-fourth anniversary of . . ." Carrie stopped in mid-sentence and began to laugh. "You're right, Hannah! How clever of you!"

"We got you a little something for your anniversary," Andrea said, removing the beautifully wrapped box from the large tote bag she'd carried in with her. "We hope you like it."

"Oh, my!" Carrie exclaimed, unwrapping it quickly and lifting off the lid. "A beautiful sweater! And it's my favorite color of blue! It's so soft and . . . is this cashmere?"

"Yes, it is," Andrea told her.

"How wonderful!" Carrie was clearly delighted. "I'd love to wear it right now, but I think I'll wait until my actual birthday." She turned to Norman. "I might just have to make a trip to the mall to buy an outfit to go with it."

"I'll go with you," Delores offered immediately. "And if you'd like, we'll go tomorrow morning. We can have lunch at that little French place and stop at the hospital on our way home to see Joe, if Doc will let us visit."

"He said it was fine," Hannah told her quickly. "Joe mentioned that he wanted to see you, and Doc says he's stable enough to have a few visitors."

"That's good news, too!" Carrie said. "This is the best anniversary of my birthday that I've ever had!"

CHRISTMAS DATE CUPCAKES

Preheat oven to 325 degrees F., rack in the middle position.

Ingredients:

2 cups chopped pitted dates or whole pitted dates *(you can usually find the chopped, pitted dates in the produce section of your grocery store during the Christmas holiday season)*
2 and ¾ cups water or cold coffee
¼ cup rum or brandy
2 teaspoons baking soda
1 cup softened, salted butter *(2 sticks, ½ pound)*
2 cups white *(granulated)* sugar
4 large eggs
½ teaspoon salt
3 cups all-purpose flour *(pack it down in the cup when you measure it)*

Hannah's 1st Note: If you can't find chopped, pitted dates, buy whole pitted dates, sprinkle them with 2 Tablespoons of flour, and then chop them in a food processor before measuring out the 2 cups you'll need.

Hannah's 2nd Note: If you don't want to use liquor in this recipe, use 3 cups of water and a teaspoon of vanilla extract.

Hannah's 3rd Note: This recipe is simple to make with an electric mixer, but you can also do it by hand with a mixing spoon if you wish.

Place the chopped, pitted dates in a medium-sized, microwave safe bowl.

Measure out 2 and ¾ cups of water or cold coffee and pour it into the bowl on top of the dates.

Add the quarter cup of rum or brandy and mix with a spoon.

Heat the bowl in the microwave on HIGH for 3 minutes or until you can see that the liquids begin to boil.

Use oven mitts or potholders to take the bowl out of the microwave and set it on a towel on the kitchen counter.

Add the baking soda to the bowl. *(Be careful – the baking soda may foam up a bit.)*

Give the bowl with the dates, liquids, and baking soda a stir with a mixing spoon.

Leave the bowl on the kitchen counter to cool.

Place 1 cup of softened, salted butter in the bowl of an electric mixer.

Sprinkle the 2 cups of white *(granulated)* sugar on top of the butter.

Turn on the mixer and beat the butter and sugar on LOW speed until they are mixed together.

Turn the mixer up to MEDIUM speed and beat the butter and sugar until they are light and fluffy. Don't stop beating until the mixture is a uniform color.

Crack the eggs and add them to the mixer bowl, one at a time, beating on LOW speed after each addition.

Add the salt to the bowl and beat that in.

Shut off the mixer and feel the bowl with the dates. If it's not so hot it could cook the eggs, turn the mixer on LOW speed.

Use a rubber spatula to gradually add the date mixture to the ingredients in the bowl of your electric mixer.

With the mixer still on LOW speed, add the flour in 1-cup increments, beating after each addition.

Turn off the mixer, scrape down the sides of the bowl with the rubber spatula, and resume beating at MEDIUM speed.

When everything is thoroughly mixed, shut off the mixer again, and let your cupcake batter sit while you prepare your cupcake pans.

You will need two 12-cup cupcake pans to bake these delicious cupcakes.

Place 2 cupcake papers in each cup. These cupcakes are moist, and if you use 2 papers, they will be easier for your guests to peel off before they eat the cupcakes.

Give the bowl with the cupcake batter a final stir by hand.

Use a spoon or a scooper to transfer the batter to the cupcake pan. Fill the cupcake papers ¾ *(three-quarters)* full. This way you will have room for the topping.

The Topping:

6 ounces *(by weight)* milk chocolate chips *(1 cup)*
½ cup white *(granulated)* sugar
½ cup chopped nuts *(use any nuts you like – I prefer walnuts or pecans)*

Place the milk chocolate chips in a bowl on the counter.

Place the white sugar in another bowl on the counter.

Place the chopped nuts in a third bowl on the counter.

Hannah's 4th Note: The reason you'll use three separate bowls is that you may have some of the topping ingredients left over. If you do, simply put the leftover chips back in their bag, put the white sugar back in its package or canister, and put the chopped nuts in a ziplock bag to use when you make another cake or cookie that calls for chopped nuts.

Sprinkle the top of each unbaked cupcake with milk chocolate chips.

Sprinkle the top of the milk chocolate chips with white sugar.

Sprinkle the top of the white sugar with chopped nuts.

When all the cupcakes have been topped, use a rubber spatula or your fingers to press the topping ingredients down gently. This will cause the topping to bake onto the cupcake batter, and not slide off when your

guests take the cupcake papers off their baked cupcakes.

Bake your Christmas Date Cupcakes at 325 degrees F. for 30 to 40 minutes. Start testing after baking 30 minutes. A cake tester or a long toothpick inserted in the center of a cupcake should come out clean when the cupcakes are done. *(If you happen to stick the toothpick in and hit a milk chocolate chip, it'll come out covered with melted chocolate—just wipe it off and stick it in again to test the actual cupcake batter.)*

Let the cupcakes cool in the pan on a wire rack. These cupcakes can be served slightly warm, at room temperature, or chilled.

Yield: 1 and ½ to 2 dozen delicious cupcakes, depending on how much batter you use per cupcake.

Chapter Ten

She knew she'd never been this cold, never in her life. She was so cold, she couldn't move. Why was it so cold? Was she outside? Had she gotten out of her warm bed, opened her condo door, and gone outside in the snow without her boots and her parka? And if she had, why? She was sure she'd never walked in her sleep before. Why now?

She shivered again. People died from exposure to the cold in the winter. Was she going to die? The only part of her body that was warm was . . . her face! Her face was nice and warm, even hot. Did she have a fever? Was she ill?

There was something on her face. She could feel it. Whatever that something was, it made her face the only part of her body that wasn't shaking with the cold. Was it a blanket? A furry, warm blanket? It made her feel like sneezing.

She attempted to reach up and feel it, but her arms

didn't seem to work. The blanket had an odor that reminded her of something, some kind of food. It wasn't a
bad odor. It was merely puzzling.

Without consciously willing it to, her nose started
twitching. That was when she realized that she felt like
sneezing. The warm, fuzzy thing, whatever it was, smelled
vaguely like fish.

She made a mental list of what she knew. There was
something warm on her face, but the rest of her was icy
cold. And the warm, furry thing smelled like . . . fish?
Yes! That was the smell. It smelled like fish and that
made her wonder if somehow, she'd traveled to Alaska.
Or perhaps she was at the North Pole on some kind of
scientific expedition. But she wouldn't be alone, if she'd
volunteered to explore some phenomenon in the frozen
North. Scientists didn't go to the North Pole alone.
They went in groups, so they could help each other sur-
vive in such a hostile environment. Why was she here?
And why was she alone? Where were the rest of the scientists?

Perhaps she wasn't alone. Perhaps one of her expedition mates had placed the fur on her face in an effort to
keep her warm. They might have harvested a walrus or
another furry arctic animal and used its fur to make a
blanket. That would certainly explain why this furry
blanket smelled like fish.

But this couldn't be a blanket. It was much too small.
It only covered her face and not even all of her face. It
was something else, something that . . . moved! The
too-small furry blanket had moved! She was sure of it!

Rather than think about a moving, furry blanket that could be a dangerous animal, she assessed the rest of her surroundings. She was lying on something hard and cold. Ice? Perhaps an ice floe? Had the others in the expedition put her on an ice floe and let her go out to sea because she was dying? And if that was the case, why had they covered her face with a small furry blanket?

The blanket moved again, and now it was making a strange noise. It sounded a bit like a car engine running, a noise caused by vibration. Could that noise be coming from the moving ice floe?

She tried to move, but her muscles didn't cooperate. She was terribly uncomfortable and she wanted to sit up to see where she was. She thought about that and concentrated until she'd managed to raise her head up slightly. That was when the furry blanket slid off and made a dreadful noise!

The noise was a yowl, a loud, protesting yowl. It reminded her of something and . . .

"Where am I?" Hannah's eyes flew open, but all she could see was inky blankness. She touched the hard surface and felt boards. She was on the floor. But which floor? And where was it?

There was a green light coming from above her. It was flashing a number, on and off, on and off, on and off. There was a four. After the four was a three and then a zero. And in between the four and the three was a colon. Four-thirty. Four-thirty in the morning. It was her digital alarm clock on the bedside table. But it was above her head, which meant that she was on the floor. Why was she on the floor? And where had that awful yowl come from?

"Moishe!" she said, reality coming in a rush. Moishe had been lying next to her, brushing against her face. But what was she doing on the floor? Had she fallen out of bed?

Slowly, a bit painfully, Hannah got to her feet. She turned to look at the bed and saw that Moishe was curled up on her pillow. Had he pushed her off the pillow and out of bed so that he could have her pillow?

The alarm clock began to beep and Hannah reached out, none too gently, to shut it off. She switched on the bedside lamp and glanced down at her furry pet. He was sleeping like an angel now that he had her expensive goose-down-filled pillow.

With a sigh, Hannah headed off to the master bathroom to take her morning shower. She'd stop at Cost-Mart today on the way home from work, and buy another pillow. It was painfully obvious that Moishe coveted her pillow and the only thing that would satisfy him was one just like hers.

Twenty minutes and three cups of strong coffee later, Hannah felt almost human again. She'd fed the cat who'd stolen her night's rest and she couldn't help but smile as she watched him attack his breakfast. This morning he was enjoying his usual kitty crunchies flavored with a generous helping of canned salmon. And now that she thought about it, and realized that his last meal had contained canned tuna, it was no longer a mystery why her moving, furry blanket had smelled like fish.

"Don't worry, Moishe," Hannah told him as she got up from her kitchen table. "I'll be home in plenty of time to fix your dinner."

As Hannah went out into the dark and took the outside, covered staircase to the underground garage, she thought about her winter schedule. It was still dark outside when she left her condo, but by the time she drove to The Cookie Jar and baked her first batch of cookies, the sky would begin to lighten. Like most people, Hannah always felt more cheerful when the sun rose and illuminated the landscape outside her kitchen window.

Veteran Minnesotans knew that winter was a season that tested their strength and determination. If you worked an eight-hour day shift inside a building, you had to drive to work in the dark, work your whole shift without going out into the sun, and drive home in the dark. In the dead of winter, the weak winter sun didn't rise until after eight in the morning and it set close to four in the afternoon. The lack of sun to brighten the day was difficult for some people to endure. If you were lucky, and you could afford to leave Minnesota in the winter and travel to some place like Florida, or Arizona, or California until the Minnesota spring arrived, you were called *snowbirds*. These were the people who left right after the first snowfall and didn't come back until the robins arrived to herald a warmer season.

The condo complex was well-lighted and Hannah

had no trouble driving up the ramp to the ground floor and navigating the circular road past the other four-unit condo buildings. It was only after she left the lights of the complex behind her that her headlights were the only guide through the dark. Her lights cut a path through the packed snow on the road and it was impossible to tell where the shoulder of the road began. The tunnel her headlights cut through the darkness was mesmerizing, and Hannah knew she had to follow the deep ruts in the snow that other cars had made to keep from driving off the road.

It seemed to take much more time than it actually did to approach the access to the highway. Here the lighting was better, and once she took her place in the irregular stream of cars traveling on the highway, she felt more at ease.

It didn't take long to reach the turnoff for Lake Eden. Hannah signaled, although there was no one behind her at the time, and turned by the Catholic church. She drove to Main Street, went down it to Third, then took the alley in back of The Cookie Jar, and parked in her spot by the back kitchen door. She took the precaution of plugging the extension cord that led to her block heater into the strip of outlets on the outer wall of her building and waded through the snow that had fallen during the night to the kitchen door.

It wasn't easy to unlock the door wearing gloves, but Hannah managed. Then she stepped inside the warm interior and flicked the switch that would turn her white kitchen walls into something that resembled a pristine snowbank reflecting the sun. She blinked a few times, because her eyes were accustomed to the darkness outside, and then she hurried to preheat her industrial oven for the morning's baking.

At precisely eight-thirty, there was a knock on the back kitchen door. Hannah gave a little sigh. It was her mother's knock, and she hoped it didn't mean that she'd have to bake extra cupcakes again.

"Hello, Mother." She ushered Delores in, and took her parka to hang on one of the hooks by the back door. "Would you like to have coffee with me?"

"Oh, yes!" Delores responded immediately, making a beeline for the work station and her favorite stool. "Thank you, dear. I didn't have time for coffee this morning."

Hannah was just about to sit down across from her mother when there was another knock at the door. This was a tentative knock, a knock that said, *Sorry to disturb you when you're working, but I hope you're not too busy to see me.* "It's Andrea," she told her mother.

Delores looked puzzled. "How do you know?"

"I recognize her knock. I'll go let her in." Hannah hurried to the door, unlocked it, and ushered in her sister. "Just hang up your coat and I'll get you some coffee."

When Hannah came back to the work station with Andrea's coffee, she didn't sit down across from her mother and Andrea. Instead, she picked up her coffee and took a big sip.

"Aren't you going to join us, dear?" Delores asked her.

"I will, but I figured I'd better answer the door first."

It was Andrea's turn to look puzzled. "But I didn't hear a knock."

"Neither did I," Hannah admitted, "but the third person should be here any minute."

"You're expecting someone else?" Delores asked.

"Yes, but I don't know who it'll be."

Don't say it! the rational part of her mind urged, and Hannah gave a little smile. Of course she wouldn't repeat one of her father's favorite superstitions, which was *Bad luck always came in threes.* There was no doubt in her mind that her mother would ask for some of her time, or that Andrea would ask for a favor that would also take her away from her work. This wasn't technically a bad thing. She didn't mind helping her family when they needed her, but holiday season was a very busy time, and she had little time to spare. She was working long hours with the baking and catering holiday parties, and when she got home at night, she was completely exhausted.

"What do you mean?" Delores asked, and for a moment, Hannah wasn't quite sure what to say. Then she remembered her remark about not knowing who her third visitor would be and responded, "I don't know who my third visitor will be, but there's an old saying that visitors always come in threes."

Not a bad cover, the rational part of her mind declared. *I wonder if your mother will buy it.*

"I think I remember hearing something like that," Andrea said, "but I thought it was something about bad news coming in threes. And Digger Gibson always says that death comes in threes."

Delores shook her head. "I wouldn't put much stock in that, dear, especially since Digger's a mortician. There are all sorts of silly superstitions. Things don't really happen in . . ." She stopped speaking, and began to frown as they heard a knock at the door.

"Or maybe they do," Hannah said with a laugh, setting her coffee down and hurrying to answer the door.

"Janice?!" Hannah couldn't hide her surprise when she opened the door and saw Janice Cox standing there. "Come in out of the cold. Do you have time for a cup of coffee before you go to work at Kiddie Korner?"

"I do," Janice said, smiling at Hannah, "and I could use a little fortification before I go down to the community center. My preschoolers haven't been able to go out on the playground for a whole week now, and they're getting more stir-crazy with each passing day."

Janice hung up her parka and spotted Delores and Andrea sitting at the work station. "Hello, Delores and Andrea." Then she turned to Hannah. "All we need is Michelle and we have the whole Swensen family here."

Hannah poured Janice's coffee, delivered it, and then she went to the baker's rack to see which of the sweet treats she'd baked earlier were cool enough to serve to her guests. "How about a Holiday Cheer Cherry Cupcake?" she asked.

"That sounds delicious!" Delores responded almost immediately. "Of course everything you bake is delicious, dear."

Your mother's trying to sweeten you up, the suspicious part of Hannah's mind decided. *Either that, or the favor she wants is a really big one.*

"That sounds great to me." Janice gave Hannah a smile. "I love cherries."

"So do I," Andrea agreed, "except I don't think I've ever had a cherry cupcake before."

"Taste it and see if you like it, Andrea," Hannah said as she set the plate she'd filled with cupcakes in front of them.

"What's the frosting?" Delores asked, beginning to peel the paper from her cupcake.

"It's a cream cheese frosting," Hannah answered.

"Is it the same one you put on your carrot cake?" Andrea wanted to know.

"Yes, except it has half of a cherry on top. I try to decorate each type of cupcake differently, so we can tell them apart if people ask us at parties."

"Smart," Janice nodded, "especially if you use frostings that look alike on some of them." She smiled and took a bite of her cupcake. "These are really good, Hannah!"

"Yes, they are!" Andrea agreed.

"Marvelous, dear," Delores added.

There was silence for a moment and Hannah knew that none of her visitors wanted to bring up the reason they'd knocked on her back kitchen door so early. It was up to her to open the subject.

"Mother," Hannah began, "I know there must be a

reason you came to have coffee with me so early. Will you tell me what it is?"

"Well . . . yes. It's Michelle. I'm worried about her."

"What's wrong with Michelle?" Andrea asked. "The last time I talked to her she sounded just fine."

"When was that?" Delores asked.

"A couple of weeks ago. What's wrong with Michelle now?"

Delores gave a deep sigh. "If I tell you, I don't want any of you to mention this."

"I certainly won't," Janice assured her.

"And neither will I," Andrea promised. "You won't mention it, will you, Hannah?"

"Of course not. What's the problem, Mother?"

"Michelle's college boyfriend wants her to go home with him this weekend to meet his parents."

"That sounds serious," Janice commented. "Is Michelle going home with him?"

Delores gave a little shrug. "Michelle told me she can't decide whether she wants to go, or not."

"Did Michelle tell you if she's serious about her boyfriend?" Janice asked.

Delores shook her head. "No. And I wasn't sure what advice I could give her. I've never been in a situation like that."

"Not even with Dad?" Andrea asked.

"No. I already knew your father's parents. I used to work summers at the café and they came in to get coffee and pie every time they drove in from the farm to shop."

"We understand, Mother," Hannah told her, and she did understand. Delores was embarrassed because she really hadn't known what advice to give her youngest daughter. "Do you want me to call Michelle?"

"Yes, but I don't want her to know that I told you about her boyfriend problem."

"I could call her," Andrea suggested.

"No," Delores said quickly. "I don't want her to know I told you, either."

Hannah thought for a moment. "I'll think of a good excuse to call Michelle and see if she confides in me."

"But what if she doesn't?" Janice asked.

"I don't know, but I'll figure something out. Maybe I'll invite her to come here to stay with me over the weekend and see what she says. And I promise I won't tell her that you told us, Mother."

Delores looked relieved. "Thank you, dear. And after you talk to Michelle, do you promise to call me to tell me what happened?"

"Yes, Mother." Hannah decided it was time to change the subject before her mother tried to extract more promises. "How about you, Andrea? You're never here for coffee this early. Is something wrong?"

"Not really. I'm really bored now that I hired Grandma McCann to help with Tracey and . . . well . . . I was hoping you'd want me to come here and help you at The Cookie Jar. I could help you in the kitchen if you teach me how to bake."

Your sister has a screw loose! Hannah's suspicious

mind retorted. *Nobody on the face of this earth could teach Andrea to bake. She can't even make a decent peanut butter and jelly sandwich!*

Truer words were never spoken, but you should still let her down easy, Hannah's rational mind advised. *She looks really serious about wanting to help you, and that's very nice of her, isn't it?*

"Yes," Hannah responded to her rational mind aloud.

"Oh, thank you, Hannah!" Andrea said.

A joyful expression crossed Andrea's face, and that was when Hannah realized that she'd spoken aloud. She glanced at Delores, who looked positively shocked, and Janice, whose eyebrows were lifting toward the ceiling. Everyone in Lake Eden knew that Andrea was culinarily challenged.

"I'm sure I could teach you to bake if I had the time," Hannah said quickly, "but there's something else that's taking up a lot of my time right now, and that's where I could really use your help."

"Really?" Andrea still looked very pleased. "What do you want me to do, Hannah?"

"I want you to help me solve a mystery."

"Oh, my!" It was clear that Andrea was awestruck. "I'd love to help you, Hannah! But what could *I* do?"

"You can run out to the hospital with me right after I finish the baking. There's someone there I want you to meet."

"And he has something to do with the mystery?"

"He certainly does." Hannah glanced at Delores

again, and realized that her mother knew exactly what she was doing. "There's a patient out there I want you to meet."

"Joe Smith," Delores said, giving a little nod. "Good idea, Hannah."

"Joe Smith?" Andrea repeated the name. "Is that this patient's real name?"

"No," Delores answered her. "We don't know his real name and that's part of the mystery."

"How did he get to the hospital?" Andrea asked.

"I'll let Hannah tell you all about him," Delores said, standing up to go. "I have to go now. Carrie and I are meeting for breakfast at the café, and then I'm going to her house to look at her antiques."

"Did you rent the building for storage?"

"Not yet, dear. We're looking at it again this morning with Al Percy. Then we're going to decide if there's enough room to store all of our things."

Hannah escorted her mother to the door, helped her get into her parka, and saw her safely outside. Then she went back to her stool at the work station and turned to Janice. "I know you have to go down to Kiddie Korner soon, Janice. It was fun having coffee with you and I hope you'll drop by again. I'm curious, though. Is there a specific reason you came to see me this morning?"

"Yes, there is," Janice replied. "I need to order some cookies for our Kiddie Korner picnic."

Hannah frowned slightly. "Are you talking about the picnic you always have on the last day before summer break?"

Janice shook her head. "No, we're having a picnic this week on Friday. Is there enough time to order four dozen cookies?"

"Yes. Of course there is. But it's not exactly picnic weather. Are you going to have a picnic in the snow?"

Janice laughed. "No, Hannah. We're going to have a picnic on the green carpet in the lobby of the community center. The kids and I decided it looks enough like grass for us."

"So it's an inside picnic?" Andrea asked her.

"Oh, yes. It's much too cold for my class to go outside. As a matter of fact, we haven't been able to use the playground for three weeks now. It's just too cold and the kids are getting a little stir-crazy."

"I can understand that. I'm feeling a bit closed in myself," Hannah said. She got up from her stool and hurried to the counter by the wall phone where she kept their order book. Once she flipped it open, she asked, "What kind of cookies would you like?"

"I'm not sure. I just know that I need something they'll really enjoy. They've been very good about staying in and playing games in the room, but that wears thin after a while."

"What are you planning for the picnic menu?" Andrea asked her.

"Hot dogs, potato chips, pickles, and lemon-lime soda," Janice answered promptly. "And just in case you couldn't tell, I had the kids vote on the menu."

"The kids voted for lemon-lime soda?" Andrea looked

puzzled. "I expected you to say root beer or orange soda."

"That's what the kids wanted. It was a tie between strawberry soda and orange soda, but then I reminded them of the rug and how we had to be careful not to spill any liquids, so they agreed they should drink something that wouldn't stain if it spilled." She turned to Hannah. "They'll be thrilled that you're making the cookies. Everybody loves your cookies, Hannah."

"That's good to hear. What kind of cookies do they like?"

"Oatmeal cookies and chocolate chip cookies are their favorites."

Hannah jotted that down. "Do they prefer milk or semisweet chocolate?"

"Milk chocolate. They all love Hershey's bars and they're milk chocolate, aren't they?"

"Yes." Hannah thought for a moment. "How about Milk Chocolate Oatmeal Cookies?"

Janice smiled. "They would be perfect! I don't remember eating any of those before and I thought I'd tasted all of your cookies at one time or another."

"You probably have, but I've never made Milk Chocolate Oatmeal Cookies before."

Janice laughed. "Wait until I tell the kids that they'll be the first ones to taste them. They'll think that's just wonderful!"

"Your picnic sounds like fun," Andrea commented.

"I hope so. I borrowed some of my mother's picnic things, so we have a big wicker picnic basket, paper plates, plastic forks, and my mother's red and white checkered tablecloths to spread out on the carpet. I just wish I had something really unusual and fun to make them say *wow* when I gave it to them."

Hannah digested that remark for a moment and then she began to grin. "I've got it!" she announced.

"What?" both Janice and Andrea asked, almost in unison.

"Lisa's Rainbow Pickles."

"Rainbow Pickles?" Janice looked puzzled. "Where do you buy those?"

"You don't. You make them, or rather, *I* make them from Lisa's recipe."

"And they're *real* pickles?" Andrea asked.

"Sort of. They're made from pickles, but you put in enough sugar to make them sweet with a tiny bit of fruit flavoring. I can make them in almost any color, except blue."

"They sound perfect for my kids," Janice decided. "Can I arrange them on a platter so they look like a multi-colored flower?"

"Absolutely. They're made from dill pickle spears and I'll make one jar in red, one in orange, and one in green. And I'll give them to you in the jars, so they'll be easier to carry."

"If you want me to, I'll come to your picnic and put them on a platter for you," Andrea offered. And then she turned to Hannah. "You can spare me that long, can't you?"

Hannah felt like laughing, but she managed to merely

smile. "Of course I can. You can go for the whole picnic, if Janice wants you. Lisa's cousin Rachael is here and she's helping Lisa in the coffee shop."

"Thanks, Hannah." Andrea turned back to Janice. "It'll be good practice for when Tracey gets older."

Janice smiled. "You and Bill will enroll her in my preschool, won't you?"

"Of course! We can hardly wait."

"Good. I imagine you'll be letting Grandma McCann go once Tracey's in preschool."

Hannah watched as a worried expression crossed Andrea's face. "Maybe. I'm just not sure."

"Then you and Bill are planning to have more children?"

"I'm not sure about *that*!"

Andrea answered so quickly, Hannah had to hide a grin. She knew how relieved Andrea had been when Grandma McCann had accepted the position as Tracey's nanny. Her sister was good with older children, but babies were another matter. Andrea was very uncomfortable around babies.

"Thanks for the coffee and cupcake, Hannah." Janice stood up from her stool. "I have to get over to the community center and put out the crayons and make sure that Danny Jeffries has a new green in his box. We're coloring a picture of a kitten today and I know that Danny will want to color it green."

"Green?" Hannah asked. "Why green?"

"I'll bet it's his favorite color," Andrea answered before Janice could.

"You're right!" Janice gave her a thumbs-up and headed toward the back door. "I'll let myself out, and thanks again, Hannah."

When Janice had left, Hannah turned to her sister. "How did you guess that green was Danny's favorite color?"

Andrea gave a little shrug. "Because it had to be. Why else would a child color a kitten green?"

Hannah smiled as she nodded. That made sense. Once Tracey was old enough to color a picture, Andrea would undoubtedly turn into a super mom!

HOLIDAY CHEER CHERRY CUPCAKES

Preheat oven to 350 degrees F., rack in the middle position.

1 cup dried cherries *(if you can't find them, use Cherry Craisins)*
¼ cup cherry liqueur *(or cherry juice)*
¼ cup pineapple juice *(apple juice will also work just fine)*
4 large eggs
½ cup vegetable oil
1 cup *(8 ounces by weight)* sour cream
1 box of white or yellow cake mix, the kind that makes a 9-inch by 13-inch cake or a 2-layer cake *(I used Duncan Hines)*
1 teaspoon ground cinnamon
5.1-ounce package of DRY instant vanilla pudding and pie filling *(I used Jell-O)*
12-ounce *(by weight)* bag of white cholate or vanilla baking chips *(11-ounce package will do, too—I used Nestlé)*

Prepare your cupcake pans. You'll need two 12-cup cupcake or muffin pans lined with double cupcake papers.

Place the cup of dried cherries in a 2-cup or larger, microwave-safe bowl. *(I used my Pyrex 2-cup measuring cup.)*

Pour the quarter-cup of cherry liqueur over the cherries.

Pour the quarter-cup pineapple juice over the cherry liqueur.

Stir the dried cherries with the liquid.

Place the measuring cup or bowl in the microwave and heat on HIGH for one minute. Open the microwave and stir the cherries and liquids again.

Heat the cherries and liquid again on HIGH for 30 seconds.

Let the measuring cup sit in the microwave for another minute.

Using potholders or oven gloves, remove the measuring cup or bowl from the microwave and set it on a towel on the kitchen counter to cool.

Crack the eggs into the bowl of an electric mixer. Mix them up on LOW speed until they are light and fluffy, and are a uniform color.

Pour in the half-cup of vegetable oil and mix it in with the eggs on LOW speed. Continue to mix for one minute or until it is thoroughly mixed.

Shut off the mixer and add the cup *(8 ounces)* of sour cream. Mix it in on LOW speed.

Feel the measuring cup or bowl with the cherries and liquid. If they're not so hot they might cook the eggs, add them to your mixer bowl.

Mix on LOW speed for one minute or until the cherries and liquid are thoroughly mixed in.

When everything is well-combined, shut off the mixer and open the box of dry cake mix.

Add HALF of the dry cake mix to the mixer bowl, but don't turn on the mixer quite yet.

Sprinkle the teaspoon of ground cinnamon over the cake mix in the mixer bowl.

Turn the mixer on LOW speed and mix for 2 to 3 minutes, or until everything is well combined.

Shut off the mixer and sprinkle in the 2nd HALF of the dry cake mix. Mix it in thoroughly on LOW speed.

Shut off the mixer and scrape down the sides of the bowl with a rubber spatula.

Open the package of instant vanilla pudding and pie filling and sprinkle in the contents. Mix that in on LOW speed.

Shut off the mixer, scrape down the sides of the bowl again, and remove it from the mixer. Set it on the counter.

Sprinkle the white chocolate or vanilla baking chips into your bowl and stir them in by hand with the rubber spatula.

Use the rubber spatula or a scooper to transfer the cake batter into the prepared cupcake pan. Fill the cups three-quarters full.

Smooth the top of your cupcakes with the spatula and place them in the center of your preheated oven.

Bake your Holiday Cheer Cherry Cupcakes at 350 degrees F. for 15 to 20 minutes.

Before you take your cupcakes out of the oven, test it for doneness by inserting a cake tester, thin wooden skewer, or long toothpick into the middle of a cupcake.

If the tester comes out clean and with no cupcake batter sticking to it, your cupcakes are done. If there is still unbaked batter clinging to the tester, shut the oven door and bake your cupcakes for 5 minutes longer.

Take your cupcakes out of the oven and set the pans on cold stovetop burners or wire racks. Let them cool in the pans until they reach room temperature and then refrigerate them for 30 minutes before you frost them. *(Overnight is fine too.)*

Frost your cupcakes with Cherry Cream Cheese Frosting. *(Recipe and instructions follow.)*

Yield: Approximately 18 to 24 cupcakes, depending on cupcake size.

To Serve: These cupcakes can be served at room temperature or chilled. They're very rich so be sure to accompany them with tall glasses of icy cold milk or cups of strong hot coffee.

CHERRY CREAM CHEESE FROSTING

½ cup *(1 stick)* salted butter, softened to room temperature

8-ounce *(net weight)* package softened, brick-style cream cheese *(I used Philadelphia in the silver package.)*

1 teaspoon vanilla extract

1 teaspoon cherry liqueur or cherry juice

4 to 4 and ½ cups confectioners *(powdered)* sugar *(no need to sift unless it's got big lumps)*

To Decorate:

Maraschino cherry halves or red decorators sugar

Mix the softened butter with the softened cream cheese until the resulting mixture is well blended.

Add the teaspoon of vanilla extract and the teaspoon of cherry liqueur. Mix them in thoroughly.

Hannah's 1st Note: Do this next step at room temperature. If you heated the cream cheese and the butter to soften them, make sure your mixture has cooled to room temperature before you complete the next step.

Add the confectioners sugar in half-cup increments, stirring thoroughly after each addition, until the frost-

ing is of proper spreading consistency. *(You'll use all, or almost all, of the powdered sugar.)*

Use a frosting knife or a small rubber spatula to place a dollop of frosting in the center of the top of your cupcakes. Then spread it out almost to the edges of the cupcake paper.

Hannah's 2nd Note: If you spread the frosting all the way out to the edge of the cupcake, your guests will get frosting on their fingers when they peel off the cupcake paper and they'll have to wash or lick their fingers. Kids enjoy this. Adults, not so much.

If you wish to decorate the tops of your cupcakes, use a half maraschino cherry *(round side up)* or sprinkle with red decorators sugar.

If you have frosting left over, spread it on graham crackers, soda crackers, or what Great-Grandma Elsa used to call *store-boughten* cookies. This frosting can also be covered tightly and kept in the refrigerator for up to a week. When you want to use it, let it sit on the kitchen counter, still tightly covered, for an hour or so, or until it reaches room temperature and it is spreadable again.

This frosting also works well in a pastry bag, which brings up all sorts of interesting possibilities for decorating cakes or cookies.

MILK CHOCOLATE OATMEAL COOKIES

Preheat oven to 325 degrees F., rack in the middle position.

1 cup salted butter *(2 sticks, 8 ounces, ½ pound)*
1 cup white *(granulated)* sugar
1 cup powdered *(confectioners)* sugar
2 teaspoons vanilla extract
½ teaspoon salt
2 teaspoons baking soda
2 large eggs, beaten *(just whip them up in a glass with a fork)*
2 and ½ cups all-purpose flour *(pack it down in the cup when you measure it)*
1 cup *(half of a 12-ounce by weight package)* milk chocolate chips *(I used Nestlé)*
1 cup dry oatmeal *(I used Quaker Quick 1-Minute Oats)*
⅓ cup white granulated sugar for rolling dough balls.

Hannah's 1st Note: This recipe is much easier to make if you use an electric mixer. You can do it by hand, but it will take some muscle.

Before you start to mix up this cookie dough, prepare your baking sheets by spraying them with Pam or an-

other cooking spray. Alternatively, you can also line them with parchment paper if you prefer.

Place the butter in a large microwave-safe bowl. *(I used a quart Pyrex measuring cup with a spout)*

Turn the microwave on HIGH and heat the butter for 1 minute. Leave it in the microwave for another minute of standing time and then check to see if it's melted. If it's not, give it another 15 to 20 seconds on HIGH with an equal amount of standing time.

When the butter is melted, set the bowl or measuring cup on the kitchen counter.

Place the 1 cup of white sugar in a large mixing bowl.

Add one cup of powdered sugar to the bowl and mix the two sugars together.

Pour the melted butter over the sugars and mix it in. Continue to mix until it is evenly blended.

Add the vanilla extract and mix that in.

Add the salt and mix that in.

Measure out the 2 teaspoons of baking soda and sprinkle that into your bowl. Then mix it in thoroughly.

Feel the sides of the mixing bowl. If it's not so hot it might cook the eggs, add them to your bowl.

Mix the eggs in thoroughly.

Measure out the flour, making sure to pack it down in your measuring cup when you measure it.

Add the flour to your mixing bowl in half-cup increments, mixing thoroughly after each addition.

Add the cup of milk chocolate chips to your mixing bowl. Stir them in thoroughly.

Measure out the oatmeal and place it in the bowl.

Mix in the oatmeal until everything is combined.

Place the ⅓ cup of sugar in a small bowl. You will use this to coat the dough balls.

Roll the dough into walnut-sized balls.

Place the balls in the bowl with the sugar to coat them.

Arrange the sugar-coated dough balls on a prepared cookie sheet, 12 to a standard-size sheet. *(If it's too sticky to roll, place the bowl in the refrigerator for thirty minutes and try again.)*

Use the palm of your impeccably clean hand to squash the cookie dough balls down slightly. That way they won't roll off the cookie sheet on their way to the oven. *(Don't laugh – it's happened to me!)*

Bake your Milk Chocolate Oatmeal Cookies at 325 degrees F. for 10 to 12 minutes. Remove the cookies from the oven and cool them on the cookie sheet for 2 minutes. Then transfer the baked cookies to a wire rack to cool completely.

Yield: 6 to 7 dozen, depending on cookie size.

These cookies freeze well if you roll them up in foil and place them in a freezer bag. They also hold together well for shipping.

RAINBOW PICKLES

Ingredients:

1 jar dill pickle spears *(I used Claussen Kosher Dill Spears)*
1 cup white *(granulated)* sugar
1 cup cold water
2 packets unsweetened Kool-Aid powder of the same flavor

Hannah's 1st Note: The jar of dill pickle spears I bought was 24 ounces by weight.

Hannah's 2nd Note: I used cherry flavor unsweetened Kool-Aid powder for the first jar of Rainbow Pickles I made. Other Kool-Aid flavors that I've used for multiple jars which also work well are orange, raspberry, and lime. I wanted a yellow so I used lemonade Kool-Aid powder, but they weren't all that different from the original color of the pickle spears. I didn't have the nerve to try grape.

Instructions:

Open the jar of dill pickle spears.

Pour all of the liquid in the pickle jar into a microwave-safe bowl, leaving the pickle spears and the pickling

spices in the jar. *(Lisa uses a Pyrex quart measuring cup with a spout.)*

Pour the cup of white *(granulated)* sugar into the bowl or measuring cup with the pickle liquid. Mix with a mixing spoon.

Add the cup of cold water to the bowl or measuring cup and mix it in.

Open the packages of unsweetened Kool-Aid powder and add the powder to your bowl or measuring cup. Stir it in with a mixing spoon.

Hannah's 3rd Note: I would NOT recommend using a wooden spoon to mix. I did this once and the wood of the spoon became colored by the Kool-Aid powder and that's why I now have a red wooden spoon.

Place the bowl or measuring cup in the microwave and heat it for 1 minute. Let it sit in the microwave for an additional minute and then, carefully, feel the sides of the bowl.

If the liquid is warm to the touch, remove the bowl or measuring cup from the microwave, place it on the kitchen counter, and give it a final stir to make sure that the sugar has dissolved.

If your bowl or measuring cup does not have a spout, use a funnel to pour the liquid back into the jar with the pickle spears and spices. Make sure you cover the pickle spears with the liquid.

Put the top back on your Rainbow Pickle jar and return it to the refrigerator. Make sure the lid is on tightly and gently shake it once or twice during the week to keep it mixed. The pickles will be brightly colored and ready to eat in a week and they will keep up to 2 weeks in the refrigerator.

Hannah's 4th Note: You may have some liquid left in the bowl after you fill the jar, just pour it down the drain.

To Serve: If you have made several jars of pickle spears in various Kool-Aid colors and flavors, arrange the Rainbow Pickles on a platter like a sunburst, alternating colors. The kids will be amazed!

Chapter Eleven

The drive to the hospital had been chock-full of questions. Hannah had filled Andrea in on the homeless man that they'd found, and Andrea had asked questions that Hannah couldn't answer. No, she hadn't asked Joe Smith how he'd learned to fix such a deep scratch on the charge nurse's desk. As a matter of fact, Hannah didn't even know if Joe's repair had worked. Could they find out this afternoon? Hannah wasn't sure. They'd have to check with Doc. The back and forth had continued right up until Hannah had parked her cookie truck, and plugged the heater into the strip of outlets on the exterior of the hospital building.

"I think it's below zero today," Andrea said, her breath coming out in a white cloud that reminded Hannah of the picture she'd seen of smokestacks on old-fashioned locomotives.

"I think you're probably right," Hannah replied. And then, a bit muffled as she held her warm scarf up over her mouth, she said, "Hurry up, Andrea! I'm practically frozen!"

"It takes longer than that to freeze a person," Andrea replied once they'd pulled open the outside door and shut it behind them.

"How do you know?"

"I know, because Bill went fishing in Canada with his father, and the fish they caught were flash-frozen on the boat."

Hannah turned to look at her sister in surprise. "But what does flash-freezing a fish have to do with freezing a person?"

"It took them a little over a half-hour to get back to the fishing lodge where Bill and his dad were staying. And when they got off the boat, the fish were completely flash-frozen. They do it at minus eighteen degrees Celsius, you know."

"I didn't know, but you didn't answer my question. What does this have to do with freezing a person?"

"I've got two answers. You're a lot bigger than a fish, and we were only out there for a couple of minutes. . . . So, there's no way you're frozen . . . yet."

Hannah opened the inner door and thought about Andrea's answer while they hung up their parkas, took off their boots, and changed to shoes. "Okay. You got me, Sis."

"You mean . . . I'm right?"

"You are if you're right about the flash-freezing temperature."

"I am. Bill's dad told me and so did Bill." Andrea

looked proud for a moment, and then she sighed. "But I just guessed about the temperature in the parking lot. I don't know how to convert Celsius to . . . whatever it is on our thermometers."

"Fahrenheit."

Andrea nodded. "That's right. Now I remember. But it's hard to convert Celsius to Fahrenheit, isn't it?"

"No, it's easy, Andrea. All you have to do is multiply the Celsius number by nine-fifths and add thirty-two."

"But I can't do math like that in my head! I don't even know if I could do it on paper. I'm not that good at math, Hannah."

"I know. I saw your grades in algebra."

Andrea gave a little sigh. "But, Hannah . . . isn't there an easier way to convert it?"

"Sure, there is."

"What is it?"

There had been real excitement in Andrea's voice, and Hannah almost relented. But her answer was too good to give up.

"*Please* tell me what it is," Andrea pleaded. "I really want to know, Hannah."

"Okay. All you have to do is ask a Canadian!"

"Ask a Cana . . . ?" Andrea stopped in midsentence and groaned. "Oh, Hannah! That's just *awful*!" Andrea was clearly vexed, but she laughed anyway. "Okay, that *was* pretty funny."

Hannah slipped an arm around her younger sister and gave her a little hug. "You can use that one on Bill when you get home."

Andrea's ensuing smile was purely sunny. "You're right! I don't think he knows the real way to convert Celsius to Fahrenheit, either." She paused and gave a little sigh. "So what's the real answer?"

"Minus eighteen degrees Celsius is zero degrees Fahrenheit."

"Really? I thought it would be much colder than that." Andrea stopped when she saw Becky Summers at the receptionist's desk. "Hi, Becky."

"Hello, girls." Becky glanced down at her roster. "Did you both come to see Joe Smith?"

"Yes, but not right away," Hannah answered. "If Doc's in his office, we'd like to see him first."

"Let me check." Becky pressed a button on her phone and a moment later she spoke. "Hello, Vonnie. I've got Hannah and Andrea out here at the desk. Both of them would like to see Doc. Is he there?" There was a pause and then Becky gave a little nod. "Thanks, Vonnie. I'll send them over to you right away."

"He's in, and he'll see us?" Hannah guessed.

"That's right. Go ahead, girls. And, Hannah . . . those were great cookies! I shared a few with the nurses and everybody loved them. Are you going to be making them down at The Cookie Jar?"

"That depends. Do you think they're Christmas-y enough?"

"Oh, definitely! Everybody wanted to know if you were going to sell them."

"Then I will. Thanks for telling me about the warm

reception they got, Becky. We'll see you later, on our way out."

It only took a few moments to walk down the hallway to Doc's office. Hannah and Andrea went in the open door and greeted Doc's secretary.

"Go right in," Vonnie told them, gesturing toward the inner door. "Doc's expecting you."

"Hello, Hannah," Doc greeted her. "And Andrea! This must be my lucky day. I have two beautiful Swensen sisters gracing my office."

Hannah knew that from anyone else, such flattery would have been insincere. But she suspected that in Doc's case, it was entirely truthful. Doc had always loved them, from the moment they'd been born to the present day.

"Sit down, girls." Doc indicated the two chairs in front of his desk. "Did you come out to see Joe Smith?"

"Yes, we did," Hannah answered for both of them. "I hope he's doing well enough to have two visitors. Andrea would like to see him, too."

Doc turned to Andrea. "So Hannah recruited you to help her find out who Joe is?"

Andrea looked a bit flummoxed. "Uh . . . yes, she thought I might be able to help."

"And you're bored at home, now that you have Grandma McCann," Doc stated, smiling kindly at Andrea. "It's nice of you to offer to help your sister, since this is always her busiest season and Hannah has a lot on her plate this year."

"Thanks, Doc," Andrea said politely, and then she began to look worried. "You don't think it's bad that I hired a nanny and didn't stay home to take care of Tracey myself?"

"Not at all. Some people are cut out for early motherhood and others aren't. I've often thought that you'd be much better with older children. Just wait until Tracey starts school."

Andrea gave a relieved smile, and Hannah smiled, too. Doc always knew the right thing to say. "How's Joe doing?" she asked, getting back to the reason they'd come.

"Better than any of us expected. A lot has happened since the last time you were here, Hannah."

"But I only missed two days!" Hannah said, feeling a bit guilty. "I had back-to-back catering jobs, and I just couldn't get out here before now."

"That's okay, honey. I just didn't want you to be shocked when you saw Joe. He looks entirely different, now that the nurses took him in hand. And physically, he's doing a lot better than any of us expected. He's still weak, but he's gained a few pounds by eating everything in sight. I think he could give someone a run for their money, if he entered that hot dog eating contest they have in New York."

"Is it all right if we visit his room now?" Andrea asked.

"It's fine, but Joe's not there. He's down in the workroom with Freddy Sawyer putting the final touches on my charge nurse's desk. You girls come with me and I'll take you down there. Then you can see for yourselves what I meant about his recovery."

Doc led the way to the elevator and pressed the button. There were only two buttons, one for the main floor and the other for the basement. The elevator came almost immediately and all three of them got in. And when the door opened to reveal the basement of the hospital, Hannah gave a little gasp of surprise.

"You painted!" she said, realizing that the basement walls were now a bright, sunny yellow.

"Freddy did. And we had new lights put in. It was pretty gloomy down here before."

Hannah gave a little shiver. She still remembered hiding in the morgue and how terrified she'd been. "It was gloomy before," she commented, hoping that her voice wasn't shaking.

"This is really pretty nice," Andrea said, stepping out onto the light blue linoleum floor. "And I love the pictures on the walls. They were taken during the construction, weren't they?"

"That's right," Doc answered, leading them toward the end of the hall. "Here's the workroom," he told them, gesturing toward a set of double doors. "We had to open both doors to move in that massive desk."

"Is it repaired?" Hannah asked, hoping that Joe had done a good job of repairing the big desk.

"Yes, and I'm sure it's never looked this good before." Doc opened one of the double doors and ushered them in. "Freddy and Joe worked on that desk for a solid day." Doc led them further into the room and around a corner. "You boys have guests," he said, smiling at Freddy and Joe.

"Hi, Hannah," Freddy greeted her. "And . . . Andrea?"

"That's right." Andrea smiled at him. "It's good to see you again, Freddy."

"Hello, Joe." Hannah walked over to stand next to the homeless man they'd found. "You're certainly looking better than the last time I saw you!"

"I am better," Joe said, smiling back at her. "Freddy says you have two sisters. Is this pretty lady one of them?"

Freddy laughed. "Joe flirts with everybody. The nurses told me that." He turned to Joe. "Isn't that right, Joe?"

"That's what they say, Freddy."

"But it's not a bad thing to say," Freddy told him, frowning slightly. "I think they like it, Joe."

"And I bet you're right, Freddy," Hannah jumped into the conversation.

Hannah motioned to Andrea to come closer. "This is my sister, Andrea," Hannah introduced them. "And this is Joe. We're not sure about his last name yet."

"Your mother said you were going to try to find someone who knew me. Did you have any success with that, Hannah?"

"Not yet, but Andrea offered to help me look. Have you remembered any more about your background, Joe?"

"Not much." He turned to Andrea. "Thank you for helping out, Andrea. Hannah's probably told you that I don't remember much about myself."

"She did tell me that. She also told me that you were fixing the charge nurse's desk."

"It's fixed," Freddy said proudly. "Would you like to see it?"

"We'd love to see it," Hannah answered. "Will you show it to us?"

"Follow me," Joe said, leading them all through a wide doorway and into another room. "We're waiting for someone to help us move it back where it belongs."

"You two girls take a look," Doc told them. "Freddy and Joe showed it to me this morning. It's quite a transformation."

"It certainly is!" Hannah said, moving closer so that she could run her hand over the smooth surface. "That scratch was really deep. How did you get it out, Joe?"

Joe smiled. "I'll let Freddy tell you what we used to do it." Joe turned to Freddy. "Do you remember the name of the paper we used, Freddy?"

"Yes. It was sand. And it had big sand on it. Joe used something he called a sand . . ." Freddy stopped speaking and sighed. "I forgot the name, Joe."

"That's all right. You got most of the name right. It was an electric sander."

"Yes. Electric," Freddy said with a smile. "I helped Joe plug it in. We had to run a longer cord."

"It took a long time to sand it down, didn't it, Freddy?" Joe asked him.

"Yes, a long time. We had to put on new sandpaper a bunch of times. Joe taught me how to do that."

"I think you should show them the kind of sandpaper we used when we started to sand the desk," Joe said to Freddy. "Can you find a piece of sandpaper like that?"

"Yes. It's the big kind," Freddy answered immediately. "I'll go get it, Joe."

Freddy went to a box on the workbench against the wall, opened it, and pulled out a sheet of sandpaper. "Here it is," he said, carrying it over to show Joe. "See how big the sand is?"

"Yes, it's very coarse," Joe added.

"That's the word! Coarse! I always forget that one. How can I remember that, Joe?"

"You could think that of *course* you'll remember it."

Freddy laughed. "That's funny, Joe. And I won't forget it now! *Of course* not."

Freddy carried it over to Hannah and Andrea so that they could see it. "It's *coarse*," he said. "This is the one we started with. Joe said it was so that he could take off more wood with this one."

"And what did I tell you about the wood, Freddy?"

"You said it was very thick and it was a different color than the rest of the desk."

"That's right. And what did we do about the color, Freddy?"

"We rubbed on something that was called *stain*. It's like when you put a leaky pen in your pocket. That happened to me once."

"I think that's happened to almost everybody, Freddy," Doc told him.

"Even you, Doc?"

"Even me, Freddy. What did you do after you put the stain on the desk?"

"Then we rubbed in something that was a little like wax, but it wasn't wax. And we rubbed and polished, and rubbed and polished, and then we rubbed and polished again."

"Exactly right, Freddy. We wanted to make sure the stain wouldn't come off when the nurse put papers on her desk."

"That's right. We had to make sure that didn't happen." Freddy ran his hand over the top of the desk. "It's smooth now. Try it, Hannah."

Hannah ran her hand over the smooth surface. "It certainly is smooth. You must have worked very hard on it, Freddy."

"Oh, we did! Joe and I did it together, and now, if another desk gets a scratch, I can fix it because Joe taught me what to do."

"We're here!" someone called out, and two of Doc's maintenance workers came into the room. "You wanted us to deliver a desk?"

"Yes," Joe said, and then he turned to Freddy. "Why don't you go with them, Freddy. You know exactly where it goes and you can tell me what the charge nurse says when she sees it."

"She'll say *wow!*" Freddy told him. "Her name is

Carole, and Carole always says *wow!* when something makes her happy."

The two men made short work of loading the desk onto a rolling dolly and Freddy went out the door with them. After the door closed behind them, Doc gave a little laugh. "Freddy's right about Carole. *Wow* is her favorite word." He turned to Joe. "You're really good with Freddy, Joe. Most people wouldn't have as much patience as you do."

"I like Freddy. He reminds me of Donnie."

"Who's Donnie?" Hannah asked quickly.

"Donnie's my . . . my . . ." Joe stopped speaking and sighed. "Sorry, Hannah. I don't remember."

"Could Donnie be your brother?" Andrea asked him.

"He could be, but I just don't know."

"How about Donnie's last name?" Doc asked him. "Do you remember that?"

"I wish I did!" Joe said emphatically. "If I knew Donnie's last name, I'd know mine."

Chapter Twelve

"**W**ow!" they all heard Carole, the charge nurse, say as they came around the corner. "This is a miracle, Freddy!"

Freddy shook his head. "No, Carole. It's just hard work and knowing what to do. Joe showed me and now I know. If you get another scratch, I can fix it."

"No way I'm going to get a scratch on this beautiful desk, Freddy! And I didn't scratch it in the first place. The movers did it when Doc had it brought here."

Freddy smiled. "I'm glad you didn't scratch it, Carole. Now, it's beautiful again."

"It sure is!" Carole ran her hand over the surface of the desk. "It's so beautiful, I don't want to put anything on top of it." She turned to Joe, who had followed them along with Hannah, Andrea, and Doc. "Thank you for teaching Freddy how to repair my desk, Joe. Who taught you how to do it?"

Joe laughed and, for a moment, Hannah thought he'd misunderstood the question.

"That was a good try, Carole. I know you and all the other nurses try to jog my memory, but I'm afraid it didn't work. All I know is that the minute I saw the desk, I knew exactly what to do to fix it."

"And that probably means you've done it before," Carole extrapolated.

"It probably does," Joe agreed.

"And you told me exactly what I needed to buy at the hardware store," Doc pointed out. "You did remember the names of the products."

"That's right!" Joe looked pleased as he considered what Doc had said. "I wonder how I remembered all that, but forgot my name and where I came from."

"Memory is a tricky thing," Doc said, giving him a kind smile. "I really think your memory will come back when you recover all of your physical stamina and relax enough to let it happen." Doc turned to Hannah. "Let's all go to the cafeteria and taste some of those bar cookies you baked. I'm getting hungry just thinking about them."

Doc led the way to the cafeteria, and Hannah joined them once she'd retrieved her pan of bar cookies from the kitchen where she'd stashed them. Carole poured coffee for all of them and Hannah carried one pan of bar cookies and a knife to the table. Carole had set out small paper plates and Hannah gave each of them two bar cookies.

"What kind of bar cookies are these?" Carole asked.

"Pineapple White Chocolate Bar Cookies," Hannah answered. "They're made with a salted crust that really sets off the sweetness."

"Now I understand!" Joe said.

"Understand what?" Carole asked him.

"Why my mother always added salt to chocolate. She said it set off the sweetness, but I was too young to understand."

"That's why my mother mixes chocolate chips and salted cashews," Hannah told him.

"That sounds good," Carole said. "I'll have to try it sometime. Your bar cookies smell really good, Hannah."

"Then go ahead and taste one," Hannah invited. "There are plenty more here, and I brought an extra pan for the nurses. This pan is ours, and you can have more if you want them."

"I think we will," Doc announced after he'd taken his first bite. "These are really good, Hannah."

"I know. I've always loved pineapple. My grandmother used to bake a pineapple upside-down cake, and the kitchen smelled so good I could hardly wait for it to come out of the oven and cool."

Andrea nodded. "I remember that. I was too young to remember very much, but I know I loved to go out to the farm."

"Was it a dairy farm?" Joe asked her.

"I don't remember," Andrea confessed, "but I think it must have been. I remember being afraid of the cows."

"We had cows and I was afraid of them, too," Joe

said. "There was one big black and white cow that didn't like me."

"A Holstein?" Hannah asked him.

"Yes. Her name was Chelsea. My mother tried to put me up on her back for a ride, but Chelsea didn't like it. The minute my mom's back was turned, Chelsea shook me off and I landed in the dirt."

"How many cows did you have?" Carole asked.

"I don't know, but I remember the big truck from the creamery coming to collect the milk cans every morning."

"Were there a lot of milk cans?" Hannah asked, realizing what Carole was trying to do.

"I think so. It used to take a while to load them all."

Dairy farm, Hannah thought to herself. *I have to remember to write down that Joe lived on a dairy farm.*

"The barn was just down the hill from the shop." Joe took another bite of his Pineapple White Chocolate Bar Cookie. "My dad said the shop was on a hill so that people could see it from the road. The shop was on one side and the lake was a little ways away on the other side of the road. When I got older, I used to ride my bike there in the summer and go swimming."

It was the first time Joe had mentioned the shop, and Hannah made a mental note to write that down in the notes she was keeping about Joe's background. "What kind of shop was it?" she asked him.

"It was . . ." Joe stopped speaking and sighed. "I don't remember, Hannah."

"Do you think that it could have been a furniture repair place?" Andrea asked.

"I . . ." Joe hesitated and then he sighed again. "It could have been, I guess. I just don't remember."

"Enough," Doc said, calling a halt to their attempts to jog Joe's memory. "You've remembered enough for one day, Joe. I want you to rest this afternoon. You need to build up your strength."

"I *am* a little tired," Joe agreed.

"I can tell," Doc said, pushing back his chair and standing up. "You three girls stay here. I'm going to walk Joe down to my office and then I'll take him back to his room."

"You want me to come to your office?" Joe asked, looking puzzled.

"Yes. There's a chair there I want you to see. It's old, but it's a favorite of mine, and I'd like your opinion on whether I should try to have it repaired, or whether I should junk it and get a new one."

Joe smiled. "Okay. Let's go, and I'll take a look at it. I think I can tell you if it can be saved."

"I'll stay and help you clean up," Carole said when Doc and Joe had left. "I'm here early and I still have twenty minutes before my shift starts."

It didn't take long to throw away the paper plates, wipe off the cafeteria table, and push in the chairs. Hannah cut the rest of the bar cookies and put them on paper plates for the nurses and the other hospital workers. Then she washed the knife, put it back in the knife holder in the kitchen, and was about ready to flick off the lights when Doc came back into the cafeteria.

"Hold on, girls," he said, walking toward them.

"Is Joe resting in his room?" Carole asked him.

"Yes. He was so tired, he fell asleep almost immediately. I just came to tell you girls the latest fact about Joe that I discovered."

"What is it?" Hannah asked quickly.

"He told me that my chair could be saved. The first thing he did was examine the mechanism. It's an old recliner with springs and wooden slats. It used to belong to Doctor Kalick's father."

"The old doctor who was your mentor?" Carole asked him.

"Yes. I love that chair, but it's been damaged. A spring has to be replaced and one of the arms has come loose. Some slats in the back need replacing, too. And the old black and gold material is terribly tattered."

"What did Joe say about it?" Hannah asked him.

"He said it was a fine piece of furniture and it could be a genuine antique."

"It's a good thing Mother didn't hear that!" Andrea exclaimed. "She'd talk you out of it in two seconds flat!" Andrea winced slightly and looked embarrassed. "I shouldn't have said that."

"Maybe not, but you're right," Hannah told her.

"You're both right," Doc said, and then he chuckled. "I don't think you girls had better tell Lori what Andrea said."

Lori! Hannah's suspicious mind repeated the name Doc had used for Delores. *That's the second time you've heard him call your mother that.*

"I know your mother," Carole said to them. "And I promise I'll never breathe a word."

"Smart move," Doc said with a laugh. "Lori's been known to shoot the messenger."

Lori, Hannah's mind repeated again. *Lori three times. Hmmm!* Hannah deliberately turned her mind to what Doc had told them. "Did Joe say he could find the right kind of spring to fix the mechanism?"

"No, Joe said he could fabricate a spring to match its mate. And he was sure he could make new slats for the ones that were missing and shore up the rest."

"Wow!" Andrea was clearly impressed. "Now I'm even more sure that he worked at a furniture repair place."

"You're on the right track, Andrea," Doc told her. "And right after he finished saying he could repair the hardware and the slats, he told me exactly how many yards of upholstery material to buy so that he could re-upholster the chair!"

"Okay." Carole sounded very sure of herself. "It's not just furniture repair. It's antique furniture reconstruction. And I'll bet that shop he talked about was his, or maybe his and his father's."

PINEAPPLE WHITE CHOCOLATE BAR COOKIES

Preheat oven to 325 degrees F., rack in the middle position.

The Crust and Topping:

2 cups (*4 sticks, 16 ounces, 1 pound*) salted butter softened to room temperature
1 cup white (*granulated*) sugar
1 and ½ cups powdered (*confectioners*) sugar
2 Tablespoons vanilla extract
4 cups all-purpose flour (*pack it down in the cup when you measure it*)

The Pineapple White Chocolate Filling:

12.25-ounce jar pineapple ice cream topping (*I used Smucker's*)
12-ounce bag (approximately 2 cups) white chocolate or vanilla baking chips (*I used Nestlé*)
1 Tablespoon sea or Kosher salt (*the coarse-ground kind*)

Before you begin to make the crust and filling, spray a 9-inch by 13-inch cake pan with Pam or another nonstick baking spray.

Hannah's 1st Note: This crust and filling is a lot easier to make with an electric mixer. You can do it by hand, but it will take some muscle.

Combine the butter, white sugar, and powdered sugar in a large bowl or in the bowl of an electric mixer. Beat at MEDIUM speed until the mixture is light and creamy.

Add the vanilla extract. Mix it in until it is thoroughly combined.

Add the flour in half-cup increments, beating at LOW speed after each addition. Beat until everything is combined.

Hannah's 2nd Note: When you've mixed in the flour, the resulting sweet dough will be soft. Don't worry. That's the way it's supposed to be.

Measure out a heaping cup of the sweet dough you've made and place it in a sealable plastic bag. Seal the bag and put it in the refrigerator.

With impeccably clean hands, press the rest of the sweet dough into the bottom of your prepared cake pan. This will form a bottom crust. Press it all the way out to the edges of the pan and a half-inch up the sides,

as evenly as you can. Don't worry if your sweet dough is a bit uneven. It won't matter to any of your guests.

Bake your bottom crust at 325 degrees F., for approximately 20 minutes or until the edges are beginning to turn a pale golden brown color.

When the crust has turned pale golden brown, remove the pan from the oven, but DON'T SHUT OFF THE OVEN! Set the pan with your baked crust on a cold stovetop burner or a wire rack to cool. Cool it approximately 15 minutes.

After your crust has cooled, take the lid off the jar of pineapple ice cream topping and put it in the microwave.

Heat the pineapple topping for 15 to 20 seconds on HIGH.

Let the jar cool in the microwave for 1 minute. Then use potholders to take the jar out.

Pour the pineapple ice cream topping over the baked bottom crust in the pan as evenly as you can.

Smooth it out to the edges of your crust with a heat-resistant spatula.

Open the bag of white chocolate or vanilla baking chips and sprinkle them over the pineapple ice cream topping as evenly as you can.

Here comes the salt! Sprinkle the sea salt or Kosher salt over the chips in the pan.

Take the remaining sweet dough out of the refrigerator and unwrap it. It has been refrigerated for 35 minutes or more, and it should be thoroughly chilled.

With your impeccably clean fingers, crumble the dough over the pineapple and white chocolate chip layer as evenly as you can. Leave a little space, so the pineapple sauce can bubble up between the crumbles.

Hannah's 3rd Note: If the pineapple topping bubbles up through the top of your bar cookies, it will look very pretty.

Return the pan to the oven and bake your bar cookies for 25 to 30 additional minutes, or until the crumbles on top are a light golden brown. Remove your bar cookies from the oven onto a cold burner or a wire rack to cool.

Hannah's 4th Note: Your pan of Pineapple White Chocolate Bar Cookies will smell so delicious, you'll be

tempted to cut it into squares and eat one immediately. Resist that urge! The bubbly hot pineapple topping will burn your mouth.

After 5 minutes of cooling time, use potholders to carry the pan to a wire rack to cool completely.

Hannah's 5th Note: When I bake these bar cookies at home in the winter, I place a wire rack out on the little table on my condo balcony and carry the pan out there. The Pineapple White Chocolate Bar Cookies cool quite fast when exposed to a Minnesota winter.

When your Pineapple White Chocolate Bar Cookies are completely cool, cut them into brownie-size pieces, place them on a pretty plate, and serve them to your guests.

Yield: A cake pan full of yummy brownie-sized treats that everyone will love. Serve with icy-cold glasses of milk, mugs of hot chocolate, or cups of strong, hot coffee.

Chapter Thirteen

Hannah walked in the door of her condo at precisely five o'clock in the evening. She set down her bag of groceries and her purse, turned the doorknob in one quick motion, and held out her arms.

"Uuuuhh!" she groaned as twenty-three pounds of orange and white feline hit her squarely in the stomach. "Hello, Moishe," she said, kicking open the door and carrying him to his favorite perch on the back of the couch. "Did you miss me?"

"Rrrrow!" Moishe looked up at her with an expression that Hannah interpreted as assent.

"I missed you, too," she told him, reaching out to scratch him in his favorite place under the chin. "Just stay here for a second, and I'll get you one of your favorite treats."

The scent that assailed her nostrils as she flicked on the lights and entered her kitchen was nothing short of remarkable. She'd started her Hunter's Beef Stew in crockpots before she'd left for work this morning and, as far as Hannah was concerned, there was no better perfume for a hungry soul than beef and onions in a rich broth.

There would be five for dinner around her combination living room and dining room table tonight, and Mike, who she suspected could eat the contents of one of her crockpots himself, would be there. Bill was also a big eater, but he was balanced by Andrea, who would eat one bowl of stew, no more. Hannah would have one bowl, perhaps a half more, and Norman would probably consume two bowls of her stew. There would be plenty of leftovers and she'd sent some home with Andrea for her nanny, Grandma McCann. Grandma McCann had promised to send one of her famous Blue Apple Pies for dessert, and all Hannah had to do to get ready for her dinner company was to add the vegetables to her stew, set the table, take a quick shower, and stick some garlic and cheese bread into the oven a half hour before her guests arrived.

"Rrrrrow!"

The impatient cry came from the living room and Hannah gave a soft chuckle. Moishe was asking for his treats. She'd deliver them first, then add the vegetables to her crockpots, set the table, take her shower, and then relax with a glass of wine after she prepared the garlic cheese bread.

Twenty minutes later, with Moishe fed a combination of his favorite tuna and dry kitty kibbles, Hannah was freshly showered and dressed in the aqua sweater that

Andrea had given her for Christmas, and her favorite dark gray slacks. A gold necklace that her mother had given her was around her neck and her combination waterproof wristwatch and timer was on her wrist. Her feet were encased in soft-soled moccasins and her unruly, curly red hair was freshly brushed. She was ready for company and all she had to do before she could sit down and have a refreshing glass of white wine was to make the garlic and cheese bread.

It only took a moment or two to cut the French bread she'd gotten at Florence's Red Owl Grocery in half lengthwise. Once that was done, she used a garlic press to mince several cloves of garlic and mixed them into a stick of softened, salted butter. She spread the garlic butter over the cut side of the top and bottom of the loaf, sandwiched the two sides together to make a whole loaf, and wrapped that loaf in heavy-duty aluminum foil. Then she stuck the wrapped loaf in the oven, turned the oven on a relatively low heat, shut the door, and went back into the living room to enjoy her wine. Once her company came, she'd take the loaf out of the oven, turn up the heat so that the bread would crisp, and sprinkle freshly grated Parmesan-Romano over the top of both sides of the loaf. Then she'd put them on a baking sheet, cut sides up and separated into two parts, and bake them until they were golden brown and crisp.

"Rrrrow!" Moishe gave a soft, little yowl, and jumped up in Hannah's lap. Hannah interpreted that as a *pet me* plea and she did. A scratch under his chin, and pet all the way down from the top of his head to the base of his tail, and a nuzzle behind both ears did the trick. Moishe began to purr contentedly and Hannah smiled. No wonder Doc claimed that petting a cat or a dog lowered both blood pressure and anxiety. She could feel the whirlwind of a busy day fading and her own contentment setting in.

Even though she was relaxed and lulled by the sound of her pet's purring, Hannah's mind was not idle. She thought about the new facts she'd learned about Joe's background today. Andrea had been very helpful when it came to asking questions. Her younger sister was never intrusive. Instead, people immediately knew that Andrea was interested in their answers, and truly wanted to know more about them. Before Bill had married Andrea, he'd once told Hannah that Andrea could charm the birds right out of the trees. This had certainly been true with Joe today. He'd told them more about his background than they'd discovered before.

Hannah had almost finished her glass of wine when her stove timer rang. Luckily, except for Moishe's contented rumbling, it was quiet in her condo. She gave Moishe a final pat and a scratch, and then she moved him to his own couch cushion so she could go to the kitchen.

Time passed rapidly when she was preparing food for company. Hannah thought about that as she put the final touches on her meal. Then she got the coffee ready to go, took out the crackers and cheese that she'd bought for an appetizer, and checked her supply of ginger ale for Norman. Mike would have Cold Spring Export beer, Bill would have a glass of red wine, and Andrea would drink white wine. Hannah checked her crockpots a final time, inhaled the rich, beefy aroma that floated up from her stew, and gave a happy smile. Everything was ready to go. All she needed now was for her company to arrive.

As if in answer to her silent request, her doorbell rang. Hannah got up to answer it and opened the door to Norman, who was carrying several bags of groceries.

"Hi, Norman," she greeted him. "What did you bring?"

"Ginger ale, white wine, red wine, and Cold Spring Export. I know you said you had them, but I thought I'd bring more so you'd have extra for the next time."

"Thanks! That was nice of you, Norman." Hannah watched as Norman carried his purchases into the kitchen and put them on the counter. "Would you like a ginger ale now, while we're waiting for everyone else to arrive?"

"I would, and I'll get it. How about you, Hannah?"

"I'm fine. I've still got wine and I really don't want more."

"Can I help you with anything in the kitchen?"

"No, thanks. I have everything ready to go."

Norman carried his glass of ginger ale to the couch and sat down next to Hannah. Moishe immediately jumped into his lap and Norman petted him. "How are you, Big Boy?" he asked Hannah's pet.

"Rrrrow!" Moishe answered.

"I love the way he does that. When I ask him a question, he seems to know he should answer."

"He's always done that. Moishe knows when someone is talking to him."

"Speaking of talking, did you visit Joe today?" Norman asked her.

"Yes, and Andrea went with me. We found out a few more things about his background, and I'll tell you after everyone else gets here."

Again, right on cue, Hannah's doorbell rang. "I'll get it," Norman said, moving Moishe over to another couch cushion and standing up. "It's probably Mike. He always gets here early when there's food involved."

Hannah knew that was true. Mike loved to eat and unfairly, as far as Hannah was concerned, he could put away multiple helpings of whatever she served and never gain an ounce.

Norman took Mike's parka, hung it over the back of a chair, and got him a Cold Spring Export. Mike took a swig of his beer and then he turned to Hannah. "Did you see Joe today?"

"Yes, and Andrea went with me. We learned a couple of new things, but I'll wait until Andrea and Bill get here to talk about it. How about some cheese and crackers while we're waiting?"

"Sounds great!" Mike answered quickly. "I'm really hungry. I didn't go to the café for coffee early enough this afternoon, and when I got there, Rose's rhubarb pies were gone."

Hannah began to smile. Mike never missed having

some sweet treat on his afternoon coffee break. "So what did you order instead?"

Mike gave a mournful sigh. "I had to settle for a couple of slices of her banana cake."

"I'll be right back with the cheese and crackers," Hannah said, rising from the couch and beating a hasty retreat to the kitchen just in time to stifle her mirth. Mike was an eating machine. He could eat anything that struck his fancy at any time of night or day and his Winnetka County Sheriff uniforms still fit, while she couldn't even walk past the Fanny Farmer candy store at the Tri-County Mall without gaining a pound or two. Life simply wasn't fair and she had to learn to accept that fact.

It only took a minute or two to lay out the slices of cheese in a nice design and surround them with crackers. Hannah was just ready to pick up the appetizer tray and serve it when she heard the doorbell ring. That meant Andrea and Bill were here, and she poured a glass of wine from the huge jug she'd purchased at Cost-Mart for her sister. Then she put the jug back, hiding it behind a six-pack of Cold Spring Export. Andrea loved the white wine that Hannah served. She thought it was expensive and hard to find. Every time she tasted it, Andrea praised it and Hannah didn't want to disillusion her by admitting that it was nothing but jug wine that cost less than a six-pack of soda.

"Hi, Hannah!" Andrea greeted her as she came breezing into the kitchen. "Do you want these two pies on the counter?"

"Yes, please." Hannah gestured toward the two wire racks she'd placed on her kitchen counter, just in case the pies were still warm from the oven. "They smell wonderful!"

"They *are* wonderful," Andrea told her. "I've had Grandma McCann's pies before and they're incredibly good." She walked over to the crockpots and peeked at the contents through the glass lids. "Hunter's Stew?"

"That's right."

"Oh, good! It's Bill's favorite!" Andrea took the glass of wine that Hannah handed her and took a sip. Then she gave a sigh of satisfaction. "I *love* this wine! It's a coquettish little temptress with a hint of sun-ripened peach and a slight undertone of crisp apple. Tell me you're ready to give up your secret, Hannah. I really want to know where you buy it."

"I can't," Hannah said, crossing her fingers behind her back to negate the lie. "The sommelier swore me to secrecy."

"Ah-ha!" Andrea looked very excited. "You had it first in a restaurant then! I'm going to ask Dick and Sally at the Lake Eden Inn if they know."

"They don't. I didn't have it there." Hannah picked up the cheese tray. "Come on, Andrea. The men are waiting to hear what we learned from Joe today."

"You didn't tell them?"

Hannah shook her head. "I wanted to wait for you. You didn't tell Bill, did you?"

"No. I decided I'd tell him when you told Mike and Norman."

"Okay . . . let's go!"

Hannah led the way, placing the cheese tray on the coffee table that sat between the two couches. "Help yourselves, everyone." She turned to Bill. "Would you like a glass of red wine, Bill?"

"Yes, I would." Bill gave her a smile. "Thanks for asking, Hannah. I'm not on call tonight, so I can have wine with dinner."

"I'll get it, Hannah," Norman said, getting up from his spot on the couch. "You've done enough for one night."

"Thanks, Norman." Hannah sat down on the couch and reached for her half-empty wineglass. "This is really nice. I can't remember the last time Sheriff Grant gave Mike and Bill the same night off duty. He usually wants one or the other of you there."

"I think it's because we haven't had a murder for a while," Bill told her.

"Bite your tongue, Bill!" Andrea said, and Hannah could tell she was only half kidding. "You shouldn't tempt fate."

"Speaking of murder, or attempted murder," Mike said, looking serious. "Has Doc figured out how Joe got that TBI yet?"

"Not yet," Hannah told him, "but he's pretty sure someone attempted to kill him."

"Is he sure enough to call Sheriff Grant and ask him to file an attempted murder charge?" Mike asked.

"I don't know. I didn't get a chance to ask him that when Andrea and I were there. And even if he does think it's attempted murder, Sheriff Grant wouldn't call you in for that, would he?"

"Probably not," both Mike and Bill answered her, almost in unison.

"He might if Joe's injury was recent," Mike added.

"And especially if Joe could name or give a description of his assailant," Bill went on to explain. "Then he might call us in."

Mike gave a nod of agreement. "In Joe's case, he can't do either one of those things. And that means there aren't that many avenues for us to explore."

Norman came back to deliver Bill's glass of red wine and everyone munched crackers and cheese for a moment. Then Bill spoke up again. "Andrea said she wanted to wait until we were all together to tell us what you two learned from Joe today. Do we have time to do that before we eat?"

"We do," Hannah answered for both of them, and she reached for the steno pad. "Joe told us a little bit about the farm where he grew up." She turned to Andrea. "Tell them what you remember, Andrea."

"He mentioned the cows, and Hannah and I decided that it was a dairy farm because the creamery truck came every morning to pick up the milk cans. Joe didn't know how many milk cans there were, but he said it took quite a while to load them all on the truck."

"The fact that it was a dairy farm isn't all that helpful," Mike told her. And then, when he saw how disappointed she was, he added, "But it's a piece of the puzzle and we can eliminate farms that don't have milk cows."

"Right," Hannah agreed. "Go on, Andrea."

"Well . . . he mentioned that he used to ride his bike to the lake to go swimming in the summer. And that made two pieces of the puzzle. The farm where he grew up must be close to a lake."

Hannah couldn't help it. She burst out laughing.

"What's so funny?" Andrea asked her.

"It's Minnesota, Andrea, the land of ten thousand lakes. Every farm is within bike-riding distance of some kind of lake!"

The men burst into laughter and Hannah winced. She hadn't meant to embarrass her sister. "Sorry, Andrea. I should have phrased it a little bit differently."

"That's okay, Hannah." Andrea gave a little laugh. "It's funny and you're right. I can't think of a single farm in this whole county that isn't within bike-riding distance of a lake."

"What else did you learn?" Mike asked.

Andrea gestured toward Hannah. "Hannah was smart. She wrote it all down while I drove back to town. Tell them about Freddy, Hannah."

"Okay." Hannah flipped to the next page of notes she had made. "When Andrea and I got to the hospital, Doc said that Joe was in the basement workroom with Freddy, and they were putting the final touches on Carole's desk."

"Carole, the charge nurse?" Norman asked.

"That's right. Doc took us down to the basement and we found Joe and Freddy in the workroom. They were waiting for a couple of Doc's maintenance men to come for the desk and take it up to Carole."

"Then you got to see it?" Bill asked.

"Yes," Andrea answered him, "and it was beautiful. The deep scratch on top was completely gone and it looked like new."

"Freddy told us what they'd done to rejuvenate it, and all three of us, Doc, Andrea, and I, were really impressed at the way Joe drew Freddy out and helped him remember the names of various things."

"Later, when Freddy had left with the maintenance men, and we were going up to the first floor to see what Carole thought of her desk, someone asked Joe how he knew how to deal so well with Freddy." Andrea turned to Hannah. "Was it you, Hannah?"

"No, it was Doc. And Joe said that he liked Freddy, and that he reminded him of Donnie."

"Did you ask who Donnie was?"

"Of course we did," Andrea said quickly. "But Joe couldn't tell us if Donnie was a relative of his, or not. We asked if he knew Donnie's last name and Joe laughed. And then he said that if he remembered Donnie's last name, he might know his own last name."

"That made me guess that Donnie could be Joe's brother," Hannah admitted. "But he could also be an uncle or a cousin. I got the feeling that Joe taught Donnie how to work in the shop."

"What makes you think that?" Mike asked her.

"I think it was because he was so good about reminding Freddy of sandpaper and the steps they'd taken to repair Carole's desk. I know it's an assumption, but I really think I could be right."

"I think so, too," Mike told her.

"So do I," Bill agreed.

"It's logical, Hannah," Norman said. "Sometimes I think we have to go with our feelings and assumptions, if there's not enough data to tell us the whole story."

Mike smiled the slow smile that always made Hannah's heart beat faster. "That's smart, Norman. Sometimes you have to go with what my mother used to call inklings."

"What are inklings?" Andrea asked him.

"Things that don't yet have any basis in fact, but that you believe are correct. At least that's the way she described it." Mike stopped speaking and gave a sigh. "How long until dinner, Hannah? I'm really starving!"

Chapter Fourteen

"I really can't eat anymore," Mike said when Hannah offered him another bowl of stew.

"Did you leave room for dessert?" Hannah asked him.

"Of course I did. I always leave room for dessert. What is it?"

"Grandma McCann's Blue Apple Pie," Andrea told him. "It's apples and blueberries mixed together and it's just incredible! I sneaked a little taste when it bubbled up through the crumble crust."

Mike looked as if the heavens had opened, and an angel had appeared. "The only thing that could make an apple and blueberry pie better would be . . ."

"I have French vanilla ice cream," Hannah offered, knowing exactly what Mike was going to say.

"Yes!" Mike's response was immediate and then he swallowed several times. This made Hannah suspect that his mouth was watering in anticipation. "Could you give me two scoops on my pie?"

"Of course I can," Hannah agreed, grateful that she'd bought a gallon. Unless Mike was feeling a bit under the weather, he'd be eating two or three slices of Grandma McCann's pie with double scoops of ice cream on each of them.

Since everyone knew that Hannah had to go to work early the next morning, once dinner was over the party broke up. Andrea and Bill were the first to leave. They were followed by Mike, who waited for Hannah to pack up a container of stew, and a piece of pie for a midnight snack.

"Are you tired, Hannah?" Norman asked, helping her load the last dish into the dishwasher.

Hannah thought about that for a moment, and then she shook her head. "I should be, but I'm not really tired. I think having company energized me. Stay for a while, Norman. I'm not going to go to sleep for a while yet."

"Okay, but I want you to promise to let me know when you get tired enough to sleep."

"All right. I promise."

"Would you like to watch a movie? I brought one of my favorites."

"That sounds good. Which movie is it?"

"*Regarding Henry.*"

"I'd *love* to see it! That's a Mike Nichols film, isn't it?"

"Yes, it is. I thought it might be appropriate because it's about a man with TBI."

"Is it sad?"

"Actually . . . no, not at all. As a matter of fact, it's a rather novel twist on a man who experiences amnesia."

"That sounds good! Should I make popcorn?"

Norman shook his head. "Thanks, but I couldn't eat another thing tonight."

"How about hot chocolate?"

"That sounds great. Do you still have those fuzzy blankets I gave you from CostMart?"

"Yes. I'll get one for each of us and we can curl up on the couch. Do you want me to turn up the heat, Norman? Now that the wind picked up, it's a little chilly in here."

"The hot chocolate and the blankets will take care of that. And if it doesn't we can always turn on your fireplace."

"Good idea. If you turn on the television and get the movie all ready to go, I'll make the hot chocolate and bring it in."

"I'll get the fuzzy blankets, too. Where do you keep them, Hannah?"

"In the old trunk on the other side of the fireplace. Just lift the lid and you'll see them. This is going to be fun, Norman."

Regarding Henry was a fascinating film and Hannah managed to stay awake for the first fifteen minutes. When she woke up, the television set was off, the living room was illuminated only by the glow of the fireplace, and Norman was gone. She sat up, rubbed her eyes, glanced at the clock on the mantel to see that it was after midnight, and smiled. Norman had brought out a pillow from her bedroom, covered her with both blankets, and there was a note propped upon her coffee table. It read, *Go to bed, Hannah. I'll be here at five-thirty in the morning to take you to breakfast, and then to work. Love, Norman.*

Even though the thought of snuggling down even deeper under the blankets and spending the night on the couch was tempting, Hannah got up, switched off the fireplace, and went in to bed. She was too tired to get into her pajamas, so she simply pulled back the covers and climbed in bed, grateful that Moishe, who'd gone to bed earlier, was sleeping on his own pillow for a change. She reached out to stroke his soft fur, curled up with the pillow she'd carried in with her, smiled a contented smile, and went back to sleep.

Morning came with a crash and Hannah sat bolt upright in bed. She switched on the light on her bedside table, looked over at the pillow where Moishe had been sleeping, and discovered that her cat was no longer there.

There was another crash and a thud. Had someone broken into her condo? A burglar? A rapist? What could she use to fight him off?

Hannah looked around her bedroom. The only thing she could see that could be used as a weapon was the heavy, cut glass bottle of perfume that she'd won at a Christmas party. It was the only thing she'd ever won, so she'd kept it. She'd opened it, taken one sniff of the perfume inside, and corked it back up again. She'd been planning to take it down to their local thrift store and donate it, but she simply hadn't gotten around to it yet.

Quietly, stealthily, Hannah felt around under the side of her bed for her moose hide slippers. She found them, pulled them onto her feet, and made her way to the dresser to get the bottle of perfume. It was heavy and she gave a little nod of satisfaction. If she moved silently and approached the intruder from the rear, she could hit him over the head with the bottle and knock him out.

There was another thud, and Hannah headed toward the sound. The intruder was in her kitchen. The guest bathroom door was open and dim light was coming in from the designer streetlights that lined the walkways outside the condo buildings. All was quiet in the hallway, and Hannah made sure she didn't trip over the fake potted plant that stood by the doorway to the living room.

There was another thud and Hannah's heart jumped up to her throat. Was she being a fool for trying to confront an intruder alone? Had he come in with a gun, or a knife that would easily best the perfume bottle she carried? Would they find her sprawled out on her kitchen floor when Lisa called the sheriff's department to report that she hadn't shown up for work?

Her eyes had adjusted to the dim interior of the living room, and the kitchen doorway was just in front of her. Should she sneak over to the couch, grab the remote phone that sat on a side table, and hurry back to lock herself in her bathroom while she called the police?

There was another thud, and that propelled her forward. No, she wouldn't call for help. This was a one-woman job and she was the woman to do it. If she took the intruder by surprise, she could do it. Rod Metcalf would write an article about her in the paper, praising her courage and presence of mind.

Another thud sealed her resolve. Hannah slipped into the kitchen, clutched the perfume bottle raised high, and prepared to tackle the person who'd dared to broach her inner sanctum.

The kitchen window was directly over one of the designer walkway lights and Hannah could see the entire room clearly. No one was standing by her stove or her refrigerator. Was he in the pantry for some reason?

The pantry door was slightly ajar, and Hannah stood behind it and inched it open. And what she saw shocked her so much, she dropped the perfume bottle on the floor.

The intruder, the rapist, the burglar was . . . Moishe! Her cat was standing on one of the shelves in the pantry, pawing at the staples she kept on the shelf above. His claw hooked a can, it came tumbling down, and hit the floor with a thud.

"Moishe!" she shouted, completely shocked. "What in the world are you *doing*?!"

She must have shocked Moishe almost as much as he'd shocked her, because her feline roommate jumped down from the shelf, raced past her like a whirlwind, and pounded down the hall to her bedroom.

"Oh, good heavens!" Hannah groaned as she flicked

on the lights and realized that the perfume bottle had lost at least half of its contents. Her kitchen now smelled like a cheap bordello, or at least the way she imagined a cheap bordello might smell.

All Hannah wanted to do was crawl back in bed and hide her head under her pillow, but sleep was impossible at this stage. She had to clean up the mess before she did anything else. First, she tackled the pantry. There were cans on the floor that needed to be picked up and put back in place. They were cans of cat food, tuna, and salmon, with one lone can of beets. Since Moishe didn't like beets, Hannah figured it must have been off-balance, and fallen when one of the other cans fell.

It didn't take long to pick up the cans and put them back where they belonged. The spilled perfume was another matter. Hannah took down a roll of paper towels, and did her best to sop it up without getting it on her hands. Of course that didn't work. The perfume soaked through the paper, and by the time she'd cleaned the kitchen floor, and filled the trash can with heavily aromatic paper towels, she smelled like she'd just emerged from work at a cheap perfume factory.

"I need a shower," she said aloud, and hurried back to her bathroom to douse herself with water and soap. It took a lot of scrubbing and rinsing before the smell of perfume seemed to diminish.

One glance at her bed and she sighed. Sure enough, her midnight marauder was stretched out on *her* pillow, fast asleep.

Mumbling about how she now knew why some people didn't have pets, she slipped into her robe and padded down the hall to put on the coffee. It was almost time to get up anyway. She'd drink a cup of coffee, eat the last of Grandma McCann's Blue Apple Pie, and watch the rest of the movie that she missed with Norman.

BLUE APPLE PIE

Preheat oven to 350 degrees F., rack in the middle position.

1 frozen deep dish piecrust *(or make your own)*

½ cup white sugar
⅛ cup *(2 Tablespoons)* all-purpose flour
⅛ teaspoon ground nutmeg *(freshly ground is best, of course)*
⅛ teaspoon cinnamon *(if it's been sitting in your cupboard for years, buy fresh!)*
⅛ teaspoon cardamom
⅛ teaspoon salt
2 cups sliced, peeled apples *(I used 2 Granny Smith and 3 Fuji or Gala)*
1 teaspoon lemon juice
1 can blueberry pie filling *(I used Comstock)*
¼ stick cold salted butter *(⅛ cup, 1 ounce)*

Prepare your crust:

If you use homemade piecrust, roll out one round. Line a 9-inch pie pan with the piecrust.

If you use frozen piecrust, buy the 8-inch deep dish kind. These come in two's, so leave one in its pan and let

it thaw on the counter. Put the other in the freezer, for the next Blue Apple Pie you bake.

Mix the sugar, flour, spices, and salt together in a medium-size bowl.

Prepare the apples by coring them, peeling them, and slicing them into a large bowl. When they're all done, toss them with the teaspoon of lemon juice. *(Just dump on the lemon juice and use your impeccably clean fingers to toss the apple slices – it's easier.)*

Dump the small bowl with the dry ingredients on top of the apples and toss them to coat the slices. *(Again, use your fingers.)*

Open the can of blueberry pie filling and add it to the coated apples in the bowl. Mix them together thoroughly.

Put the apple and blueberry mixture in the pan with the piecrust. Smooth the top with a rubber spatula.

Cut the cold butter into 4 pieces and then cut those pieces in half. Place the pieces on top of the apple and blueberry mixture in the piecrust.

Put your pie on a baking sheet with sides that will catch any drips.

Make your French Crumble now.

French Crumble:

1 cup all-purpose flour
½ cup cold butter
½ cup brown sugar
½ teaspoon cinnamon

Put the flour into the bowl of a food processor with the steel blade attached. Cut the stick of butter *(½ cup, 4 ounces, ¼ pound)* into 8 pieces and add them to the bowl. Cover with the ½ cup of firmly packed brown sugar and sprinkle in the cinnamon.

Process with the steel blade in an on-and-off motion until the resulting mixture is in uniform small pieces.

Remove the mixture from the food processor and place it in a bowl.

Pat handfuls of the French Crumble in a mound over your pie. With a sharp knife, poke several slits near the top to let out steam.

Bake your pie at 350 degrees F. for approximately one hour, or until the top crumble is a nice golden brown and the apples are tender when you pierce them

with the tip of a sharp knife. If they're not, bake your pie in 10-minute increments until the apples are cooked.

Yield: 8 regular or 6 large pieces of very tasty pie.

Serve with plenty of strong coffee, or icy cold milk. If you wish, top the pie slices with vanilla ice cream or sweetened whipped cream.

Chapter Fifteen

"A new perfume?" Norman asked her when she answered the door and he stepped inside.

"Yes. It's called Eau de Moishe."

"What?"

"Eau de Moishe. He's responsible for the perfume I'm still wearing after last night. And I've got to tell you that I don't like it, either. I tried to get rid of it, I really did. But three soapings and rinsings last night didn't do it, and neither did the long, hot shower I took this morning."

"Put on your parka, Hannah. I'm going to take you to the Corner Tavern for breakfast. And once you have a couple more cups of coffee, you can tell me all about it."

Forty minutes later, fortified by coffee and the stimulus of Norman's company, Hannah felt almost like her normal self. "I thought it was an intruder, Norman," she told him.

"You thought *what* was an intruder?" Norman asked her.

"Moishe."

Norman laughed. "Okay, Hannah. Start from the beginning, so that I can catch up."

"Right," Hannah agreed. "It's like this, Norman. When I woke up, you were gone and I was still on the couch."

"I know that part. Go . . ." He stopped speaking and waved at the person who'd just come into the Corner Tavern. "Hold off on your explanation, Hannah. Mike just came in and he's joining us for breakfast."

"Mike's here this early?" Hannah asked in surprise. "I thought he had the day off today."

"He does, but he worked all night after he left your place. He'll explain when he gets here."

"Hi, Hannah . . . Norman," Mike greeted them, and then he stopped to stare at Hannah as he sat down. "Is that a new perfume, Hannah?"

Both Hannah and Norman burst into laughter. It took a full minute before Norman could say, "Hannah told me it's Eau de Moishe."

"Huh?"

"I'll explain in a minute," Hannah said, taking another sip of her coffee.

"Coffee, Mike?" the waitress asked, hurrying over to their table.

"Definitely," Mike said, smiling at her. "I need something to wake me up."

"You're up really early, Mike," Hannah commented.

"I'm not up early. I'm still up," Mike told her. "I worked all night, Hannah."

"But . . . I thought you didn't have to go in to work last night."

"I didn't. I *chose* to go in to work. I had things I needed to do after I talked to you and Andrea last night."

"You mean . . . about the case?"

"That's right. I'll tell you about it, right after you tell me about Eau de Moishe."

Hannah took a deep breath, and then she smiled. "It was just me being silly," she admitted. "I thought I heard someone breaking into the condo last night. There was a crash that woke me up, and then I heard another couple of thuds."

Mike looked shocked. "And you didn't call me?"

"I . . . no. I probably should have, but I thought I could handle it."

"How?" It was Norman's turn to ask a question.

"Well . . . I looked around for a weapon, and I found one."

"A weapon?" Mike asked, looking alarmed. "I didn't know you had a gun, Hannah."

"I don't."

"Then what kind of weapon are you talking about?" Norman asked for clarification.

"I found something heavy, something I thought I could use to sneak up on an intruder, and knock him out."

Both men were silent for a moment, and then Norman asked, "Are you talking about Eau de Moishe?"

"Yes." Hannah tried not to laugh. "You both have to remember that I was tired, and more than a little sleepy. I wasn't thinking clearly, so I grabbed the first heavy object I could find."

"A perfume bottle?" Norman guessed.

"Yes. I won it last year at a Christmas party."

"And you went to confront an intruder with nothing but a *perfume* bottle?" Mike asked.

Hannah couldn't help it. She laughed. Mike sounded absolutely dumbfounded. "I know it's silly, but that's exactly what I did. I went out in the hallway, and there was another thud. And then I realized that the noises were coming from the kitchen. So I went in there and found the pantry door was open slightly. So I pushed it open and . . ."

"Moishe was in there!" both men spoke in tandem.

"That's right. He was up on a shelf knocking cans to the floor. Things like cat food and cans of salmon and tuna. I was so shocked, I dropped the perfume bottle and it spilled all over the kitchen floor."

"And that's why you smell like a French . . . whatever," Mike said, not finishing his thought. "Really, Hannah! If anything like that happens again, call me."

"Or me," Norman added. "Just hole up somewhere safe, and call us for help."

"Thank you," Hannah said, and she meant it. It was nice to have two protectors on white steeds ready to ride out and save her from danger . . . not that she couldn't protect herself from any danger that she encountered. But of course she wouldn't tell them that.

"Why were you working all night, Mike?" she asked instead, hoping to change the subject.

"I was using the office computer. It's hooked up to several databases that I can't get privately."

"You were looking to see if you could find out something about Joe?" Hannah asked him.

"That's right. Sheriff Grant has rules about who can and can't use the computer, and what they're allowed to access. And I haven't really been able to do much of a search before."

"Did you tell him that Doc thought Joe's injury could have been done intentionally by someone attempting to hurt or kill him?"

"I did, but he said that was conjecture, that there was no proof of that. And since Joe didn't remember how it happened, there was no reason for me to investigate it."

"That figures," Norman said with a sigh.

"Anyway . . ." Mike continued, "I decided to do a little research on my own, when the sheriff wasn't around. And last night Marjorie Hanks came to clean the office. That meant it was open, so when I left your place, I went in to the office, to see if Sheriff Grant was there."

"And he wasn't?" Norman guessed.

"No. Marjorie told me he'd just left. I told her I had to finish some reports, so she cleaned around me and I looked up all the entries for missing persons in the past year."

"Did you find anything?" Hannah leaned forward eagerly.

"No. I tried the hospital to see if Doc was still there, and got him on the phone. He said he couldn't pin down Joe's injury time-wise and all we could do was hope that Joe would remember something about what had happened to him."

"So you didn't learn anything new," Norman concluded.

"That's right. I put in all the variables we knew, and guessed at some of the others, but nothing interesting came up." He turned to Hannah. "I'm sorry, Hannah. I was really hoping to find out something for you."

"It's okay, Mike. I really appreciate the effort. I guess all we can do is hope that Joe remembers more, and something he tells us gives us a clue."

"What are you having for breakfast, Mike?" Norman asked him. "I'm buying."

"Thanks. I think I'll see what's new. I looked at the menu board when I came in, and it said they had a new Christmas special every week. Last week's was really great."

"What was it?" Hannah was curious.

"It was called the Jack Frost."

"Eggs and Jack cheese?" Hannah guessed.

"That's right! It was sausage, pepper Jack, and red and green bell peppers inside so it was Christmas-y."

"That's clever," Norman said, turning to their waitress, who had just come up to refill their coffee cups. "Do you have a Christmas special today?"

"We do, and I think it's my favorite. It's called Santa's Christmas Wreath Pancakes."

"That sounds interesting," Hannah said. "Do the pancakes look like wreaths?"

"They do, and they're really pretty. They're cinnamon and sugar pancakes. The chef makes three big pancakes, slathers them with butter, and puts them on a plate. Then he uses a round cookie cutter to cut out the middle of the pancakes."

"So what's left looks like wreaths?" Hannah asked.

"Exactly right. He decorates the top wreath with powdered sugar and dots it with red and green candied cherries. It's really pretty."

"What does your chef do with the part of the pancake he cut out?" Hannah asked her.

"That's the fun part. He unstacks the middles and puts them on a second plate. And then he sprinkles the tops with more cinnamon and sugar, makes a circle of powdered sugar frosting in the centers, and puts a strawberry on top of the circle with the point up. And for a final touch, he squirts whipped cream all the way around the bottom of the strawberry and a little on the tip, so it looks like the tassel of a cap. They look like little Santa hats, and the kids think they're great!"

"That sounds like a lot of work," Norman commented.

"Not really. The waitresses decorate the middles and

all the chef has to do is decorate the wreath. And the nice thing about it is you can order one wreath—that's one pancake only—two wreaths, or three wreaths."

Hannah figured, "And each wreath comes with a Santa hat?"

"That's right," the waitress said.

Mike nodded. "That's smart and you convinced me. I'm ordering Santa's Christmas Wreath Pancakes."

"And you want three pancakes, right?" the waitress asked him.

"Yeah. I'm hungry this morning."

The waitress turned to Hannah. "How about you, Hannah?"

"I'll have the same, but I only want one pancake."

"And you?" she asked Norman.

"I'll try those, but I only want two."

"Got it!" the waitress said, flipping her order pad closed and stashing it in her apron pocket. "Let me top off your coffee, and I'll be back in less than five minutes with your pancakes."

"Wait a second," Mike stopped her. "Do those pancakes come with bacon, or sausage, or any kind of meat?"

"No, but you can order a side. We've got bacon, sausage, or ham."

"Perfect. Give me a side of . . ." Mike hesitated for a moment and then he sighed. "I can't make up my mind between sausage or bacon."

"You can order both if you want to," the waitress told him.

"Yeah. That'd be good. I'll have both. And you might as well throw in an order of ham, too. I'm practically starving."

Hannah judiciously avoided Norman's eyes. She knew that if she glanced at him, she'd start to laugh. Mike was an eating machine, no doubt about it.

SANTA'S CHRISTMAS WREATH PANCAKES AND SANTA'S HAT PANCAKES

(This recipe can be doubled if you wish.)

Ingredients for Santa's Christmas Wreath Pancakes:

1 Tablespoon brown sugar
1 Tablespoon baking powder
1 Tablespoon ground cinnamon
½ teaspoon salt
1 and ¼ cups all-purpose flour *(pack it down in the cup when you measure it)*
1 large egg
1 and ¼ cups half and half *(light cream)*
1 teaspoon vanilla extract
½ stick *(2 ounces, 4 Tablespoons)* salted butter, melted

Ingredients for Cinnamon Powdered Sugar Glaze:

¼ stick *(2 Tablespoons)* salted butter
1 to 1 and ½ cups powdered sugar *(pack it down in the cup when you measure it)*
½ teaspoon ground cinnamon
1 to 2 Tablespoons milk or light cream

Ingredients to Decorate Santa's Christmas Wreath Pancakes and Santa's Hat Pancakes:

16 red and/or green candied cherries *(If you can't find candied cherries, you can substitute maraschino cherries.)*

4 large strawberries *(You can substitute frozen strawberries if you thaw them the morning you plan to make the pancakes.)*

To Make Santa's Christmas Wreath Pancake batter:

Place the Tablespoon of brown sugar in a large bowl on the counter.

Add the Tablespoon of baking powder and mix well.

Sprinkle in the cinnamon and salt. Mix them in thoroughly.

Measure out the all-purpose flour. Make sure you pack it down in the measuring cup when you measure it.

Mix the flour in thoroughly.

Crack the egg in another bowl. Use a whisk to mix the yolk and the white together. Mix until the egg is frothy.

Add the cup and a quarter of half and half. Mix it in thoroughly with the egg.

Mix in the vanilla extract.

Melt the half stick of salted butter in a small bowl in the microwave. Set the bowl on the counter and let it cool to room temperature.

Add the melted, salted butter to the bowl with the egg and light cream. Mix it in thoroughly.

Make a well in the center of the bowl with the dry ingredients.

Drizzle the liquid ingredients into the well in the bowl of dry ingredients, stirring constantly. Mix until everything is blended together. This forms your Santa's Christmas Wreath Pancake batter.

Cover the bowl with plastic wrap and put it in the refrigerator overnight. Your Santa's Christmas Wreath Pancake batter will be ready to make for breakfast in the morning.

Hannah's Note: Pancake batter improves if it sits in the refrigerator overnight. Bubbles may form on the surface, but that's fine. You'll mix it up again in the morning before you make it.

In the morning, take the bowl of pancake batter out of the refrigerator, and let it sit on your kitchen counter while you make the Cinnamon Powdered Sugar Glaze.

To Make the Cinnamon Powdered Sugar Glaze:

Place the quarter stick of salted butter in a small, microwave-safe bowl.

Heat the butter on HIGH in the microwave for 30 seconds.

In another bowl, mix up the powdered sugar and cinnamon.

Pour the melted butter into the bowl with the powdered sugar and cinnamon mixture.

Add the milk or light cream, in small increments, until the glaze reaches drizzling consistency.

To Fry Pancakes:

Lightly spray a nonstick frying pan with Pam or another nonstick cooking spray. Alternatively, put an ounce of butter in the center of a nonstick frying pan. *(I used a 12-inch Teflon frying pan).*

Turn the burner on MEDIUM heat. If you used butter, use a spatula to move the butter around in the frying pan so the whole bottom is coated.

When you think your frying pan is hot enough, test it by sprinkling a few droplets of water in the pan from the tips of your impeccably clean fingers. If the droplets of water "dance" around in the pan, your frying pan is ready.

Give your pancake batter a final stir. Then ladle approximately ⅓ to ½ cup of batter into the center of the heated frying pan.

Quickly, using a heat-resistant spatula or the back of a wooden spoon, spread the batter around in the pan, so that it makes an 8-inch to 10-inch circle.

Let the large pancake cook approximately 2 minutes, or until you notice little bubbles begin to form on the top of the pancake and the edges look slightly dry. This means it's time to turn the pancake over and fry the other side.

Slide the blade of a heat resistant spatula under your pancake to loosen it from the pan. Then use it to flip the pancake over so that the uncooked side is on the bottom.

Fry another 1 to 2 minutes more, or until the center is cooked, and the bottom is slightly browned.

Remove your pancake from the pan and put it on a serving plate. (Unless you're Mike, or someone at your breakfast table insists that they're starving, the normal serving is 1 to 2 pancakes.)

To make your pancakes into Santa's Christmas Wreath Pancakes, use a round cookie cutter to cut out the center of the plated pancakes.

Remove the centers of the pancakes, and put them on smaller plates. They will eventually become Santa's Hat Pancakes.

To Decorate Santa's Christmas Wreath Pancakes:

Either sprinkle the top of your "wreath" with powdered sugar, or drizzle on Cinnamon Powdered Sugar Glaze.

Dot the top side of the "wreath" with red and/or green candied cherries to resemble the berries on a wreath.

To Decorate Santa's Hat Pancakes:

Spoon a small circle of Cinnamon Powdered Sugar Glaze in the center of each small pancake.

Cut the stem part off a fresh *(or frozen and thawed)* strawberry to give it a flat bottom to sit on. Be sure to leave the tip of the strawberry intact. *That's the top of the Santa's Hat.*

Place the strawberry, point up, in the center of the circle of glaze. Then drizzle a little more glaze around the base of the strawberry so that it looks like the white fur on the bottom of Santa's hat.

Dab a little more glaze on the tip of the strawberry so that it resembles the tassel on the tip of Santa's hat. You can also decorate Santa's Hat Pancakes with whipped cream if you wish.

Yield: Makes approximately 4 Santa's Christmas Wreath Pancakes and 4 Santa's Hat Pancakes.

Chapter Sixteen

There was a knock at her back kitchen door and Hannah knew exactly who it was. It was a tentative knock, as if her early-morning caller was desperately hoping he wasn't disturbing her, and that meant it had to be Joe Smith.

"Come in, Joe." Hannah opened the door and greeted him. "Pour yourself a cup of coffee, and I'll get you a couple of my new Christmas Coconut Crunch Cookies for breakfast."

"Sounds great, Hannah," Joe said quickly, hanging up the parka Delores and Carrie had given him. "Do you think it'll ever warm up?" he asked her, rubbing his hands together as he headed for the kitchen coffeepot.

"Probably not for another month," Hannah answered, putting a generous helping of cookies on a plate for him.

"You're probably right," Joe said with a sigh, carrying two cups of coffee to the work station and taking a seat across from Hannah's favorite stool. "After all, the Minnesota spring doesn't usually come until April at the earliest, and the end of May at the latest. I guess we should stop talking about the cold weather, and be grateful that we'll probably get a white Christmas." He smiled at Hannah as she came over to sit down. "I love Christmas, don't you?"

"I do. The reflection of the lights on the snow is so beautiful. And if the weather's not really awful, everyone goes out at night to visit neighbors and go to holiday parties."

"And you cater those parties?" Joe asked. And then an expression she couldn't interpret crossed his face.

"What did you just think of, Joe?" Hannah asked him.

"Your catering. I used to help my mother with parties. We always had the neighbors over for Christmas. Relatives too. And my mother always invited anyone in our township over for one of her parties, so that everyone was included."

"That was nice," she said, making a mental note to write down the word *township* on the list she was keeping about what Joe had remembered. "Do you recall the name of your township?"

"It was Lake something, or maybe something-Lake. All I can remember is that *Lake* was in the name. Everyone loved my mother's holiday parties."

"And you said that you helped with those parties?"

"So did Donnie, but there was only so much he could do."

"Because he was slow?"

Joe shook his head. "Not really. He knew all the neighbors and remembered their names. And he helped them with odd jobs before Dad started the shop. After that, Donnie was too busy learning how to refinish furniture and reupholster sofas and chairs. He loved to work in the shop, Hannah. He said it made him feel smart."

"Did you help to teach Donnie how to work in the shop?"

"Yes. Donnie had trouble when it came to things like reading and adding numbers together, but he loved to make things look like new again. And he had a real talent for it. Dad used to ask Donnie which material to use on chairs and sofas, and he told me that the patterns and colors that Donnie chose were perfect. When Dad died, and Donnie and I kept the shop open, I used to ask Donnie for advice when it came to choosing upholstery material."

"Do you remember Donnie's last name, Joe?"

"Yes, it's the same as . . ." Joe stopped speaking and looked startled, as if he were waking from a dream. "I . . . I have a terrible headache, Hannah." He reached in his pocket and pulled out a vial of pills. "Doc gave me some pills. Do you mind if I get a glass of water?"

"Of course not! Just stay right where you are, Joe. I'll get it for you."

As Hannah ran water into a glass, she decided to call Doc the moment Joe left and tell him what had happened. It was clear that Joe's memory was coming back, and the things he remembered were painful to him. She needed Doc's guidance on which questions she could ask and which subjects she should avoid.

As Hannah delivered Joe's glass of water and watched him take one of the pills from his prescription bottle, she thought about everything that had taken place over the past week.

The first bit of news she'd received from Doc was startling. Joe and Freddy had completely reupholstered his recliner, including replacing the wooden slats that had broken. Hannah had seen it the next time she'd gone to the hospital to see Joe, and it was a thoroughly professional job. Joe and Freddy were a good team.

The next change had been instigated by Delores and Carrie. Once they'd seen the work that Joe and Freddy had done at the hospital, Delores had purchased the storefront, where their combined antiques were stored, turned on the electricity and heat, and fashioned a small "apartment" for Joe to live in while he regained his memory.

The next big change had come from Joe himself. Of course, he was grateful for Delores and Carrie's largess. He'd offered to work renovating their antiques during the day for them, if they agreed to hire Freddy to help him with the heavy lifting and provide a small salary for food and necessities.

Of course, Hannah's mother had been delighted to accept Joe's offer and Joe and Freddy had begun to work in the storefront two doors down from Hannah. She had invited Joe to stop by at The Cookie Jar for coffee every morning, and he'd gratefully accepted her offer.

Hannah readily admitted that there was an ulterior motive to her offer of coffee and some of her bakery goods. Having morning coffee with Joe every day provided her with the opportunity to ask him questions about his former life. Hannah hoped, if things went well and Joe's memory came back, she'd be able to find the family he'd left behind, including the person she suspected was his brother Donnie.

"Which piece of furniture are you working on now, Joe?" Hannah asked him, giving him time to talk about something that wouldn't cause his headache to recur.

"Your mother's davenport," Joe responded immediately. "It was in bad shape, Hannah, but I think Freddy and I got a handle on it. Did you know that it converts into a sofa bed?"

"No!" Hannah was surprised. "I had no idea. And I don't think Mother knew either. Is that why it's so heavy?"

"Yes. The carriage under the mattress is made of steel, and so are the inner springs. Steel is great for durability, but adds a lot to the weight of the davenport. Unfortunately, the mattress is a total loss."

"No wonder it was so heavy!" Hannah said, remembering how much strength it had taken to move the davenport out far enough for her to climb up and out of the space. "What happened to the mattress? Did someone remove it?"

"No. It was still there . . . in pieces. There were still chunks of padding."

"Rats?" Hannah guessed.

"It had to have been something like that, perhaps mice, or possibly an opossum tearing it up to make a bed for her young." Joe gave a little shrug. "It was so far gone, it was impossible for me to tell what had gotten into it."

"Can the mattress be replaced?"

"Yes, but it'll have to be a custom job. There was enough of the mattress left to measure how thick it was and where it was sectioned to fold, and I had the frame under it to go by."

"Can you make a new mattress?" Hannah asked him.

Joe laughed. "No, not me. That's way beyond my skill set. But your mother and Carrie are looking for a place that can make a mattress that size."

"Mother's good at finding things like that," Hannah told him.

"I noticed. She's also very good at choosing which antiques to buy. Carrie will occasionally fall for the cheap imitations, but your mother won't. She's got a good eye."

"That's nice to know." Hannah felt a rush of admiration for her mother's talents. Her dad had always said that Delores was great at finding rare antiques.

"She's also very good at choosing upholstery material, almost as good as Donnie was." Joe stopped and looked sad. "I'm really glad Freddy works with me part-time. He reminds me of Donnie, and I really miss my brother." Joe popped the rest of the last cookie into his mouth and smiled at her. "I don't suppose there are more of these, are there, Hannah? All your cookies are great, but I think these Christmas Coconut Crunch Cookies are the best."

Once Joe left for the morning, with a bag of take-out cookies and a cup of coffee in one of Hannah's to-go containers, Hannah glanced at the clock. It was still too early to call Doc to tell him that Joe had called Donnie his brother. Chances were that he was up by now, but if he wasn't, she didn't want to disturb his sleep.

She baked three more batches of cookies, rinsed out the metal bowls she used for cookie dough, and put them in her industrial dishwasher. Once that was set and activated, she poured herself another cup of coffee and sat down to go through her recipe book to decide what she should bake next.

The Christmas rush was upon Hannah and Lisa at The Cookie Jar, and Hannah was coming in early to bake almost double the cookies they usually sold. Either Hannah or Lisa was busy almost every night with a party to cater, or a special delivery for a Christmas dessert, and it would become even more intense before the holiday season was over. That made Hannah think of what Joe had said about helping his mother with parties. While she had Doc on the phone, she would ask his advice about whether she should offer Joe the chance to help her with catering parties. They could always use an extra pair of hands at large gatherings.

While Hannah sat with a fresh cup of coffee, she paged through her loose-leaf recipe book and thought about what she wanted to bake next. They really needed another Christmas cupcake, but she was fresh out of ideas. It should probably be a chocolate cupcake of some sort. At parties, chocolate cookies, chocolate pie, chocolate-filled cream puffs, and chocolate cupcakes seemed to be almost everyone's favorite. Whatever she decided to create, Hannah knew it should probably be something with chocolate.

As she paged through her recipe book, she came across the first recipe she'd ever created for her mother. It was Chocolate-Covered Cherry Cookies and Delores loved them. And Delores wasn't the only one who loved the combination of chocolate and cherries.

The moment the idea popped into her head, Hannah set about to make up a new cupcake recipe with a chocolate-covered cherry in the center.

The thing Hannah considered was how the cupcake should taste. It should be rich with enough chocolate to satisfy even the most addicted chocolate lover. Her model was Delores. Hannah had once found her mother's stash of chocolate candy in a drawer in her kitchen. The drawer had been full, but a month later, when Hannah had looked again, it was almost empty. Delores prided herself on maintaining her weight. She liked to tell people that her wedding gown still fit her perfectly. She also bragged that she was the same weight she'd been when she was a senior in high school. How could her mother eat all that chocolate and still maintain her girlish figure? Hannah had pondered that question many times, and she'd come to the conclusion that Delores had probably made a pact with the same devil that Mike had made. Oh, of course she knew she was being ridiculous, that it was a matter of body chemistry and basal metabolism, but she did wonder why her mother and her sisters, Andrea and Michelle, had no trouble maintaining their weight, when she struggled constantly with the problem.

The next decision Hannah had to make was what she should call her new cupcake. She didn't want to use the words Chocolate-Covered Cherry in the name because she planned to hide the candy in the middle of the cupcake and using it in the title would take the surprise part away. The baker would know, of course, but someone tasting the cupcakes for the first time would be deliciously surprised.

Twenty minutes later, after making the cupcake batter as rich with chocolate as she possibly could, Hannah slipped the first batch onto the shelves of her industrial oven. Luckily, she'd found the box of chocolate-covered cherries that she'd been planning to put under the Christmas tree for her mother, still wrapped and in the pantry.

There was nothing like baking to clear her mind, and now she was ready to call Doc Knight to ask him what he'd prescribed for Joe's headaches, and whether Joe could help her cater Christmas parties.

CHRISTMAS COCONUT CRUNCH COOKIES

DO NOT preheat oven—dough must chill before baking.

Hannah's 1ˢᵗ Note: This recipe makes approximately 10 dozen cookies. If you like, you can reduce the yield to approximately 5 dozen, by cutting each ingredient by half.

2 cups melted butter *(4 sticks, 16 ounces, 1 pound)*
2 cups powdered sugar *(don't sift unless it's got big lumps and then you shouldn't use it anyway)*
1 cup white *(granulated)* sugar
2 eggs
1 teaspoon vanilla extract
1 teaspoon coconut extract
1 teaspoon baking soda
1 teaspoon cream of tartar *(critical!)*
1 teaspoon salt
2 Tablespoons all-purpose flour
1 cup sweetened coconut flakes
1 cup white chocolate or vanilla baking chips
4 additional cups flour *(don't sift—pack it down in the cup when you measure it)*

½ cup white decorators sugar in a small bowl *(for coating dough balls)*

Melt the butter in a microwave-safe mixing bowl. Place the mixing bowl on your kitchen counter.

Add both of the sugars and mix thoroughly. Let the mix cool to room temperature.

Stir in the eggs, one at a time, mixing after each egg is added.

Add the vanilla extract and coconut extract. Mix them in thoroughly.

Sprinkle in the baking soda, cream of tartar, and salt. Stir until they are well mixed in.

With the steel blade in place on your food processor, sprinkle in 1 Tablespoon of flour.

Measure out the sweetened coconut flakes and add them to the food processor on top of the flour. Now add the white chocolate chips on top of the coconut.

Sprinkle the remaining Tablespoon of flour on top of the white chocolate chips.

Use an on-and-off motion with the steel blade to process the coconut/white chocolate chip mixture. Continue to process until everything has been chopped into very small pieces.

Hannah's 2nd Note: One of the reasons that some people don't care for coconut in cookies is that the coconut flakes stick between their teeth. Chopping the coconut up into tiny pieces eliminates that problem.

Transfer the finely chopped, flour-coated coconut/white chocolate chip mixture to your mixing bowl. Stir thoroughly.

Add the remainder of the flour in half-cup increments, mixing after each addition.

Use your impeccably clean hands to round up the cookie dough into a ball.

Place the cookie dough in a sealable plastic bag and refrigerate it for at least one hour. *(Overnight is fine, too.)*

When you're ready to bake, preheat oven to 325 degrees F. with the rack in the middle position.

Prepare your cookie sheets by spraying them with Pam or another nonstick cooking spray. Alternatively, you can line them with parchment paper, leaving a little ear at the top and a little ear at the bottom so that you can easily pull the parchment paper, cookies and all, to a wire rack after they are baked.

Place the white decorators sugar in a shallow bowl.

Use your impeccably clean hands to roll the dough into walnut-sized balls.

Roll each dough ball in the bowl of decorators sugar to coat it.

Place the sugar-coated dough balls on the cookie sheets you've prepared, 12 cookies on each standard-sized cookie sheet.

Flatten the dough balls with the back of a metal spatula or the palm of your impeccably clean hand.

Bake your Christmas Coconut Crunch Cookies at 325 degrees F. for 10 to 15 minutes. *(The cookies should have a tinge of light golden brown on the tops and outer edges.)*

Remove the cookies from the oven and transfer them, still on the cookie sheets, to cold stovetop burners or wire racks on the kitchen counter.

Cool the cookies on their cookie sheets for 2 minutes and then remove them to wire racks to cool completely.

Yield: approximately 8 to 10 dozen buttery, sugary cookies.

Chapter Seventeen

Hannah hung up the phone, and walked to the kitchen coffeepot. She'd learned a lot from her conversation with Doc. The prescription he'd given Joe was nothing but a mild analgesic, something anyone could buy over the counter at a pharmacy. As for Joe helping her with the catering, Doc was completely in favor of it! He thought it would be good to get Joe out with people again.

She picked up the coffeepot, to pour herself another cup, and thought better of it. She'd had too much coffee already this morning. All coffee'd out by this time, Hannah was just sitting down on her stool at the work station when there was a knock at her back kitchen door. She recognized the knock immediately and hurried to let Andrea in.

"Ooooh! What smells so good?" Andrea asked as she stomped the snow from her boots, put them on the rug by the door, and hung her coat on a hook.

"Chocolate Surprise Cupcakes."

"What's the surprise?" Andrea asked, as Hannah went to the kitchen coffeepot and poured her sister a cup.

"You'll have to figure it out for yourself. They come out of the oven in fifteen minutes and they have to cool for at least half that time before I can frost them."

"I'll taste one unfrosted," Andrea offered quickly. "I was out of unflavored yogurt this morning, so I didn't have any breakfast."

Hannah worked hard not to look as disgusted as she felt. Unflavored yogurt was a fine ingredient in many recipes, but she couldn't imagine eating it straight out of the carton.

"I'm glad you stopped by this morning," Hannah said, sitting down across from her sister. "I have a little research project for you."

"Does it involve Joe Smith's identity?" Andrea asked eagerly.

"Yes. He was in for coffee this morning and he mentioned that the farm where he lived was in a township. I asked him if he remembered the name of the township and he said it was *Lake Something* or *Something Lake*, but he couldn't remember anything more about it."

"No problem," Andrea said quickly, taking her cell phone out of her pocket and pressing some keys. "Lake-something or something-Lake. Is that right?"

"That's what he said."

Hannah watched as Andrea pressed more keys on her

phone. For one brief moment, she wished that she had a newer cell phone, one that could connect with the internet, but then she thought better of it. She had trouble enough searching for things on her home computer. Learning another whole system that involved a new cell phone would take time and one-on-one instruction. Right now, in the midst of the Christmas rush, she didn't have enough minutes to spare for either of those things.

"Uh-oh!" Andrea said, looking down at the screen on her phone.

"Uh-oh what?"

"There's a ton of them!"

"Townships?"

"Yes. And a lot of them have *Lake something* or *something Lake* in their names."

"So it's not really a clue?"

Andrea sighed. "It is, but only if we can pair it with another variable. Then I can search for a name with both variables."

Hannah opened her steno pad and paged through the list she'd made. "How about if Joe knew the name of the lake by his farm, the one he used to ride to on his bike to go swimming?"

"That might help."

"Might?"

"Yes. Remember what you pointed out to me? Minnesota is the state with ten thousand lakes?"

"Yes. I didn't mean to embarrass you by saying that, Andrea."

"You did embarrass me, but only for a second. Then I realized how funny it was. Do you know the name of Joe's lake?"

"I do. He remembered it the other day. It's Long Lake."

It took a full minute for Andrea to respond, and then she sighed again. "I'll try, but it could be a lost cause."

"Why?"

"I'll tell you in a few seconds." Andrea clicked more keys on her phone and it beeped several times. Then she got up from her stool, walked around the table, and showed the screen to Hannah.

"Here's why," she said.

Hannah glanced down at the screen and gasped. "There are over one hundred fifty Long Lakes in Minnesota?!"

"Yes, it's the second-most common lake name."

"What's the most common name?"

"Mud Lake. This website says there are over two hundred Mud Lakes."

"Wonderful!" Hannah said sarcastically. "That's the other lake name I wrote down. Joe said that Mud Lake was closer than Long Lake, but his mother wouldn't let him go swimming there because of the leeches."

Andrea laughed. "That's another one."

"*What's* another one?"

"Leech Lake! That's another common lake name. I think we'll have to give up on the lake names until we can get more information from Joe."

It was Hannah's turn to sigh. "You're right. We're

going to need more . . ." She stopped speaking as they heard a knock at the door. "That's Mike," she said.

"You recognized his knock?"

"Yes. It's impatient and demanding. It's like he's saying, if you don't get to this door fast, I'll break it down."

"Do you think he would?"

"No, at least not unless he was convinced there was something wrong. Then I'm sure he would."

Andrea nodded. "Me too."

"I'll let Mike in, and then I'll frost a couple of the cupcakes I just made. Will you get coffee for Mike?"

"Sure," Andrea agreed, "but you'd better rethink that."

"Rethink what?"

"Frosting a couple of cupcakes. A couple won't be enough for Mike."

Hannah laughed. "You're right, of course. I'll frost as many as I can, while you get him settled at the work station."

The frosting she'd made earlier was in a covered bowl on the counter and Hannah gave it a stir. It was the right consistency and that meant it was ready to use. She got out her favorite frosting knife, and frosted a half dozen cupcakes quickly. Andrea was still talking to Mike at the work station and she could hear their conversation.

"I'm hungry as a bear this morning," Mike said to Andrea. "I went to work early, so I could use the computer before anyone else came in."

"You mean Sheriff Grant?" Andrea asked him.

"Yeah. And I have to be a little careful around the new secretary that he just hired."

Hungry as a bear this morning. Mike's words alerted Hannah and she frosted a few more cupcakes. Then she put them on a plate, covered the bowl with the frosting, and headed for the work station to appease the hungry bear.

"Have a Chocolate Surprise Cupcake, Mike," she invited, setting the plate on the table. "You too, Andrea."

"These are new, aren't they?" Mike asked.

"Yes. I just came up with the recipe this morning."

"What's the surprise?"

"You'll find out," Hannah told him. "The surprise is in the middle of the cupcake."

"All right then. I'll just have to bite into one," Mike said, reaching for a cupcake, peeling off the paper, and taking a huge bite. He took a second bite and a surprised expression crossed his face. "Kmmmjpy," he said unintelligibly.

"What?" Andrea asked, winking at Hannah to show that she was teasing Mike.

Mike swallowed. "Candy!" he said clearly. "And it's got something in the middle . . . hold on." Hannah and Andrea watched while Mike took another bite. "Chmmmmphy," he said.

Both Hannah and Andrea shook their heads.

Mike swallowed again and then he started to grin. "Chocolate-covered cherries," he said.

"Absolutely right," Hannah told him. "There's a chocolate-covered cherry inside each cupcake."

"Cute idea," Mike pronounced, reaching for another cupcake. "And they're good, too. I love that frosting, Hannah."

"What is it?" Andrea asked, reaching for her own cupcake.

"Chocolate Fudge Frosting made with maraschino cherry juice instead of vanilla extract."

Andrea bit into her cupcake and gave a sound of satisfaction. Unlike Mike, she swallowed before she tried to speak. "Really good!" she said. "The frosting is just like fudge."

"It's a little softer than fudge, but it's almost the same," Hannah told her.

"Have you made these for Mother yet?" Andrea asked.

"She hasn't tasted these yet, but you know how crazy she is about Chocolate-Covered Cherry Cookies."

Mike looked interested. "Have I tasted those?"

Hannah thought about it for a moment. "I'm not sure, but I think you must have. They're a staple here at The Cookie Jar."

"What do you do if you can't get chocolate-covered cherries?" Andrea asked. "Florence doesn't always carry them at the Red Owl, does she?"

"Not always, but she stocks them around the holidays. I guess you could use some other kind of candy and still call them Chocolate Surprise Cupcakes."

"Peanut Butter Cups!" Mike suggested. "Or if those are too big, you could use Reese's Pieces."

"I think they make a miniature peanut butter cup, too," Andrea told them. "I've seen it at CostMart."

"That would work," Hannah agreed. "And instead of putting the two Tablespoons of cherry juice in the frosting, you could use vanilla extract."

"How about caramels?" Mike asked. "Most people love chocolate and caramel."

"You'd have to be a little careful with that," Hannah told him. "Hard caramels wouldn't necessarily soften in the oven, but you could use something like a soft caramel coated with chocolate."

"Those are called Rolo candies," Andrea said quickly. "I think they'd work fine, Hannah. The next time I'm at CostMart, I'll pick up some and you can try them."

"I'll taste-test those," Mike offered quickly.

Andrea nodded. "So will I. I love Rolo candies."

Hannah just stared at her perfect model-size sister and sighed. Andrea was another person who inhaled food and never had to diet. Why hadn't she inherited that particular gene when both of her sisters had?

"Hey, Mike . . . I heard you say you went to work early this morning," Hannah said, changing the subject. "Were you doing something on the computer for Joe?"

"Yes. I was checking the database again. I'm sorry, Hannah. I put in all the info I could think of, but nothing came up. And then I looked at all the photos."

"Photos?" Andrea asked.

"Yes. When someone reports a missing person, we always ask for a recent photo. No one in our five-state area looked at all like Joe."

Hannah was silent for a moment, and then she shook her head. "I just don't understand it. Doc doesn't think Joe's been missing for that long. He told me he thought the outer limit was six or seven months."

"I went back a year the first time I checked. This time I went back two years. There's nothing there."

"Is it possible that Joe went missing and no one reported it?" Hannah asked.

"Sure. Maybe no one missed him. Or maybe someone thought he left of his own accord. That happens. When I worked in Minneapolis, this would happen every once in a while. It was like the husband that went out for a pack of cigarettes one night and just didn't come back home."

"That's frightening," Andrea said, and Hannah noticed that she gave a little shiver.

"Yes, it is," Hannah agreed, "but that's not what happened in Joe's case. He's here and he's alive. He just doesn't remember who he is."

"Do you think we should get Rod to run his photo in the paper?" Hannah suggested. "He could have a caption that said something like, *Can Anyone Identify This Man?*"

Mike shook his head. "Maybe, but only as a last resort. Doc told me he thinks someone might have tried to kill Joe. And if that person's still out there and he sees Joe's photo, he could come after Joe again."

"You're right," Andrea said. "We can't do anything that might jeopardize Joe."

"But it could be the only way we can find out who

Joe really is," Mike pointed out. "And that's something all of us, including Joe, want. Isn't that right?"

"Give me some time to think about that," Hannah said. "If it's the only way, we'll have to, but we'll have to think of some way to protect Joe. He's starting to remember now. Just give it another week, and maybe he'll be able to tell us something that'll help us." She stopped and frowned slightly. "We've got a little time, don't we?" She waited until both of them nodded. "You'll keep checking that computer database, won't you, Mike?"

"Yes. Sheriff Grant's going to a conference tomorrow and he'll be gone for three days. That'll give me free access to the database."

"And you'll join me for coffee with Joe in the morning, won't you, Andrea?"

"Of course I will! I want to help him just as much as you do, Hannah."

"Good." Hannah smiled at both of them. "And I'll use Joe for this week's catering. Maybe he'll remember something about his mother's holiday parties that'll provide us with a clue."

They sat there sipping their coffee and eating cupcakes for several moments, each lost in their own thoughts. Then Andrea began to smile.

"What?" Hannah asked her.

"I got it. I know exactly what you can use."

Hannah was thoroughly confused. "You know exactly what I can use for what?"

"For your Chocolate Surprise Cupcakes. If you can't find chocolate-covered cherries, or Reese's Peanut Butter Cups, or Rolo candies, you can use Fanny Farmer creams!"

"Good idea!" Mike praised her. "Fanny Farmer soft centers are really good and they make them in lots of flavors."

Hannah thought about that for a moment and then she nodded in agreement. "I could always buy an assortment. They're all chocolate-covered and they have pineapple, lemon, orange, soft chocolate, vanilla, coconut, soft caramel, and a lot of other flavors."

"And there's another benefit," Mike added. "They're assorted, so if someone has more than one cupcake, the second one will still be a surprise."

CHOCOLATE SURPRISE CUPCAKES

Preheat oven to 350 degrees F., rack in the middle position.

4 large eggs
½ cup vegetable oil
½ cup heavy cream *(whipping cream)*
8-ounce *(by weight)* tub of sour cream *(I used Knudsen)*
1 Tablespoon chocolate syrup *(I used Hershey's)*
1 box of chocolate cake mix, the kind that makes a 9-inch by 13-inch cake or a 2-layer cake *(I used Pillsbury)*
5.1-ounce package of DRY instant chocolate pudding and pie filling *(I used Jell-O.)*
12-ounce *(by weight)* bag of chocolate mini chips *(11-ounce package will do, too—I used Nestlé)*
1 box of chocolate-covered cherry candy *(you will need 24 pieces)*

Hannah's Note: Lisa discovered another kind of chocolate-covered cherry that also works well in these cupcakes. They're made by Dove, the people who make Dove Bars. Their chocolate-covered cherries don't have a sweet liquid around the cherry. Either variety will work well in these cupcakes.

Prepare your cupcake pans. You will need 2 twelve-cup pans lined with double cupcake papers.

Crack the eggs into the bowl of an electric mixer. Mix them up on LOW speed until they're a uniform color.

Pour in the half-cup of vegetable oil and mix it in with the eggs on LOW speed.

Add the half-cup of heavy cream. Mix it in at LOW speed.

Scoop out the container of sour cream and put it into a small bowl. Add the Tablespoon of chocolate syrup and stir it in.

Add the sour cream and chocolate syrup mixture to your mixer bowl. Mix that in on LOW speed.

When everything is well combined, open the box of dry cake mix and sprinkle it on top of the liquid ingredients in the bowl of the mixer. Mix that in on LOW speed.

Open the package of DRY instant chocolate pudding and sprinkle in the contents. Mix it in on LOW speed.

Shut off the mixer, scrape down the sides of the bowl, remove it from the mixer, and set it on the counter.

Sprinkle the mini chocolate chips in your bowl and stir them in by hand with a rubber spatula.

Use a mixing spoon or a scooper to fill the cupcake papers ONLY HALF FULL.

Place one piece of chocolate-covered cherry candy in the center of each cupcake, pushing it down slightly with the tip of your impeccably clean finger.

Use the mixing spoon or scooper to add more cupcake batter until the chocolate-covered cherry candies are covered and the cupcake papers are three-quarters full with batter.

Bake your Chocolate Surprise Cupcakes at 350 degrees F. for 20 to 25 minutes, or until a cake tester, wooden skewer, or long toothpick inserted a half-inch from the center of the cupcake comes out clean.

Take your cupcakes out of the oven and set the cupcake pans on cold stovetop burners or wire racks.

DO NOT remove the cupcakes from the pans. If you remove them from the pans while they are too warm, they may lose their shape.

Let the cupcakes cool in the pans until they reach room temperature. Then remove them from the pans

and refrigerate them for at least 30 minutes before you
frost them.

(Recipe and instructions follow.)

Yield: 18 to 24 rich, chocolate cupcakes with a piece of
chocolate-covered cherry candy hidden in the center.

CHOCOLATE CHERRY FROSTING

2 cups semisweet *(regular)* chocolate chips
  (a 12-ounce package)
¼ teaspoon salt *(it brings out the flavor of the
  chocolate)*
14-ounce can of sweetened condensed milk
1 small jar of maraschino cherries in juice
1 ounce *(2 Tablespoons)* salted butter

Hannah's 1st Note: If you use a double boiler for this frosting, it's foolproof. You can also make it in a heavy saucepan over low to medium heat on the stovetop, but you'll have to stir it constantly with a wooden spoon or a heat-resistant spatula to keep it from scorching.

Set a strainer over a bowl in your sink.

Drain the maraschino cherries in the strainer, reserving the juice.

Fill the bottom part of the double boiler with water. Make sure the water doesn't touch the underside of the top.

Put the chocolate chips and the salt in the top of the double boiler, set it over the bottom, and place the dou-

ble boiler on the stovetop at medium heat. Stir occasionally until the chocolate chips are melted.

Stir in the can of sweetened condensed milk and cook approximately 2 minutes, stirring constantly, until the frosting is shiny and of spreading consistency.

Shut off the heat, remove the top part of the double boiler to a cold burner, and quickly stir in 2 Tablespoons of maraschino cherry juice. *(It may sputter a bit, so be careful.)* Then add the butter and stir it in until it melts.

Your frosting is ready to use.

Hannah's 2nd Note: If you want to keep this frosting soft for several minutes, place the top part of the double boiler over the hot water again. This will enable you to use the frosting for ten minutes or so before it hardens.

If your frosting begins to harden and you're not yet ready to frost your cupcakes, simply heat the water in the bottom part of the double boiler again and place the top part over the reheated water. Give it a couple of minutes and then stir the frosting to soften it again.

Once you have frosted your cupcakes, give the pan to your favorite person to scrape with a spoon and eat.

Another alternative is to frost soda crackers, salt side down, or sugar cookies for snacking.

If you wish, you can cut the maraschino cherries in half, lengthwise, and place a half cherry, rounded side up, on top of each cupcake before the frosting hardens.

Hannah's 3rd Note: Once this frosting cools, it's just like fudge.

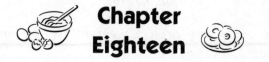

Chapter Eighteen

"Would you care for more coffee, Miss Jackson?" Joe asked, carrying the silver carafe of coffee to the nearest table.

"Thank you, Joe. I'd love another cup."

Hannah watched Betty Jackson smile at Joe as he poured her coffee. Betty looked happy that someone was paying attention to her.

"And was that one sugar and two creams, Miss Jackson?"

"Why, yes!"

Hannah had trouble keeping a straight face. Betty was acting as if Joe were the most clever man she'd ever met, simply because he'd remembered how she took her coffee.

"Did you enjoy Hannah's Strawberry Cupcake?"

"I certainly did! I decided that two cupcakes would be my limit at this party, but now I can't decide if I want another strawberry or if I want to try the German Chocolate Cupcakes."

Joe smiled down at her. "I can help you make your decision, Miss Jackson. Why don't you have a half and half?"

Betty looked surprised. "A half and half?"

"Yes. I'll cut a Strawberry Cupcake in two and do the same with a German Chocolate Cupcake. Hannah brought some extra cupcake papers with her and I'll put both halves in a new paper and deliver it to you."

Betty looked absolutely delighted. "That would be perfect! But what if no one wants the half cupcakes that are left?"

"I'll have the other half and half," Janice Cox, who was sitting across from Betty, volunteered. "What a great idea, Joe! I want cupcakes at my wedding reception, but Drew and I can't agree on which cupcakes we want. Do you think Hannah will make us half and half of vanilla cream and chocolate fudge?"

"I'm willing to bet she will. Of course it might cost a little extra because it's more work for her."

"That's okay," Janice said quickly.

Joe told her, "Why don't you ask Hannah later tonight and put in your order if she says yes?"

That idea was a stroke of genius, Hannah's rational mind told her. *And Joe even mentioned that it would take more time and cost extra. He's a very good businessman.*

Hannah watched as Joe cut the two cupcakes in half, arranged the halves in two pristine cupcake papers, and delivered them to Betty and Janice. Both women looked as if they were delighted with their new treat. Now that she thought about it, Joe had charmed every woman at the holiday party, and the men seemed to like him, too. No wonder Joe's mother had been happy for his help at her parties! There was no doubt about it. Joe was a like-able, personable guy and there had to be people out there who loved him and missed him dreadfully. She had to find them quickly, so that Joe could go back home again.

The party was over and Hannah stood at the door with the hostess, Irma York, wishing the guests good-bye and a safe trip home. While she was helping Irma with her hostess duties, Joe was busy packing up dishes, plates, silverware, and the cupcakes that were left. Irma had already told Joe to pack the cupcakes up in a box and leave them with her. She planned to take them to a meeting of the Lake Eden Regency Romance Readers the next afternoon and serve them the way Joe had developed for Betty Jackson and Janice Cox.

"It was a lovely party, Irma," Hannah told her, as Irma closed the front door behind the last guest. "I love the decorations you used on the card tables."

"My aunt Carolyn did those. If you have time, Hannah, she'd like a word with you."

"Of course I have time," Hannah responded immediately, glancing at the food table and seeing that Joe was still busy packing up their things. "Will you introduce me? I don't think I've ever met your aunt before."

"You haven't. Aunt Carolyn doesn't get out that much. She lives in a senior care facility for patients with memory problems."

"I'm sorry to hear that."

"It's not so bad. She's still herself and she remembers a lot, especially about the old days. Gus and I have had wonderful evenings with her, talking about old times. And Gus gave her a haircut that she absolutely loves."

"I'll remember to compliment her on that. Give me a clue, Irma. What sort of thing does your aunt want to discuss with me?"

"She wants to ask about Joe. Delores told me that you were investigating Joe's background and Aunt Carolyn thinks she might know something about that."

"Really?" Hannah felt a surge of excitement. She'd been hoping that someone at one of the holiday parties, a relative who might be visiting Lake Eden from some other locality, would provide a clue to Joe's former life.

Irma led Hannah over to an easy chair next to the fireplace. "Here's Hannah, Aunt Carolyn."

Irma's aunt gave Hannah a friendly smile. "Your cupcakes were wonderful, dear."

"Thank you. And your table decorations were simply beautiful."

"I'm glad you enjoyed them. Irma asked me to help and I did my best for her. She's a sweet girl, don't you think?"

"Yes. Irma's a good friend of my mother's. They belong to several of the same clubs." Hannah glanced over at Joe, who was almost through packing up. It was time to ask what she might know about Joe. "Irma tells me that you might know something about Joe's background."

"Oh. Well . . . I'm not sure, dear. My memory isn't as good as it used to be. It's not easy getting old, you know."

"Please tell me what you remember. It could be important when it comes to finding where Joe came from, and if he has relatives that are looking for him."

"Yes. Yes, of course. I don't exactly remember Joe, but I did notice that he looks a lot like one of my former neighbors. It was a long time ago, dear, so I think that neighbor was probably Joe's father, or maybe even his . . ." She turned to Irma. "What's the name of the brother of someone's father?"

"Uncle?" Irma asked.

"Yes. That's it. This neighbor could have been Joe's uncle."

"How long ago was this, Aunt Carolyn?" Irma asked her.

"A long time, dear. It was right after I was married. We had to live with his parents until our house was ready. We were there for several months, and let me tell you, it wasn't easy! His mother was . . . well . . . it's a good thing I can't remember the word for what she was! Let's just say that she didn't approve of me at all!"

"How close was this neighbor to your mother-in-law's place?" Hannah asked.

"The building was on the top of the next hill. That was where they did the work."

"What work was that?" Irma asked her.

"It was something to do with furniture. They fixed it. And then they sold it. My husband's mother had her big oak table refin . . . fixed."

"So, they refinished furniture?" Hannah asked, providing the word that Irma's aunt hadn't been able to complete.

"Yes! And they did the cloth on chairs and sofas, too. That's called a word like the other one."

"Reupholstered." This time, Irma provided the word.

"That's the word. I went to the building on the hill with my father-in-law to pay for the table they had refinished."

"And that's where you saw Joe's father or his uncle?" Hannah asked.

"Yes. He looked just like Joe except I think Joe is even a little bit more good-looking. His ears are better. I always notice a man's ears."

Hannah glanced at Joe again. He was carrying out the last load of party supplies and it was time to ask Irma's aunt the crucial question. "Where did your husband's parents live?"

"Miles away from the house we bought, thank goodness!" Irma's aunt responded immediately.

"Was it in Minnesota?" Irma asked her.

"Oh, yes. The land of ten thousand lakes. And there was a lake right there next to their farm."

"Do you remember the name of the lake?" Hannah asked.

Irma's aunt laughed. "I certainly do! It was Mud

Lake, and my husband's father told me that fishermen made the mistake of fishing there."

"The mistake?" Hannah asked.

"Yes. There weren't any fish except dogfish, and everybody in Minnesota knows you need gloves to take dogfish off the hook because of the spines." Irma's aunt laughed. "They're really ugly, Hannah."

"Were there any good fishing lakes nearby?" Hannah asked.

"Yes, but it wasn't the closest lake."

"Do you remember the name of that lake?" Irma asked her.

"I want to say Clear Lake, but that was somewhere else. I think it was Long Lake or . . . Round Lake! That was it! I'm almost sure that the lake where the neighborhood kids went swimming was Round Lake."

It only took a few moments to finish loading up the cookie truck, and soon Hannah and Joe were heading to The Cookie Jar.

"Did you think it went well, Hannah?" Joe asked her.

"It went very well. Irma was pleased, and everyone seemed to have a good time."

"Was I . . . okay?" Joe asked tentatively.

"You were more than okay. Everyone was glad you were there, Joe. You're very good with people. You seem to instinctively know the right thing to say. Everyone really liked you."

Joe gave a relieved sigh. "That's good. I was a little worried. I haven't done this sort of thing for a long time and I was much younger then." He paused and cleared his throat. "I saw you talking to Miss Carolyn. She said she thought she knew me, but she wasn't sure."

"That's right." Hannah turned into the alley and parked in her usual spot by the back kitchen door. "Come in for a cup of hot chocolate, Joe. I think both of us have had enough coffee for the day. We'll relax a bit, and I'll tell you exactly what Irma's aunt said."

Once they'd carried in all the party things, Hannah made them both a cup of hot chocolate and motioned to a stool at the work station. "Sit down, Joe. I know you're anxious about Irma's aunt. She said she thought she knew you at first, but then she realized that you were much too young to be the person she thought she remembered."

"Oh." A strange combination of expressions crossed Joe's face. At first he looked relieved, and then he appeared disappointed. "What else did she say, Hannah?"

"She told me about living with her in-laws when she was first married. And she described a place very like the one you said you lived in when you were growing up."

"Really?"

"That's right. She even mentioned that there was a building next door that was on top of a hill."

Joe began to look hopeful. "That sounds like where I grew up, all right. Was this in Minnesota?"

"Yes, she told me about two lakes, and they sounded like the lakes you described to me."

"I wonder if . . . oh, Hannah! Maybe she knew my parents!"

"That's what I was thinking. The only problem is that Irma's aunt has trouble with her memory. Before we left, Irma called me aside and said that her aunt had brought some papers and photo albums with her and she promised me that they would go through them in the morning."

"Did Miss Carolyn remember any names?" Joe asked.

"A couple. She said her husband's parents were Ed and Bertha. Does that bring back any memories for you, Joe?"

Joe shook his head. "No, not really. I'm almost sure the people on the next farm weren't named Ed and . . . oh!"

As Hannah watched, Joe's face turned pale and beads of sweat broke out on his forehead. "Sara!" he gasped.

"Who's Sara?" Hannah asked quickly.

"The next farm. My friend . . . growing up . . . her name was Sara!"

"And you just remembered that?"

"Yes. But her parents' names were Ed and Bertha. They were . . . were . . . something else." Joe reached up to hold his head in his hands. "I need a pill, Hannah! My head! It feels like it's going to burst open!"

"Just a minute, Joe. I'll get you a glass of water." Hannah rushed over to the sink to run a glass of water, while Joe drew the vial of pills from his shirt pocket.

"Here you are," she said, setting the glass down on the surface of the work station.

Joe shook out a pill, popped it into his mouth, took a drink of water, and swallowed. And then he gave a relieved sigh. "I should be getting used to this by now. Whenever I remember something important, I get an awful headache. Sara is important, Hannah. She lived on the next farm. I'm sure of that now. Sara takes care of Donnie. I have to find them. And I . . . I love Sara!"

STRAWBERRY CUPCAKES

Preheat oven to 350 degrees F., rack in the middle position.

4 large eggs
½ cup vegetable oil
½ cup strawberry liqueur
1 cup *(8 ounces by weight)* sour cream
1 Tablespoon strawberry jam
Box of strawberry cake mix, the kind that makes a 9-inch by 13-inch cake or a 2-layer cake *(I used Pillsbury)*
5.1-ounce package of DRY instant vanilla pudding and pie filling *(I used Jell-O.)*
12-ounce *(by weight)* bag of white chocolate or vanilla baking chips *(11-ounce package will do, too—I used Nestlé)*

Prepare your cupcake pans. You'll need two 12-cup cupcake or muffin pans lined with double cupcake papers.

Crack the eggs into the bowl of an electric mixer. Mix them up on LOW speed until they're a uniform color.

Pour in the half-cup of vegetable oil, and mix it in with the eggs on LOW speed.

Add the half-cup of strawberry liqueur *(or milk)*. Mix it in at LOW speed.

Scoop out the container of sour cream and put it into a small bowl. Add the Tablespoon of strawberry jam and stir it in.

Add the sour cream and strawberry jam mixture to your mixer bowl. Mix that in on LOW speed.

When everything is well-combined, open the box of dry cake mix and sprinkle it on top of the liquid ingredients in the bowl of the mixer. Mix that in on LOW speed.

Open the package of instant vanilla pudding and pie filling, and sprinkle in the contents. Mix it in on LOW speed.

Shut off the mixer, scrape down the sides of the bowl, remove it from the mixer, and set it on the counter.

If you have a food processor, put in the steel blade and pour in the white chocolate or vanilla baking chips. Process in an on-and-off motion to chop them in smaller

pieces. *(You can also do this with a knife on a cutting board if you don't have a food processor.)*

Sprinkle the chopped white chocolate or vanilla baking chips in your bowl and stir them in by hand with a rubber spatula.

Hannah's 1st Note: If you don't want to use strawberry liqueur in this recipe, use whole milk. Hank, down at the Lake Eden Municipal Liquor Store, told me that any alcohol used in cooking will break down at 160 degrees F.

Hannah's 2nd Note: The reason the white chips in this recipe are chopped in smaller pieces is that regular-size chips are larger and heavier, and they tend to sink down to the bottom of your cupcakes.

Use the rubber spatula or a spoon to transfer the cupcake batter to the prepared cupcake pan. Only fill them ¾ full.

Place the cupcake pans into the center of your preheated oven.

Bake your Strawberry Cupcakes at 350 degrees F. for 20 to 25 minutes.

Before you take your cupcakes out of the oven, test for doneness by inserting a cake tester, thin wooden skewer, or long toothpick. Insert it into the middle of a cupcake. If the tester comes out clean, with no cupcake batter sticking to it, your cupcakes are done. If there is still unbaked batter clinging to the tester, shut the oven door and bake your cupcakes for 5 minutes longer.

Take your cupcakes out of the oven and set the pans on cold stovetop burners or wire racks. Let them cool in the pans until they reach room temperature and then refrigerate them for 30 minutes before you frost them. *(Overnight is fine, too)*

Frost your cupcakes with Strawberry Cream Cheese Frosting. *(Recipe and instructions follow.)*

Yield: Approximately 18 to 24 cupcakes, depending on cupcake size.

To Serve: Serve with tall glasses of ice-cold milk or cups of strong coffee.

STRAWBERRY CREAM CHEESE FROSTING

½ cup *(1 stick)* softened, salted butter
8-ounce *(net weight)* package softened, brick-type
  cream cheese *(I used Philadelphia in the silver
  package.)*
1 Tablespoon strawberry jam
4 to 4 and ½ cups confectioners *(powdered)* sugar
  (no need to sift unless it's got big lumps)

Fresh strawberries to decorate. (Alternatively, you can sprinkle red decorators sugar on top of each frosted cupcake if desired.)

Mix the softened butter with the softened cream cheese.

If your strawberry jam has big pieces, cut them into small pieces with a sharp knife. Then add the strawberry jam and beat until the mixture is smooth.

Hannah's 1ˢᵗ Note: Do this next step at room temperature. If you heated the cream cheese or the butter to soften it, make sure it's cooled down to room temperature before you continue.

Add the confectioners' sugar in half-cup increments until the frosting is of proper spreading consistency. *(You'll use all, or almost all, of the powdered sugar.)*

Using a frosting knife *(or rubber spatula, if you prefer)*, spread frosting from the center of your cupcakes out to the edges.

If you managed to find fresh strawberries, cut off the tops and place one, cut side down, on top of each cupcake. Tell everyone that they're Santa Hats. If you couldn't find fresh strawberries, sprinkle your cupcakes with red decorators sugar and call it good.

Let the frosting "set" at room temperature. After it "sets," cover your cupcakes loosely with foil and then refrigerate them.

If you have frosting left over, spread it on graham crackers, soda crackers, or what Great-Grandma Elsa used to call *store-boughten* cookies. This frosting can also be covered tightly and kept in the refrigerator for up to a week. When you want to use it, let it sit on the kitchen counter for an hour or so until it reaches room temperature and it is spreadable again.

You can also color this frosting with a drop or two of food coloring. If you make these cupcakes at Hal-

loween, a drop of yellow and a drop of red will make a nice orange frosting. On Valentine's Day, use just one drop of red and your frosting will be pink. Use green for St. Patrick's Day, and alternate between red and green for Christmas.

Hannah's 2nd Note: This frosting also works well in a pastry bag.

Chapter Nineteen

Hannah had just unlocked the back kitchen door of The Cookie Jar when Andrea pulled up in her car. She stopped in her tracks, and turned to look at her sister in disbelief. She waited until Andrea had got out of her car and walked over to her. "What's wrong?" she asked.

"Nothing. Why?"

"Because you never get up before eight unless you absolutely have to."

"I absolutely had to."

"Why?"

"Because I wanted to find out how Joe did at Irma York's last night. Did the guests like him?"

"They adored him. Have you had breakfast yet?"

Andrea shook her head. "Of course not. I just got out of bed and came straight over here. Have you?"

"No. Let's go over to the café, and I'll treat you to one of Rose's omelets."

"With bacon?"

"Yes, if you want it."

"I want it." Andrea grabbed Hannah's arm, and the two sisters began to walk down the alley. It was only a block to the café, but it was a cold morning and both of them were chilled by the time they got there.

"Andrea?" Rose greeted her. "Is something wrong?"

"No." Andrea turned to look at Hannah, and both of them began to laugh. "Do you mean because I'm here so early?" Andrea asked.

"Well . . ." Rose paused and looked uncomfortable. "Yes. Yes I do. I know that Hannah goes to work early, but I don't usually see you this time of the morning."

"That's true," Andrea agreed. "There's nothing wrong, Rose. I just wanted to see Hannah early to ask her how Irma York's Christmas party went last night."

"It was great!" Rose said. "And now I understand why you're working so hard to try to find out more about Joe. He's really a nice man and I'm sure there are people out there who miss him."

"Irma's aunt thought she recognized him," Hannah told her.

"Really?" Andrea looked very excited. "Why didn't you tell me, Hannah?"

"Because I haven't had a chance to tell you." Hannah turned to Rose. "If you'll get us cups of coffee and join us, I'll tell both of you everything that Irma's aunt said."

Once Rose delivered their coffee and slid into the booth beside Andrea, Hannah told them everything she'd learned.

"That's all?" Andrea asked, when Hannah had finished.

"I'm afraid so. Irma told me that her aunt brought some papers and old photo albums with her on her visit, and they were going to go through them together this morning."

"So Irma's coming in to The Cookie Jar to tell you today?" Rose asked.

"Yes, if there's anything to tell. And I promise I'll come down to tell you if there's any news."

"Oh, good!" Rose slid out of the booth and pulled out her order pad. "What would you two girls like for breakfast?"

"I'll have a bacon and cheese omelet," Andrea said. "And wheat toast, please."

"Make my omelet ham and cheese," Hannah decided quickly. "And I'd like an English muffin, if you have one, Rose."

"I do. I'll get started on your omelets right after I refill your coffee," Rose said, slipping the order pad in her pocket and heading for the counter to get the coffee carafe.

"That looks like Mother's car," Andrea said, pointing to the car that was parked in back at the vacant storefront next to Bertie Straub's Cut 'n Curl beauty shop.

"I think you're right," Hannah agreed, unlocking the back kitchen door of The Cookie Jar and flicking on the lights. She went straight to her oven to preheat it, and then she came back to join Andrea. "I'd better hurry and put on the coffee. And then I'd better get started on the baking. I'm trying out a new cookie this morning. I mixed up the dough last night."

"What's this one called?" Andrea asked, following Hannah into the warm interior of the kitchen.

"I don't know yet. I'll think of a name right after we taste them. We didn't have any dessert at the café."

"Dessert for breakfast?" Andrea asked.

"Why not? We have dessert with lunch, and dessert with dinner. There's no reason why we can't have dessert with breakfast."

"That sounds like something I hope you don't tell Tracey when she grows up!" Andrea watched as Hannah put on the coffee, and retrieved a bowl of cookie dough from the walk-in cooler. "What kind of cookies are you making?"

"It's a basic chocolate chip cookie dough with cashews, chocolate chips, and crushed potato chips."

"They sound really good!"

"We're about to find out." Hannah finished rolling the cookie dough balls and placed them on cookie sheets. Then she slipped the cookie sheets into the racks of her industrial oven, set the time for twelve minutes, poured them both a cup of coffee from the kitchen coffeepot, and went back to the work station to join Andrea.

"Vegas Cookies, Hannah."

"What?"

"Vegas Cookies. That's what you should call them."

"Why Vegas Cookies?" Hannah asked, clearly puzzled.

"It's a pun on the ingredients, Hannah. Cashew Chips In," Andrea said, her lips turning up in a grin that Hannah could only categorize as devilish.

"Oh, Andrea! That's just awful!"

"I know. Bill says I'm getting a lot better at making up puns. You'll call them Vegas Cookies, won't you, Hannah?"

Hannah smiled. "Yes, I will. From now on, these are Vegas Cookies."

"Good!" Andrea's smile was like the sun coming out on a rainy, dreary day. "Thanks, Hannah."

"Don't thank me. You thought of the pun. I can use it, can't I?"

"Of course!" Andrea spoke so fast, Hannah could tell she'd been hoping that her pun would be used.

Just then the timer went off, and Hannah got up to see if her newly named Vegas Cookies were ready to come out of the oven. She walked over to look at them, and turned back with a smile. "They're done. Now all we have to do is let them cool for a few minutes and we can . . ."

Hannah stopped speaking as a knock came at the door. It was an authoritative knock, a knock she recognized immediately. "Will you let Mike in and pour him a cup of coffee, Andrea?"

"Yes, but . . . oh, I get it. You recognized his knock."

"Right. And keep him away from here. I'm about to take out oven-hot cookies, and I don't trust him not to snatch one and burn his fingers."

"Don't worry. I'll keep him away," Andrea said, jumping up and rushing to the back kitchen door to let Mike in.

"Oh!" she gasped in surprise, as she opened the door. "Hi, Norman. I didn't know that you were here, too."

"Of course not," Mike said. "I knocked and there's no way you could know that Norman was here, too. I've got to remember to get someone to install a peephole in Hannah's kitchen door."

"You're right," Norman agreed. "Even if it's a knock she doesn't recognize, she opens the door to see who it is."

"Hold the door!" A voice came from behind Norman, and Hannah recognized it. Delores and Carrie were here.

"Where's Joe?" Hannah asked, when everyone had come in.

"He said to tell you that he'll be over later this afternoon," Carrie reported. "We brought him takeout from the Corner Tavern."

"Right after he ate and drank his coffee, he started sanding my dining room table. He said he wanted to get down to the wood before he went anywhere."

"Please get everyone coffee, Andrea," Hannah instructed. "I'll make more, just as soon as I get these cookies on the cooling racks. We'll be six, is that right?"

"That's right, and it'll be crowded at the work station," Andrea said. "Shall we go to the big table against the back wall of the coffee shop, Hannah?"

"That's a good idea. Get everyone settled, and I'll take care of the baking just as soon as I can."

Hannah breathed a sigh of relief as Andrea led Mike, Norman, Delores, and Carrie into the coffee shop. "Hi, Lisa," she heard Andrea say, and she knew that Lisa had come in early to set up the coffee shop for the morning rush.

"Hi, everyone," Lisa greeted the group as they entered the coffee shop. "I see you've got coffee already. That's good. I'll put on one of the big pots in here, and we'll be all set."

A few moments later, Lisa entered the kitchen. "I see you got hit with company this morning," she said, walking over to look at the cookies on the bakers rack. "Those look good, Hannah. And they smell good, too. What are they?"

"Vegas Cookies," Hannah said, careful not to expound on her answer. "Andrea named them and you'll have to ask her why they're called Vegas Cookies."

Lisa looked puzzled, but she nodded. "Okay. What can I do for you in here?"

"Absolutely nothing. Just keep them entertained while I bake. I'm sure that, with such a big group, they've got lots to talk about."

"How did Joe do last night at Irma's party?"

"He was wonderful. Everyone loved him and he was

a big help to me. Joe's great with people, Lisa. You should have seen him with Betty Jackson and Janice. And Irma told me that he was especially good with her aunt Carolyn."

"I'm glad to hear that. I really like Joe. Did anyone happen to recognize Joe?"

"Yes and no. I'll tell you about it later. And don't forget to ask Andrea why she called our new cookies Vegas Cookies."

"I'll get a platter and take it in," Lisa said, taking a serving platter from the cupboard and beginning to plate the cookies. "I'll be back to hear what happened at the party later."

The baking went smoothly once Hannah didn't have to play hostess and chief coffee-maker. She smiled as she heard a burst of raucous laughter coming from the coffee shop. Andrea had obviously told everyone at the big table her pun.

Dozens of sheets of cookies later and Hannah had filled the shelves on her baker's rack. She was just taking the last pan of cookies out of the oven when she heard another knock on her back kitchen door.

It was a knock she didn't recognize, but Hannah opened the door anyway. Paranoia was not a particular failing of hers. Perhaps she should be a little more cautious, as Mike urged her to be, but she knew almost everyone who lived in Lake Eden, and she wasn't as security minded as Mike was.

"Hi, Irma!" she said as she recognized the parka-clad

figures standing there. "And you, too, Aunt Carolyn. It's good to see both of you again. Come in and have a cup of coffee with me."

"Thanks, Hannah." Irma ushered her aunt in and hung their parkas up on the hooks by the back door. "It always smells so wonderful in here."

"Thank you." Hannah glanced at Irma's aunt. "I'm sorry to be blunt, but I'm so eager about Joe. Did you remember anything?"

Irma's aunt gave a frustrated sigh. "No, dear. I'm so sorry, but I can't seem to recall the name of that township. If it does come back to me, I'll tell Irma right away and she can call you. I really wanted to help that nice man, but I simply can't remember."

After Irma and Aunt Carolyn had left, carrying a bag of Vegas Cookies to share with Irma's husband, Hannah sat down at the work station again and cupped her hands around a fresh cup of coffee. She really didn't want more coffee, but the heat of the cup was comforting.

For one long minute that seemed to take much longer than sixty seconds to pass, Hannah was deeply depressed. Joe had remembered the name of the woman he loved, but how could she find Sara and Donnie without a last name or a location?

As always, in times of crisis, Hannah stood up and took out a mixing bowl. She would bake. That seemed to clear her mind and perhaps she she'd think of a way to help Joe.

"Something new," she said to herself softly. "Bake something you've never baked before, and that might help your mind work out a solution."

A new cupcake was what she needed. They always sold lots of cupcakes during the holiday season, and she needed something like White Chocolate Eggnog Cupcakes, something that reminded everyone of the holiday season. Eggnog was a holiday drink. What other beverages did people drink over the holidays?

As she sat there, an old memory surfaced. She was a child sitting next to her father and mother at the kitchen table. She had a cup of warm milk with sugar in it and they had mugs of something they called hot buttered rum. It smelled wonderful and she wanted a taste, so her father dipped his spoon in his cup and gave her a tiny taste. She remembered being disappointed that hot buttered rum didn't taste as good as it smelled, and that gave her an idea. She would make a new cupcake that would taste just as good as the mugs of hot buttered rum had smelled.

The moment she thought of it, Hannah got up and began to assemble ingredients. She'd take the easy way out and use a spice cake mix for the base of her cupcakes. They would be holiday rum cupcakes with cinnamon and all the other related spices. Golden raisins would be perfect with the sweet cupcake batter she planned to make. And if people didn't want to use actual rum in their Golden Raisin Rum Cupcakes, they could use rum extract.

As she mixed up the batter and prepared her cupcake

pans, Hannah realized that she was smiling. Baking was acting as her salvation again. She felt happy when she was baking good things for people to eat. It was almost impossible to be sad or depressed when someone offered you a warm, fresh-baked cookie, or a sweet, delicious confection.

As she filled the last cupcake pan, Hannah realized that there was something she was missing, something important. The moment she slipped her new cupcakes in the oven, she'd go back over the notes she'd taken about what Joe had told them, and find out what had eluded her.

Her steno pad was in her drawer and Hannah took it out. She flipped to the notes she'd made and read them over. She wasn't looking forward to telling Joe that Irma's aunt had failed to remember the name of the township where she'd lived. It was too bad she didn't have his mother's recipe for German chocolate cake. If she had it, she could bake one for him to soften the disappointment he was bound to feel.

Hannah flipped back to the first notes she'd taken, right after she'd first invited Joe into her kitchen for coffee. He'd told her all about his mother's cake and how it was his favorite. He'd even mentioned going with his mother and father to the grocery store in the middle of a snowstorm to buy what his mother needed for the cake. Joe had mentioned the ingredients his mother had purchased. She'd bought fresh cake flour, German chocolate, coconut flakes, pecans, and . . .

"An orange!" Hannah gasped, staring down at the page. Joe's mother had bought an orange! There was no orange in German chocolate cake . . . unless Joe's mother had been creative with the standard recipe.

Joe had mentioned that after his mother took off the peel, she'd cut orange slices that looked like wheels for him to eat. What had Joe's mother done with the peel? Had she thrown it away as most people would? Or had she somehow used it in her cake, or the frosting?

Joe had told her that the recipe his mother had used was her favorite, and she'd shared it with friends and neighbors. Were there any copies of that recipe out there? She couldn't very well ask everyone in Minnesota if she had a recipe for German chocolate cake that used orange zest.

"The library!" Hannah said loudly. "That's it!"

"What's it?" Lisa asked, coming into the kitchen just as Hannah was jumping to her feet.

"Do you know what time Marge is opening the library at the community center today? And if she still has that shelf of Minnesota cookbooks?"

Lisa glanced at her watch. "Marge is probably unlocking the door right now. And if you're talking about the women's club cookbooks and the church cookbooks, she still has them. There's even more now. She told me that every group sends her a cookbook when they publish one."

"Do people check them out?"

"No. Marge won't let them. She tells them that they

can make a copy on the copy machine if they want to, but the cookbooks can't leave the library."

"Because people keep them?"

Lisa nodded. "Yes, and this is Marge's private collection. It's just like the yearbooks she collects from all the Minnesota schools. She just lets people look at them and make copies, that's all."

VEGAS COOKIES
(CASHEW CHIPS IN COOKIES)

Preheat oven to 350 degrees F., rack in the middle position.

1 cup softened, salted butter *(2 sticks, ½ pound, 8 ounces)*
1 cup white *(granulated)* sugar
1 cup brown sugar
2 large eggs *(just whip them up in a glass with a fork)*
¼ teaspoon salt
1 teaspoon baking soda
2 teaspoons vanilla extract
2 and ½ cups flour *(pack it down in the cup when you measure it)*
1 and ½ cups finely crushed plain potato chips *(measure AFTER crushing)*
1 cup finely chopped salted cashews *(measure AFTER chopping – I used Planters)*
1 to 2 cups semisweet chocolate chips
⅓ cup white *(granulated)* sugar *(for coating dough balls)*

Hannah's 1st Note: Use regular potato chips, the thin, salty ones. Don't use baked chips, or rippled chips,

or chips with the peels on, or kettle fried, or flavored, or anything that's supposed to be better for you than those wonderfully greasy, salty, old-fashioned potato chips.

In a large mixing bowl or in the bowl of an electric mixer, beat the butter, white sugar, and brown sugar together.

Add the eggs and mix them in thoroughly.

Sprinkle in the salt, baking soda, and vanilla extract. Mix everything up together.

Add the flour in half-cup increments, mixing thoroughly after each addition.

If you haven't done so already, crush your potato chips and add them to your bowl. Mix them in thoroughly.

If you have a food processor, use it with the steel blade to chop the salted cashews into small pieces. Then add them to your bowl and mix them in.

If you are using an electric mixer, scrape down the sides of the bowl and take the bowl out of the mixer.

Give the bowl a thorough stir by hand with a wooden spoon or a mixing spoon.

Add the chocolate chips, mixing them in by hand.

Put the final third-cup of white sugar in a small bowl. You will use this to coat your cookie dough balls after you form them.

Form one-inch dough balls with your impeccably clean hands and place them in the bowl with the sugar, no more than two balls at a time. Roll them around with your fingers until they are coated with sugar.

Place the coated cookie dough balls on an UN-GREASED cookie sheet, 12 to a standard-sized sheet.

Hannah's 2nd Note: You can also line your cookie sheets with parchment paper, but be sure to leave little "ears" at the top and the bottom of the paper. That way you can simply pull the paper, cookies and all, over to your wire racks after they are baked.

Flatten the cookie dough balls a bit with the palm of your hand so that they won't roll off on their way to the oven.

Bake your Vegas Cookies at 350 degrees F., for 10 to 12 minutes, or until the cookies are starting to turn light golden brown at the edges.

Remove the baked cookies from the oven and place the cookie sheets on cold stovetop burners or wire racks on the kitchen counter.

Let the cookies cool on the cookie sheets for 2 minutes.

After the 2-minute cooling time, remove the cookies from the cookie sheets and place them on wire racks to cool completely.

Yield: Between 6 and 8 dozen crunchy, very tasty cookies that your guests will love. They will also groan loudly when they ask about the name and you tell them Andrea's pun.

Serve these cookies with tall glasses of milk or strong black coffee.

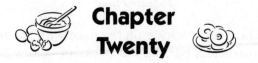

Chapter Twenty

Of course, everyone had wanted to help, so fifteen minutes later, Hannah, Mike, Norman, Andrea, Delores, and Carrie were seated around a table in the community library with Marge's community cookbook collection stacked in front of them.

"Most of them have indexes," Marge explained. "Just turn to the page and see if they list the recipes. Most of them are either alphabetical by recipe title, or in sections."

"Sections?" Mike asked.

"Yes, like Cakes, Cookies, Desserts, Pies, Candies . . . categories like that. Since Hannah is looking for a specific cake, look under the cake section and see if there's a German chocolate cake listed."

"Got it," Mike said, reaching for a cookbook and then turning to Hannah. "What do you want us to do if we find a German chocolate cake?"

"Put this yellow stickie on the page with the recipe," Marge instructed, passing out packs of yellow stickies. "Then pass the cookbook to Hannah. She'll read through the recipes you find to see if she can locate the right one. I'll help, too. I won't have any library visitors this early in the morning."

Except for the turning of pages and the occasional sigh of frustration, the library was quiet. Hannah watched as everyone looked for something that might, or might not, be there.

There were dozens and dozens of cookbooks. Marge had amassed a huge collection over the years. There were enough people working and Hannah did her best to keep up with the recipes that they gave her, going through the ingredient list and looking for a German chocolate cake that listed an orange as an ingredient. For the first half hour, she found nothing that fit the description that Joe had given her.

"Try this one next, Hannah," Andrea said, putting the cookbook she'd been examining on the top of Hannah's pile. "It's from a township that has the word *lake* in its name."

Hannah felt a tingle of excitement as she read through the recipe, but the list of ingredients didn't include an orange. She glanced at the end of the recipe to see if orange zest might be listed as an optional ingredient, and blinked several times to make sure she'd read the line correctly.

"What is it?" Norman asked, noticing Hannah's excited expression. "Did you find something?"

Hannah gave a little nod and, at the same time, managed to keep from sounding too excited. "Maybe," she told him. "This German chocolate cake has orange zest as an option in the chocolate frosting."

"Whose cookbook is it?" Marge asked her.

"It's the Sweetwater Lake Township," Hannah told her, glancing at the title on the cover. "And it's called the Sweetwater Lake Township Farm Cookbook."

"Call Irma and see if her aunt recognizes the name," Andrea urged. "Maybe this is it!"

Hannah rummaged in her purse for her cell phone, but then she remembered leaving it plugged in an outlet to charge in The Cookie Jar kitchen. "I don't have my phone," she said.

"I'll call," Norman, who was sitting next to her, offered. "Just as soon as Irma answers, I'll hand the phone to you."

Hannah waited until Norman looked up Irma's number and dialed it. A moment later, he gave Hannah a nod as he greeted Irma. "Hi, Irma. It's Norman. Hannah's with me and she'd like to talk to you."

"Thanks," Hannah told him, taking the phone and holding it up to her ear. "Is your aunt with you, Irma?"

"She's right here," Irma said, her voice sounding very far away from Hannah's ear.

"Would you ask her if the name of the township could be Sweetwater Lake Township?"

"Hold on. I'll ask her," Irma replied.

Hannah held on, wishing she'd thought to cross her fingers. She was afraid to do it now because Norman's phone had buttons and indentations on the sides and she was worried that she might cut off the call by mistake.

"Hannah?" Irma came on the line again.

"Yes?"

"Aunt Carolyn says that's it! She's sure that was the name! And she thinks that Edith was the name of Joe's mother."

A huge smile spread over Hannah's face, and she realized that the name on the recipe was Edith's German chocolate cake. "Give your aunt a hug from me," she said quickly. "If she's right, and this is Joe's mother's recipe, we may have solved the riddle of Joe's identity!"

Of course Carrie and Delores had wanted to go, but Hannah had promised that she'd call the minute that they knew something. Of course, they'd picked up Joe and he rode in the passenger seat of Norman's car while Hannah and Andrea sat in Norman's spacious backseat. Mike insisted on going along, just in case they needed law enforcement, and he followed Norman's car in his Winnetka County Sheriff's Department cruiser.

"Does it look familiar yet, Joe?" Hannah asked as they passed a lake, golden light shining on its surface.

"I think so . . . I'm not completely sure. Are we in Sweetwater Lake Township yet, Norman?"

Norman glanced down at the map that was displayed on his GPS. "We'll be coming up on it in about five minutes. The map shows that it'll be on your side, Joe."

They rode in silence for another few minutes and then Joe sat forward and stared intently out the window. "This looks like the hill on the way to our farm, Norman. I can't be completely positive, but . . . everything looks very familiar."

Another few minutes passed and Joe gave a little nod. "Yes. I'm almost sure now. This is the road that leads to our farm. And once we come down this hill, if this is it, we should be able to see the shop!"

Hannah crossed her fingers for luck. Joe seemed almost certain that they were approaching the place where he'd lived.

"There it is!" Joe said as the next hill came into view. "See that red building on top of the hill?"

"I see it," Hannah said, breathing a sigh of relief that she hadn't brought them all on a wild goose chase.

"I see it, too," Andrea said, peering out her car window. "Is that your farmhouse behind it?"

"Yes. We're passing our pasture right now."

Norman drove up the hill, and stopped at the red building Joe had identified as the shop. "Is this it, Joe?" he asked.

"Yes. Do you see the sign on the peak of the roof?"

"Yes," Norman answered. "It says Warner Restoration."

"And that's my last name," Joe told them. "My full name is Joseph Eaton Warner. Eaton was my mother's maiden name."

Norman stopped the car, and Joe hesitated a moment

before he made a move to open his door. "I'm really nervous," he said, "and I'm not sure why. I know this is the right place."

"I'll go see if there's anyone inside," Norman offered, opening his door before Joe had time to agree, and walking up to the front of the building. He tried the door, but it didn't open. Then he walked around the side of the building and peered through the window.

"There's no one there," he reported when he came back to the car.

Joe looked confused. "Not even my stepbrother? Dad left me the business, but he gets paid to work by our father's trust!"

"Who's your stepbrother, Joe?" Hannah asked.

"Jake! He lived with his mother when Dad got divorced, but we work together, so we try to get along."

Andrea frowned. "Don't you like him, Joe?"

Joe shrugged. "Not much, but he should have been here! Maybe he's down at the house."

"Do you want me to drive to the farmhouse, Joe?" Norman asked him.

Joe swallowed before he answered, and then he nodded. "Yes, please. Thanks, Norman."

"I'll go knock this time," Hannah said, getting out of the car the moment Norman stopped in front of the farmhouse.

"And I'll go with you," Andrea agreed, opening her door and sliding out. "You just sit tight, Joe. We'll find out if anyone's home."

"Joe was shaking," Andrea said, as she joined Hannah. "I'm glad we're going up to the house. He looked like he was really nervous."

"I know," Hannah agreed. "It could be because he doesn't know what kind of welcome he'll get from his stepbrother."

Hannah went up the steps, and knocked on the door, but there was no answer. She knocked again, louder this time, but again, no one answered the door. "I don't think anyone's home," she said.

"Let's look through the window," Andrea suggested, already heading around the side of the house.

Both sisters peered in the kitchen window. No one was sitting at the table and there was no movement of any kind.

"Deserted," Andrea said.

"But there was someone here recently," Hannah pointed out. "There are dishes in the sink and someone put them in a pan of soap and water. There are still a couple of bubbles left on the surface."

"Do you think we should check the barn?" Andrea asked.

"We can, but I don't think it'll do any good. When we passed the pasture, the cows were out and it's not milking time. I really doubt there's anyone in the barn."

"Then we should go to the nearest neighbor and ask," Andrea suggested.

"Good idea. Come on, Andrea. Let's go tell Joe that we know someone was here this morning, but they're gone now."

The neighboring farm was only a mile or two away and, as Norman turned in the driveway, they saw a man standing by the house.

"Good! Someone's here!" Andrea said.

"It's Vern," Joe told them. "Vern and Letty live here. I'll go ask him what's happening. And maybe he knows where Jack is."

"We'll go with you," Hannah said quickly, motioning for Mike, who'd just driven up in his cruiser, to follow them. "Come on, and let's meet Joe's neighbor."

As Joe rushed up to his neighbor, Hannah noticed that Vern's face paled.

"Joe?!" he gasped, looking as if he'd seen a ghost.

"Yes, Vern. I'm back and we just came from my place. Where is everybody?"

"I . . . I . . . I gotta sit down!" Vern said, almost falling into the rocker that was on his front porch. "Is it really you, Joe?"

"It's me, Vern. Where are Sara and Donnie?"

Vern took a moment to recover his equilibrium, and then he sighed deeply. "It's a long story, Joe. Everyone thought you were dead. And Jake tried so hard to find you."

"Who's Jake?" Mike asked him.

"He's Joe's stepbrother," Hannah explained, realizing that Mike hadn't heard their earlier conversation.

Joe nodded. "That's right. We worked together at the shop."

Hannah reached out to put her arm around Joe as he grabbed his head and groaned.

"It's beginning to come back to me now," he told them. "Jake was always in love with Sara."

"Joe's neighbor," Hannah explained.

"That's right. But Sara told him she loved me." Joe's face turned pale. "That didn't matter to Jake. He still wanted Sara."

Hannah tightened her arm around Joe's shoulders as she turned to Vern. "You said you thought Joe was dead," she reminded him. "Why did you think that?"

"We *all* thought that. A day or so after Joe disappeared, Jake told the sheriff he'd found a broken guardrail on the bridge that goes over the river. The roads were icy the night Joe drove off and it was snowing like crazy. Jake said he was worried that Joe had slid off the road, gone through the guardrail, and crashed into the river." He turned to Joe. "They looked for you everywhere, but nobody could find you."

"Did the sheriff drag the river?" Mike asked him.

"Yeah. A couple of divers went down looking and they found Joe's car. But they never found . . . you know . . ."

"So they gave up?" Mike asked him.

"Pretty much. We only have two divers, and the water was cold. They couldn't go down for very long at a time. And then, about a week later and a couple of miles downstream, Jake found Joe's Minnesota Vikings cap."

Joe took a moment to process that information. Then

he asked, "Are you talking about the stocking cap that Sara gave me for Christmas?"

"Yes, and Sara said you were wearing it the night you drove off to get the things she needed to make your mother's German chocolate cake."

Joe nodded. "I remember that. It's all coming back now. Jake offered to go with me, but we'd been arguing and I said I'd rather go by myself."

Vern sighed. "That's what he told the sheriff. And we all assumed the worst."

"That I slid off the road, crashed through the guard-rail, into the river and drowned?" Joe asked.

"That's right. And then, a couple weeks later, all you-know-what broke loose. Sara was living at your place to take care of Donnie, but someone reported her! That's when the county came to get Donnie."

"Is Donnie okay?" Joe asked quickly.

"Yes, and he'll be even better when Sara can get him out of that place they put him in, take him back home, and . . ." Vern stopped and a panicked expression crossed his face. "You have to get to town right away! The county people said it wasn't right for Sara to take care of Donnie."

"Why?" Hannah asked Vern.

"Because Sara wasn't Donnie's relative, so she couldn't be the caretaker for a teenage boy. They took him away, Joe, and Donnie was miserable, even though Sara went to be with him every day. Sara told my wife that she just had to rescue Donnie and she read a copy of the county rules. She didn't want to do it, but the only way she could get Donnie back was to marry into the family. And the only family Donnie had left was . . ."

"Jake?" Joe asked, and he clenched his hands. "My stepbrother, Jake?!"

Vern jumped to his feet and grabbed Joe by the arms. "You've got to get to town, Joe! Sara's at the church right now, and she's going to marry Jake! You have to stop the wedding!"

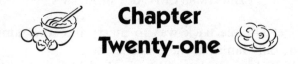

Chapter
Twenty-one

As they pulled up in front of the church, Hannah rolled down her window. The front doors were open slightly for ventilation, and they could hear strains of wedding music coming from the interior.

"It's Mendelssohn! The bride is marching down the aisle!" Andrea exclaimed.

"Oh, no! Does that mean we're too late?" Joe asked.

"No," Andrea explained. "That's when the bride starts her walk down the aisle. It's okay, Joe. The ceremony hasn't started yet, but we'd better hurry!"

By the time Norman had stopped the car, and they'd hurried to the foot of the steps leading up to the church, the music had stopped. With Joe in the lead, they hurried through the double set of doors and found themselves in the back of the church.

The church was packed with people. The minister at the front of the nave was reading the vows and Hannah heard the groom say, "I do." Then the minister turned to the bride, a lovely vision in a white wedding dress and a veil.

"Do you take this man to be your lawfully wedded husband?" he asked her.

"Say no, Sara!" Joe shouted out, racing down the aisle.

The bride turned, and Hannah could see her shocked expression. For a moment she looked as if she were about to faint, but then her mouth opened and she gasped *"Joe!?"*

"It's me, Sara!" Joe ran up to the altar and grabbed her arm. "Say no!"

"No!" Sara's voice was loud and clear. "No, I won't marry you, Jake!"

"Hallelujah!" Hannah heard the minister say under his breath, and there was a collective sigh of relief from the entire congregation.

"Joe?" Jake's mouth fell open in shock, and he looked as if he couldn't believe his eyes. "It can't be you! You're dead! I killed you!"

Mike pushed Andrea out of the way and raced down the aisle. Before Jake could try to make a move to flee, Mike had him down on the white carpet runner that the church used for weddings. He clicked on the handcuffs before any of the congregation could do more than gasp at what they'd just heard.

A moment later a tall, burly man rushed up to Mike. "Thanks, fella," he said. "I'm the sheriff here and I'll take over now. Everybody here heard him confess to attempted murder."

"Let's go in my squad car," Mike said, hauling Jake to his feet. "We'll put him in the back."

There were a few moments of stunned silence, as the sheriff and Mike left the church, dragging Jake behind them. Then Joe took Sara in his arms. "I love you, Sara," he said, and then he got down on one knee. "Will you marry me?"

"Yes!" Sara's response was immediate and the minister began to smile. "Hallelujah!" he declared, as he helped Joe to his feet. "Everyone here was expecting a wedding."

Sara locked eyes with Joe. "Now?" she asked softly.

"Now," Joe answered.

"Oh!" Carrie breathed. "How wonderful!"

"It was wonderful," Hannah agreed. "I've never seen Joe look so happy. And Sara was radiant."

"Of course she was." Delores took a small bite of the Golden Raisin Rum Cupcakes that Lisa had placed on the large table in the back of The Cookie Jar. "These are wonderful cupcakes, Hannah."

"Thank you."

"They remind me of hot buttered rum," Doc commented.

"I agree," Rachael said, and they all turned to look at her.

"How do you know?" Lisa asked her cousin.

"I don't, at least not from personal experience," Rachael said quickly, "but my father used to make hot buttered rum for my mom on New Year's Eve."

"Good save," Hannah, who was sitting next to Rachael, said under her breath. "Can anyone guess the first thing that Joe and Sara did right after the wedding?"

"They went to get Donnie," Doc said quickly, and everyone else nodded.

"You're right," Norman confirmed it. "They got him and brought him to the reception."

"Donnie didn't have to go back again, did he?" Lisa asked.

Hannah shook her head. "No. Since Joe was Donnie's brother, and he was married to Sara, the woman at family services closed Donnie's case with the agency."

"That's a relief!" Carrie said. "Did you get a chance to meet Donnie?"

"Just briefly," Mike said. "He sat with both of them at the head table, and he was so happy, he kept hugging Joe and Sara. The sheriff and I locked Jake in a cell at the jail, and we came back for the reception."

"I forgot to tell you something," Norman said. "Joe wanted Hannah and I to be their witnesses at the wedding. We stood up with Joe and Sara at the altar."

"How wonderful!" Carrie gave a pleased nod. "Was it a beautiful wedding?"

"Yes. One of the ushers lent Joe his suit to wear, and Sara was already in her wedding gown," Andrea explained.

The moment those words were out of Andrea's mouth, Hannah realized that Delores was staring at her in shock. "What is it, Mother?"

"You stood up at the altar in those clothes?" Delores asked her.

"Yes." Hannah shrugged, glancing down at her jeans and sweatshirt.

"And you stood up in front of all those people in *that* outfit?"

"Yes." She tried her best not to give in to the additional reply that occurred to her, but she couldn't resist. "I guess I could have taken these off, but I didn't have anything else with me. And I don't think the minister and the congregation would have approved of that."

Doc was the first to begin laughing, and a moment later, Mike, Andrea, Carrie, Lisa, Rachael, and Norman joined in.

"Come on, Lori," Doc said. "You know you deserved that, and I can see your lips twitching. Go ahead and laugh with the rest of us."

It took a moment, but Delores burst into laughter along with everyone else. "That's my Hannah," she said.

GOLDEN RAISIN RUM CUPCAKES

Preheat oven to 350 degrees F., rack in the middle position.

1 cup golden raisins *(regular raisins will work, too)*
¼ cup dark rum *(I used Bacardí rum)*
¼ cup pineapple juice *(apple juice will also work just fine)*
4 large eggs
½ cup vegetable oil
1 cup *(8 ounces by weight)* sour cream
1 teaspoon ground cinnamon
1 box of spice cake mix, the kind that makes a 9-inch by 13-inch cake or a 2-layer cake *(I used Duncan Hines)*
5.1-ounce package of DRY instant vanilla pudding and pie filling *(I used Jell-O.)*
12-ounce *(by weight)* bag of white chocolate or vanilla baking chips *(11-ounce package will do, too—I used Nestlé)*

Prepare your cupcake pans. You'll need two 12-cup cupcake or muffin pans lined with double cupcake papers.

Place the cup of golden raisins in a 2-cup or larger, microwave-safe measuring bowl. *(I used my Pyrex 2-cup measuring cup.)*

Pour the quarter-cup of rum over the raisins.

Pour the quarter-cup pineapple juice over the rum.

Stir the raisins with the liquids.

Place the measuring cup or bowl in the microwave and heat on HIGH for one minute. Open the microwave and stir the raisins and liquids again.

Heat the raisins and liquids again on HIGH for 30 seconds.

Let the measuring cup sit in the microwave for another minute.

Using potholders or oven gloves, remove the measuring cup or bowl from the microwave and set it on a towel on the kitchen counter to cool.

Crack the eggs into the bowl of an electric mixer. Mix them up on LOW speed until they are light and fluffy, and are a uniform color.

Pour in the half-cup of vegetable oil and mix it in with the eggs on LOW speed. Continue to mix for one minute or until it is thoroughly mixed.

Shut off the mixer and add the cup (8 ounces) of sour cream. Mix it in on LOW speed.

Feel the measuring cup or bowl with the raisins and liquids. If they're not so hot they might cook the eggs, add this to your mixer bowl.

Mix on LOW speed for one minute or until the raisins and liquids are thoroughly mixed in.

When everything is well combined, shut off the mixer and open the box of dry spice cake mix.

Add HALF of the dry cake mix to the mixer bowl but don't turn on the mixer quite yet.

Sprinkle the teaspoon of ground cinnamon over the cake mix in the mixer bowl.

Turn the mixer on LOW speed and mix for 2 to 3 minutes, or until everything is well combined.

Shut off the mixer and sprinkle in the 2nd HALF of the dry cake mix. Mix it in thoroughly on LOW speed.

Shut off the mixer and scrape down the sides of the bowl with a rubber spatula.

Open the package of instant vanilla pudding and pie filling and sprinkle in the contents. Mix it in on LOW speed.

Shut off the mixer, scrape down the sides of the bowl again, and remove it from the mixer. Set it on the counter.

If you have a food processor, put in the steel blade and pour in the white chocolate or vanilla baking chips. Process in an on-and-off motion to chop them in smaller pieces. *(You can also do this with a knife on a cutting board if you don't have a food processor.)*

Sprinkle the white chocolate or vanilla baking chips into your bowl and stir them in by hand with the rubber spatula.

Hannah's 1st Note: If you don't want to use rum in this recipe, use whole milk or water with a teaspoon of rum extract mixed in for flavor. If you don't have and don't want to buy rum extract, use vanilla extract or even coconut extract.

Use the rubber spatula or a scooper to transfer the cake batter into the prepared cupcake pan. Fill them three-quarters full.

Smooth the top of your cupcakes with the spatula and place them in the center of your preheated oven.

Bake your Golden Raisin Rum Cupcakes at 350 degrees F. for 15 to 20 minutes.

Before you take your cupcakes out of the oven, test it for doneness by inserting a cake tester, thin wooden skewer, or long toothpick into the middle of one of the cupcakes. If the tester comes out clean and with no cupcake batter sticking to it, your cupcakes are done. If there is still unbaked batter clinging to the tester, shut the oven door and bake your cupcakes for 5 minutes longer.

Take your cupcakes out of the oven and set the pans on cold stove burners or wire racks. Let them cool in the pans until they cool to room temperature and then refrigerate them for 30 minutes before you frost them. *(Overnight is fine, too.)*

Frost your cupcakes with Cinnamon Cream Cheese Frosting. *(Recipe and instructions follow.)*

Yield: Approximately 18 to 24 cupcakes, depending on cupcake size.

To Serve: These cupcakes can be served at room temperature or chilled. They're very rich so be sure to accompany them with tall glasses of icy cold milk or cups of strong hot coffee.

CINNAMON CREAM CHEESE FROSTING

½ cup *(1 stick)* salted butter, softened to room temperature

8-ounce *(net weight)* package softened, brick-style cream cheese *(I used Philadelphia in the silver package.)*

1 Tablespoon molasses *(I used Grandma's Molasses)*

1 teaspoon ground cinnamon

1 teaspoon rum extract *(if you don't have it, use vanilla extract)*

4 to 4 and ½ cups confectioners' *(powdered)* sugar *(no need to sift unless it's got big lumps)*

Mix the softened butter with the softened cream cheese until the resulting mixture is well blended.

Add the Tablespoon of molasses and mix it in thoroughly.

Sprinkle in the teaspoon of ground cinnamon. Mix it in thoroughly.

Hannah's 1ˢᵗ Note: If your ground cinnamon is as old as the hills, you'd better toss it out and buy new. Cinnamon loses its flavor after a year in a spice jar.

Add the rum extract and mix it in until everything is well blended.

Hannah's 2nd Note: Do this next step at room temperature. If you heated the cream cheese and the butter to soften them, make sure your mixture has cooled to room temperature before you complete the next step.

Add the confectioners' sugar in half-cup increments, stirring thoroughly after each addition, until the frosting is of proper spreading consistency. *(You'll use all, or almost all, of the powdered sugar.)*

Use a frosting knife or a small rubber spatula to place a dollop of frosting in the center of the top of your cupcakes. Then spread it out almost to the edges of the cupcake paper.

Hannah's 3rd Note: If you spread the frosting all the way out to the edge of the cupcake, your guests will get frosting on their fingers when they peel off the cupcake paper and they'll have to wash or lick their fingers. Kids enjoy this. Adults, not so much.

If you wish to decorate the tops of your cupcakes, you'll have to work quickly before the frosting hardens. You can make swirls in the frosting with the tip of your

frosting knife or spatula to make a design. Another alternative is to press the edge of a small spatula into the frosting, pull it up, and make little tips in the frosting just as you might do with meringue. You can also sprinkle the frosting with your favorite kind of ground nuts.

If you have frosting left over, spread it on graham crackers, soda crackers, or what Great-Grandma Elsa used to call *store-boughten* cookies. This frosting can also be covered tightly and kept in the refrigerator for up to a week. When you want to use it, let it sit on the kitchen counter, still tightly covered, for an hour or so, or until it reaches room temperature and it is spreadable again.

This frosting also works well in a pastry bag, which brings up all sorts of interesting possibilities for decorating cakes or cookies.

Index of Recipes

Baking Conversion Chart

These conversions are approximate, but they'll work just fine for Hannah Swensen's recipes.

VOLUME:

U.S.	Metric
½ teaspoon	2 milliliters
1 teaspoon	5 milliliters
1 Tablespoon	15 milliliters
¼ cup	50 milliliters
⅓ cup	75 milliliters
½ cup	125 milliliters
¾ cup	175 milliliters
1 cup	¼ liter

WEIGHT:

U.S.	Metric
1 ounce	28 grams
1 pound	454 grams

OVEN TEMPERATURE:

Degrees Fahrenheit	Degrees Centigrade	British (Regulo) Gas Mark
325 degrees F.	165 degrees C.	3
350 degrees F.	175 degrees C.	4
375 degrees F.	190 degrees C.	5

Note: Hannah's rectangular sheet cake pan, 9 inches by 13 inches, is approximately 23 centimeters by 32.5 centimeters.